Only With a Bargepole

Eddie Brown is confused. He knows he is debonair, suave, cultured, intelligent and fatally attractive to women. Why, then, does Life keep coming apart in his hands?

For reasons which the government is not yet prepared to disclose, Eddie – ex-schoolmaster and fluent Russian linguist – is a member of the Special Overseas Directorate. Known to initiates as the S.O.D., this is an organization specializing in industrial espionage and it is, incidentally, on Our Side.

Spying is a very nerve-racking business and when Eddie is entrusted with a perfectly simple courier job, he does rather tend to see sinister figures lurking under every bed. He responds in a typically Eddie way, using his initiative in situations where a modicum of elementary horse-sense might have been more appropriate. Before he knows what's happening, his primary mission of delivering a small parcel to an address in Vienna sinks without a trace and Eddie finds himself flashing around Europe, hopelessly in league with a gang of kidnappers. The kidnappers' victim is Miss Muriel Drom, the daughter of Eddie's boss at S.O.D. At first Miss Drom is strangely resistant to Eddie's charisma but eventually as they get to know one another and face death side by side, her attitude undergoes a mysterious change.

Finally . . . Well, everybody loves a happy ending, don't they?

also by Joyce Porter

Dover One
Dover Two
Dover Three
Sour Cream with Everything
Dover and the Unkindest Cut
  of All

The Chinks in the Curtain
Dover Goes to Pott
Neither a Candle Nor a Pitch-
  fork
Rather a Common Sort of Crime
Dover Strikes Again

A NOVEL BY

Joyce Porter

Only With a Bargepole

WEIDENFELD AND NICOLSON

5 WINSLEY STREET LONDON W I

Copyright © 1971 by Joyce Porter

SBN 0297 00368 2

Printed in Great Britain by
Bristol Typesetting Co Ltd, Bristol

To Pat and Mostyn Thomas, with much affection,
and as a small return for borrowing their house

One

My boss, Sir Maurice Drom, is a moody sort of fellow. Bears grudges, too. Of course, as head of the Special Overseas Directorate and thus one of the big wheels in industrial espionage, he's entitled to a few foibles but he does carry things a bit too far at times.

Like not speaking to me for four weeks after the last job I did for him.

Childish behaviour in a grown man, don't you think? I mean, it's not as though the mission had been a total failure. It hadn't been a total success either and I'd be the first to admit it but, as I pointed out to Sir Maurice when he debriefed me, nobody in their right senses could hold *me* responsible for that. We had quite an argument about it, actually, and it was after that he relapsed into the sulks and relegated me to sorting out old files in the basement.

All now, though, was apparently forgotten and forgiven and I was summoned once again up into the sunshine of his presence.

As soon as I got into the room I hastened to let him know that I, for one, was prepared to let bygones be bygones. I began panting heavily.

Sir Maurice fell for it. He looked up from behind his desk. 'What's the matter with you?'

' It's the altitude,' I gasped, ' and all this daylight and fresh air. I'm not used to it.' I could see his apoplexy coming on so I continued quickly, just in case the attack proved to be fatal this time. 'Did you know that mouldy old cellar of yours is absolutely riddled with rising damp?'

'It doesn't seem to have had much effect on you,' Sir Maurice observed sourly.

'Well, you know me, sir, always merry and bright!' I swung myself nonchalantly into the posh armchair he likes to reserve for his VIP visitors.

'Yes,' he agreed heavily, 'I know you, Brown. And you needn't bother making yourself comfortable! What I've got to say won't take more than a couple of minutes.' He reached for a TOP SECRET file which he'd got all ready laid out and waiting on his desk.

'My leave?' I asked with the unquenchable optimism of youth. 'Well, and not before time, if you don't mind my saying so. I've got at least three weeks due to me but every application I put in comes back with "not approved" scribbled all . . .'

'Not your leave!' he snarled impatiently because the subject had been a bone of contention between us for some considerable time. 'I've got a job for you.'

I assumed a more serious mien, some of the jobs that Sir Maurice had lumbered me with being no laughing matter. For either of us. 'Is that wise?' I enquired gently.

'This is something so simple, Brown, that even you couldn't muck it up.'

My nostrils twitched suspiciously. 'You're not proposing to send me abroad again, are you?'

Sir Maurice sighed. 'Brown, you and I are supposed to be engaged – God help us! – in industrial espionage. I should be interested to know how you think we could possibly operate without going abroad.'

'How about stealing secrets from the firms in this country,' I came back bright as a button, 'and flogging them to our foreign competitors?'

He didn't, as they say, vouchsafe me the courtesy of a reply.

Having counted under his breath up to ten he opened his file and read a bit of it gloomily. 'This is a perfectly straightforward courier job.'

'Oh, I've heard that one before!' I said. And if I was bitter, who's to blame me? I've had some very unnerving experiences since I became the Board of Trade's most unwanted spy.

'You've just got to deliver a small parcel to Vienna.'

'When?'

He consulted his watch. 'Your plane leaves in a couple of hours. Miss Ross has all your tickets.'

'Who to?'

His eyebrows winced at the grammar but he was too keen on getting shot of me to pretend he didn't understand the question. 'There's no need for you to know all the details. Just do as you're told and everything will be perfectly all right. Now, listen carefully, because I have no intention of repeating your instructions. You'll be in Vienna by mid-afternoon today. You are to proceed directly to your hotel and remain there until it is time for you to leave for your rendezvous. Allow yourself ample time and don't be late.'

'You can trust me, sir!' I leered.

'At 7.45 p.m. you are to be – with the parcel, of course – in the Hundemuseumstrasse opposite Number 475. Miss Ross has a street map of Vienna for you and she will show you where Hundemuseumstrasse is. It isn't at all difficult to . . .' His voice broke off on a note of pure horror. 'Brown, what in God's name are you doing?'

I wiggled the ball point pen and the used envelope in the air. 'Just taking a few notes of your instructions, sir.'

He catapulted himself out of his chair, charged across the room and snatched the offending articles out of my hands. 'You bloody, thick-headed moron!' he screamed, looking more like a pink blancmange than ever in his fury. 'Don't you ever learn anything?' He crushed the envelope in a podgy paw and hurled it into a corner. The ball point pen went clattering after it. 'How many times have you been told that *nothing* – I repeat, *nothing* – is to be committed to writing? The veriest tyro in this game knows that!'

I drew myself up. Cut to the quick but dignified with it. 'I was going to eat the envelope immediately afterwards, sir, I do assure you. And the pen, too,' I added with a forgiving smile.

For a minute I thought he was really going to hit me but Sir Maurice hadn't got his knighthood for nothing. He swallowed hard, and, after a pregnant pause, stalked back to his desk. 'You are to wait outside Hundemuseumstrasse 475 on the opposite side of the road,' he continued in a tone of icy restraint. 'You will find a lamp-post there. Stand under it and wait. Eventually you will be contacted.'

My trouble is that I can't leave ill alone. 'I'll bet there's a password!' I chortled. 'Oh, goodie-goodie! Just like when I was in the Brownies!'

Sir Maurice's face went a very nasty colour as he choked out the admission that there was indeed to be an exchange of passwords. 'We don't know who will be making the pick-up,' he explained defensively, 'and, of course, there must be some means of mutual identification. The contact will approach you and say' – he cleared his throat – '"Rule Britannia, Britannia rules the waves".'

For once I didn't utter a dickie bird.

Sir Maurice hurried on, red-cheeked. 'And you will reply, "There'll be bluebirds over the white cliffs of Dover".'

Biggles couldn't have done better.

'You will then hand over your parcel and return to your hotel where you will pass the night. Miss Ross has booked you on to a flight back here to London early tomorrow morning.'

'And that's all?'

Sir Maurice wriggled crossly in his chair. 'One cannot cover every eventuality,' he admitted with reluctance. 'These people in Vienna are extremely important to us and, whatever happens, I don't want them upset. They may possibly want some further assistance from you – I don't know – but, if they do, you are to co-operate to the best of your ability.'

Neither of us cared much for the sound of that.

'Suppose,' I asked, ever careful of my own skin, 'something goes wrong?'

'Where you are concerned, Brown, that is always a distinct possibility,' snapped Sir Maurice, perking up as he seized on the chance to be nasty. 'We have not overlooked it. Should you not have made contact by 22.45 hours or should you get yourself into any other difficulties, you are to ring Vienna 75 51 17 and identify yourself by means of your password. Use a public call box and do not telephone except in a case of extreme urgency. Is this all quite clear?'

'As mud,' I said, descending to depths of cliché I rarely plumb.

'Good!' Sir Maurice put his TOP SECRET file away and pulled out another one with a green cover. 'Well, I have a great deal of work to get through this morning so I shall not detain you. Report directly to me when you get back.'

However not even Knight Commanders of the British Empire get rid of little old me as easily as that. 'What's in this parcel?'

Sir Maurice busied himself in not looking at me. 'That's none of your business! Your job it just to deliver it, intact and with the seals unbroken.'

'Suppose I get stopped going through Customs?'

'You won't!' His irritation was beginning to show again.

'You've fixed it, have you?'

Sir Maurice threw his pencil down on the desk. 'No, I have not fixed it! This business is extremely delicate and I'm not having it broadcast to the world and his wife. If we warn the British Customs and the Austrians, we might as well put an advertisement on the back page of *The Times* and have done with it. Besides,' – he picked up the pencil again – 'you won't have any trouble. We've had the package done up so that it looks like a box of those man-sized paper handkerchiefs. No Customs official is going to be in the slightest bit interested.'

I wasn't so sure. Morever, Sir Maurice's office was nice and comfortable and I'd got oodles of pointless bickering still left in me. The good Sir Maurice wasn't, unfortunately, blessed with my stamina and had already jabbed his thumb on the bell-push.

His secretary, Miss Ross, appeared in the doorway as if by magic. The wicked-old-witch kind.

'Ah, Miss Ross!' Sir Maurice bestowed a benign smile where it would be most appreciated. 'Brown and I have have concluded our little briefing. I believe you have his documentation outside.'

'Yes, I have everything ready, Sir Maurice.' Saccharine dripped from every word. She only turned the old acid on when she addressed me. 'Would you come this way, Mr Brown?' It isn't easy to turn a simple invitation into an imprecation but Miss Ross managed it. She knew full well that Sir Maurice loathed my guts and that was good enough for her.

'Good-bye, Brown,' – Sir Maurice was already scribbling deathless notes on his scratch pad – 'and good luck!'

I cut my losses and made a dignified exit through the door that was being held open for me. Well, riling the boss is an occupation that soon palls and I thought I'd give Miss Ross a twirl for a change.

She closed the door reverently behind me and then fled for cover behind her desk. Having read my personal file, Miss Ross laboured under the misapprehension that I habitually raped any woman who was foolish enough to approach within grappling distance. I gave her a leer to keep her spirits up.

She went white, the silly cow, and fended me off with a sheaf of airline tickets. 'In accordance with Sir Maurice's instructions,' – the genuflection was barely perceptible – 'I have booked you on one of these all-inclusive holiday tours to Vienna. Sir Maurice thought you would be less conspicuous as a member of a group. We are arranging to have an urgent telegram despatched to your hotel to explain your sudden departure tomorrow morning. It will state that your father is dangerously ill, so kindly don't tell your fellow holiday-makers that you are an orphan.'

I grunted my acknowledgement of the warning and glanced through the papers that Miss Ross was poking at me. They were providing me with the thinnest of covers, I noted. A phoney passport but with my own name on it. Occupation: shop assistant. Charming! Trust them not to boost my ego by making me a TV producer or a heart surgeon or something. When I glanced through the brightly illustrated literature from the travel firm, though, I realized why I hadn't been elevated in the social scale. The leaflet, as furnished by the Good-bye Tourist Agency (Good-bye Tours are a GOOD BUY!), told the whole grisly story. Eight, Glorious, Memorable, Fun-packed days in Gay Vienna, it promised, for twenty-two pounds ten shillings per person, inclusive of smooth-as-silk air travel by Sooper-dooper jet and seven slumber-sound nights in the luxurious surroundings of Das Gasthaus und Pension Schlumberger situated in the Austrian capital's most salubrious district.

I looked up, somewhat breathless, to find Miss Ross still keeping her weather-eye on me. 'Very high class!' I sneered.

She bridled so violently that I heard her corsets squeak. 'The Board of Trade doesn't have money to throw around,' she informed me tartly. 'We had another circular from the government only the other day calling for the utmost economies in all our expenditure. We have to pay for the whole week, you know, even though you'll only be there for one night.'

I got my fingers free from the sticky label which I was requested to affix in a prominent place on my suitcase.

'Your baggage is over there in the corner,' sniffed Miss Ross, obliged to give me every assistance for Sir Maurice's sake. 'The packet is inside.'

Single-handed I transferred the sticky label to the lid of a cheap fibre suitcase and then opened it. A large box of tissues lay on top of a pile of my own neatly laundered smalls. What organisation! They must have sent somebody over to rifle my flat. I picked up the box and weighed it thoughtfully in my hand. It looked perfectly innocuous and perfectly genuine but it was at least twenty times heavier than the real thing. If one of them Revenooers should pick it up . . .

'What's in it?'

I'd little hope of catching Miss Ross like that. 'You should have a tie-on label for your lapel,' she twittered. 'I'm sure I gave you one with all the other things.'

'It's here,' I said and held up a vulgar bit of pasteboard which proclaimed in over-large letters: City of Your Dreams! Gay Vienna!! Foreign Frolic Tour 571. Good-bye Tours are a GOOD BUY!!!

Miss Ross smirked maliciously.

I tied the damned thing on with my best devil-may-care air, and with the little suitcase on the floor by my feet, sat and waited until it was time for me to leave for my rendezvous with the other Foreign Frolickers at Heathrow. Miss Ross, having decided that since I had restrained my bestial instincts thus far I could probably be trusted to keep my distance, got on with her work. She began thrashing her typewriter with such enthusiasm that it made me tired to watch her. I closed my eyes and, good little espionage agent that I am, began to review my instructions. I had just managed to recall the time of the meeting – 7.45 p.m. – and the name of the street – Hundemuseum – and was dreamily groping for the number of the house when we had a diversion. One of the official messengers came creaking in with a trayful of the morning's mail.

Miss Ross made a great fuss of the old codger and beamed indulgently when he all but ruptured himself laughing at me and my label. (I did not, by the way, look in the least like an East End kid awaiting evacuation in 1939.) The outcome of all this uncalled-for jollification was that, between them, they dropped the tray of letters. Miss Ross snapped back to her old vinegary self. Those were Sir Maurice's precious missives on the floor!

A picture postcard, stamp-side downwards, aeroplaned across to land by my foot. Always the perfect gentleman, I bent down to retrieve the same, only to have it torn out of my hand by an infuriated Miss Ross.

'That's mine!' she gasped, holding the postcard to where her bosom should have been and frantically trying to brush off the contamination left by my unworthy fingers. 'It's personal!'

The messenger, mistakenly scenting sex, switched allegiances and winked roguishly at me. 'From the boy friend, is it?'

'Of course not!' simpered Miss Ross, obviously rather flattered. 'It's from Muriel.'

'Muriel?'

Miss Ross returned to her desk. 'Muriel Drom. Sir Maurice's daughter. His only child, actually. He calls her his little ewe lamb, you know. Such a dear, sweet girl!' She gazed in adoration at the postcard. 'She never forgets me when she goes on holiday. Of course,' – with modest pride – 'I've known her ever since she was just a toddler.'

The messenger, understandably, was losing interest. He picked up his tray and began edging towards the door. 'Having a nice time, is she?' he asked with more charity than I would have shown.

'Just a minute!' Miss Ross, all a-quiver with excitement, adjusted her glasses and began reading.

The messenger remained patiently standing with one hand on the door knob. He caught my eye and gave me another wink. A pitying one this time.

'Yes!' exclaimed Miss Ross with enough emotion to have done justice to the Annunciation itself. 'She says she's having a simply marvellous time.'

'That's nice,' said the messenger.

'And they're having simply marvellous weather, too.'

'Good,' said the messenger.

'She says the hotel is simply marvellous and so's the food.'

'It makes all the difference, doesn't it?' said the messenger and, having done his good deed for the day, took his leave.

Miss Ross nodded a vague farewell and re-read her postcard. Then, tossing me a gratuitously triumphant look, tucked it away reverently in her handbag and returned to her type-writer.

Now, you'd not think to look at me that I was the worrying type, would you? Or nervous? Or over suspicious? Well, I didn't used to be, that's for sure. Before I got myself mixed up with the Special Overseas Directorate and all its works I had a markedly trusting and open nature. The only reason I haven't bought the Eiffel Tower from a friendly stranger in a pub is that I've never had the wherewithal on me at the time. Things are different now, though. Taught by bitter experience, I wouldn't trust the Archbishop of Canterbury alone either with my old Aunt Winifred or with the collection plate.

So, as Miss Ross tickled the plastic keys, my head was spinning with deep and dark forebodings. This simple little trip that Sir Maurice had blithely laid on for me had suddenly acquired a most sinister aspect. I chewed my bottom lip in anguish. Could my revered lord and master be plotting to pull yet another fast one on me?

The old cerebral cog-wheels churned away as I tried desperately to work out the angles. What the blazes was he up to this time? I knew he'd consider the sacrifice of his right arm a small price to pay for getting rid of me, but would he really go in for anything as tricky as this? With an effort I pinned my feverish imagination down and decided that my downfall was more likely to be a welcome spin-off than be Sir Maurice's primary target.

My thoughts were getting as turgid as my prose so I took a deep breath and tried again.

Sir Maurice was sending me to Vienna to deliver a small package (contents unknown) to a certain party (identity un-known). Well, there was nothing unduly alarming about that. Indeed, it was the footling sort of mission that was only too typical of S.O.D.'s operations. What was hustling me into a nervous decline was the 'coincidental' presence in Vienna of Sir Maurice's only daughter, the fair Muriel of the thought-ful postcard.

Conscientious readers will marvel as to how I had acquired this startling piece of intelligence – skippers are advised to turn back a page or two – because Miss Ross at no point indicated by word or deed the current location of Miss Drom and the postcard had only been in my possession, stamp-side down, for the merest sliver of a second!

Well, that's where training comes in, isn't it? And an extensive general knowledge and a highly developed deductive skill and the eyesight of a veritable eagle. Granted I hadn't seen any postmark or stamp on the card but I had seen the picture on the other side. A fat white horse standing on its back legs. It hadn't taken me a million light years to identify that.

Der Lipizzanerhengst! Die Spanische Hofreitschule! That spelt Vienna. As did Caprioles and Levades and Piaffes and Courbettes and Croupades and Mezairs und so weiter. The Austrian tourist attraction par eminence – especially for the English who love horses except when they come done up in sausages.

I could just picture Miss Muriel Drom spotting the postcards on a stand and deciding that one of the famous white stallions from the Spanish Riding School would do simply marvellously for poor old Miss Ross in Daddie's office. Scribble a few conventional lines, stick a stamp on and there's your reputation for thoughtfulness!

But, enough of all this equine talk! What really mattered was that the ewe lamb of Sir Maurice was in Vienna and this same Sir Maurice was using me to deliver a highly mysterious package, also to Vienna. Food for thought.

What could he be sending her? Money? Cannabis Resin? A set of clean undies? It must be something that he considered too risky to entrust to the post.

Miss Ross was watching me again. I flashed her my second-best smile. 'How long has Miss Drom been abroad?' I asked innocently.

'Who,' demanded Miss Ross, 'said she was abroad?'

One of the troubles of working in the heady atmosphere of

top level espionage is that people get too bloody security minded for their own good.

I stopped trying to pump Miss Ross and returned to my ruminations. No, it was too much of a coincidence. Sir Maurice must have some dark design though I still hadn't decided by the time it came for me to leave for the airport whether it was to fix me or assist his daughter.

S.O.D. and the parsimonious Board of Trade did me proud, delivering me to the wrong departure hall in an old butcher's van. Constructive thought during a journey spent fending off aggressive legs of New Zealand lamb was naturally quite impossible and I'd resolved none of my problems when I began lugging my suitcase the odd couple of miles across Heathrow's broad, rolling acres.

The crux of the matter, I told myself, is that parcel. One way or another there's something highly illegal about it. And, if the balloon goes up, guess who's going to be caught red-handed holding the baby?

I dragged my stomach in as a taxi zoomed past me at ninety miles an hour and, before I had the opportunity of returning the driver's two-fingered salute, a Rolls Royce whipped up behind and all but cut me off in my prime. Clutching fast to the traffic bollard which had probably saved my life, I came to the conclusion that at the moment I had other things to worry about. Like reaching the opposite pavement all in one piece.

The lady with the pram who joined me on my island was my salvation. Under her protection I finally made it across the carriageway and through the swing doors.

Two

Inside the hall thirty million people were thrashing round and every single one of them wore a lapel badge similar to mine. The harassed airport staff cowered fearfully behind their counters while, here and there, a travel agency courier sank with pitiful cries beneath the relentless boots of his clients.

The phlegmatic English were off on holiday.

Although normally the soul of courtesy, I had my cover to maintain and I just couldn't afford not to join in the fun. In no time at all I had notched up a pregnant woman, two kiddies and a frail old gentleman who should have stayed in his geriatric ward. To begin with I swung my suitcase rather at random but before long I picked up the object of the game. It was Find Your Courier. There were no rules.

Good-bye Tours must have taken over this part of London Airport for the day. Dotted around the hall their representatives struggled in the madding crowd to hold aloft small placards fixed on poles. Each placard bore a large-size replica of the lapel badges with which all we Frolickers had been issued. These banners were our rallying points and, like soldiers on an eighteenth-century battlefield, we were supposed to hack our way towards them. It was a good idea and it might have worked if there hadn't been one small snag. The lettering on the placards was totally illegible at anything over ten paces.

So, up and down the hall we fought only to meet with one bitter disappointment after another. Now it was: Gay Paree! The World's Naughtiest City!! Foreign Frolic Tour 294. Then, wobbling precariously as an exhausted middle-aged lady bound for Majorca reached her limit and bit the courier: Mysterious Rotterdam! City of the Sea!! Foreign Frolic Tour 162. A final effort, a last slash with the sharp edge of the suitcase and – Costa Brava! Sunshine, Sea and Sand!! Foreign Frolic Tour 97(b).

Oh, Gawd!

Me, if I'd been just a simple holiday maker, I'd have packed it in there and then. But I wasn't, and duty called. I girded up my loins, set my sights on yet another placard and kicked off. The throng appeared to be thinning out a bit as several bedraggled crocodiles shambled off in the direction of the departure lounge. I twisted round to clobber some sadist who'd caught me a cruel blow in the kidneys and found that my Guardian Angel was putting in a bit of overtime. There, right next to me, was the placard I'd been searching for. I was home and dry.

The courier for Foreign Frolic Tour 571 (City of Your Dreams! Gay Vienna!!) was a brutal looking woman who, in happier days would have been running her own concentration camp. She had a lovely touch with stragglers from other tours who tried to infiltrate her group and one couldn't but admire the telling kicks she administered with her number nines. I queued up to report. Number, rank, name. Chin up, stomach in, thumbs down the seam of the trousers.

I could see she wasn't impressed by the way she held my tickets up to the light to check for forgeries.

'Got your passport?'

I nodded and produced the required article for inspection.

'I'll keep that!' She whipped the passport out of my hand and added to the pile already stuffed in her handbag. 'Luggage?'

'Just the one suitcase, ma'am!' I held that up, too.

'Stick it with that lot over there!' Her bark arrested me as I was in the middle of executing a very smart about-turn. 'And just watch it, sonnie?'

'I beg your pardon?'

'After twenty years in this business,' she informed me grimly, 'I can spot trouble-makers a mile off. There's one on every tour and, unless something even more horrible turns up, you're ours. So – I'm warning you. Watch it!'

'By heck,' – an elderly man in a cloth cap who had over-heard this exchange grinned at me – 'she's none taken a fancy to thee, lad!'

'Apparently not,' I agreed distantly. 'And now, if you'll excuse me, I must get rid of my suitcase.'

He was quite unsnubbable. 'There's no hurry. There's half an hour's delay. These bloody charter flights are all t'same. They kept us cooling our heels for three bloody hours when we went to t'Algarve last year. I reckon I'll just pop into t'toilet while I've got chance.'

I watched him shuffle off without regret. You can easily have too much of the globe-trotting proletariat.

It was as I was shoving my way over to the pile of luggage that I had one of my bright ideas. Suppose Sir Maurice really was trying to smuggle something out to his daughter? For all I knew, the girl might easily be a drug addict or what-have-you and I could well be carrying a right packet of trouble in my suitcase. I began getting quite nervous. How long did you get for trafficking in drugs these days?

Well, luckily I've reduced the business of looking after Number One to a fine art. If the Customs men should by any chance make a swoop, it wasn't going to be my head on the chopping block. No, sirree!

I worked my way unobtrusively round to the lee side of the luggage pile. Kneeling down I opened my suitcase and began scratching around in it with a most convincing air. Nobody appeared to be paying any particular attention to me so I quietly transferred my attentions to the suitcases of my fellow travellers. What a suspicious lot of peasants they were!

Had nobody had the decency to leave just one measly piece of luggage unlocked? I trimmed off a badly damaged thumb nail with my teeth and reached for a flashy looking, powder blue job. Aha! The catches yielded with a couple of gratifying clicks to my questing fingers.

I took another surreptitious glance around before I raised the lid and unleashed the five and a half pounds of mixed confetti which some joker had deposited on top of a frothy pink nightdress. Well, that explained everything! Tittering happily to myself I removed the box of paper hankies from my case and inserted it delicately under the nightdress. Then I shovelled the greater part of the confetti back in, closed the powder blue suitcase, dusted off my knees and stood up.

It was like the Charge of the Light Brigade. Across the heap of luggage I saw the entire contingent of Foreign Frolic Tour 571 bearing down on me. For one awful moment I thought I had been rumbled but then I realized that our courier had merely given us the off. Some hundred and twenty of us fought over that mound of suitcases like jackals over the kill and bore our battered booty with triumphant cries across to the weighing-in counter. Once we had got rid of our luggage we raced for the departure lounge and the duty free shop. No Customs or Passport official had the nerve to stem our stampede.

By the time we actually boarded the aircraft I, for one, was feeling pretty whacked. Talk about the survival of the fittest! If we hadn't been given reserved seats I doubt if I would ever have made it to Vienna. As things were there had been a pretty sharp skirmish as we fought for space to stow our coats, hand luggage, bottles of booze and cartons of cigarettes.

I fastened my safety belt with trembling fingers and vowed that, next time I ventured on holiday, I was going to take a course in body building first.

'By gum, it's a relief to take the weight off your feet!'

I turned to find that I'd got the old man sitting next to

me – the one who'd witnessed my initial brush with the lady courier.

Well, I wasn't going to have him yacking at me for the entire journey. 'Yes,' I said shortly and, leaning back, closed my eyes.

He inserted a bony finger between my third and fourth ribs. 'T'lass is coming round with t'sweets,' he informed me and after that there was no holding him. He insisted on treating me to a lengthy résumé of his entirely uneventful and uninteresting life with the result that I could cheerfully have throttled him long before we crossed the French coast.

'You're a single, too, are you?' he asked. 'Travelling by tha'self, I mean? I'm in t'same boat. We ought to pal up together.'

Over my dead body.

'I've a list of all t'best brothels in Vienna,' he went on with a knowing snigger. 'Pal of mine at t'Darby and Joan Club give it me. By heck, he'd a right old time out there last year! He was under t'doctor for three weeks when he come back. Nervous exhaustion, he said. But, like I told him, it weren't his nerves that was exhausted, it were his . . .'

'I happen to be going to Vienna because I'm interested in ecclesiastical Baroque architecture,' I said primly.

That had the old fool rolling round in the aisles. 'Now pull t'other one!' he guffawed delightedly. 'A fine, upstanding young buck like you? Eh, I'm not so green that I'm cabbage-looking, tha' knows!'

'I assure you that I never for one moment imagined that you were.'

'Eh? Oh, well, never mind about me. It's you we've got to get straightened out. Here,' – he glanced at me suspiciously – 'tha's never one of them pansy bastards?'

Somewhat grimly I set his revolting mind at rest on that point.

'Well, that clinches it then. It must be t'girls!'

'No!' I snarled, beginning to lose my cool.

'Aw, come off it, son! I've been watching thee, tha' knows.

That buxom wench on t'other side there! You've none taken your eyes off since you got on t'plane!'

The fact that this observation was perfectly true didn't make it any less irritating. Of course I had been watching the young lady occupying a seat three or four rows further up the plane. Unless I was much mistaken, she was the owner of the powder blue suitcase and thus the temporary and unwitting custodian of my precious package. My deduction was based on the following carefully noted clues. One: she was arrayed in the type of brand new outfit only sported by brides when they are 'going away'. Two: she had a powder blue make-up bag which matched the suitcase. And, three: if she and the young gentleman sitting next to her weren't just newly married, they damned well ought to have been. Even my dirty old man was taken aback (though not to the point of speechlessness) by their uninhibited goings-on.

'By gum,' he gasped, eyes popping in disbelief, 'he's never going to . . .'

Since the benedick in question clearly was, I averted my gaze and looked out of the plane window. 'Ah, the Alps!' I said brightly before I realized that it was merely an oddly shaped cloud formation.

The old man beside me sucked his breath in. 'Aye,' he croaked, 'and that young bugger there's damned well scaling 'em! By heck,' – he ran his tongue over parched lips – 'there ought to be a law against it!'

Actually there was, but the arrival of afternoon tea saved all our blushes and the young gentleman's hands became temporarily otherwise occupied.

My next door neighbour soothed his savage breast with airline tea and fruit cake and then started chattering again. I put my sun-glasses on. It was the only defence I had, short of homicide.

'Espionage!' he proclaimed triumphantly.

The sun-glasses came off with a jerk. 'I beg your pardon?'

'It's got to be one or t'other, lad.'

'What has?'

'You coming to Vienna! If tha's none interested in t'women, tha' must be a spy.' He let me have the point of his elbow in the ribs again, just to show this was all a bit of harmless joshing. 'There's nowt else in Vienna.'

'Oh, come now!' I protested feebly.

'I'm telling thee! Vienna's t'spy capital of the world. Everybody knows that. They're all there – Russians, Germans, French, English, American, Chinese – you name 'em, Vienna's got 'em.'

'Rubbish!'

Mild opposition was just what the cantankerous old devil wanted and he went on rambling on and on about the CIA and SMERSH and MI5 and spies coming in from the cold and third men and licences to kill while I sat miserably and sweated.

Looking back, I reckon this ridiculous conversation marked the beginning of things getting out of hand. I put my sunglasses back on and mentally kicked myself for not having thought of the possibility before. Nobody knew better than I that Sir Maurice didn't trust me as far as he could spit and never had. Having placed a package of some value in my care, what could be more natural than that he should send someone else along to keep an eye on me and make sure that I carried out my instructions?

Once I'd got this far the rest was too easy. Look how this old buffer had forced his attentions on me at the airport! Sat next to me on the plane! Quizzed me about my interest in the owner of the powder blue suitcase! Brought up the subject of espionage! No, there was no getting away from it – he was one of Sir Maurice's watchdogs.

And that conclusion opened up vast new possibilities. I stopped thinking about little presents being sent to Miss Drom. Sir Maurice wouldn't have gone to all this trouble and expense it he hadn't thought that I might – possibly – do a bunk with his precious parcel. And I would only do a bunk if the parcel really were precious. Like gold or diamonds. I felt my stomach muscles contract with greed. Blimey, that box of paper handkerchiefs might be worth a king's ransom! Why on earth hadn't I thought of that before shoving it in somebody else's luggage?

Heady dreams of an early retirement and the Bahamas kept me going for the remainder of the flight. It was only after we'd actually landed at Schwechat and were taxi-ing along the runway that another explanation occurred to me: maybe this boring old buffer wasn't Sir Maurice's man at all but One of Theirs. That would still make the package worth stealing of course but I wasn't keen on getting involved in any rough stuff. Some of those foreign secret agents just don't know where to stop, you know.

So, it was with mixed feeling that I joined in the scrummage to leave the aircraft. A silken couch or a marble slab? When you come to think about it, there's a lot to be said for a boring, humdrum existence.

As we straggled across the tarmac I found myself, accidentally, next to the courier lady who had been so brusque with me in London.

I gave her an ingratiating smile. 'What about our luggage?' I asked timidly.

Travel hadn't broadened her mind. 'What about it?'

'I was wondering when we'd get it back, that's all.'

'You dratted trippers are all the same! Forever worrying about your luggage!' She relieved herself with a withering laugh. 'I can't imagine why. No self-respecting thief would touch most of it with his gloves on.'

'I was thinking about the Customs,' I murmured.

'The Customs? You don't really think the Austrian Customs are interesed in what you lot are bringing in, do you?' She really had a most unpleasant laugh. 'You'll find your precious suitcase in your room when you get to the hotel, so stop fussing about it!' A subversive movement somewhere behind her caught her attention and she swung round. 'What's that blasted woman doing now? Hey!' Her raucous voice cut across the windy wastes of the airfield. 'Come on, you! Get a move on.'

A faint cry, as if for mercy, came wafting back to us. I didn't get the gist of it but our courier did.

'Arthritis and a dislocated hip joint!' she muttered crossly as she stormed back to round up the straggler. 'I suppose the fool thinks that's an excuse for holding everybody up!'

Das Gasthaus und Pension Schlumberger brought a sudden hush to the Foreign Frolickers as we de-bussed outside its seedy portals.

'By heck,' said my old friend, who'd sat next to me in the coach in spite of all my manoeuvrings, 'they've none sent us to the Ritz, have they?'

I agreed and we followed the others inside.

I must admit I'd been counting on a scene of wild confusion in the hotel lobby as Foreign Frolic Tour 571 sorted itself out, with angry scenes as the management got the allocation of the bedrooms all wrong, frantic demands for the loo and pots of tea, and piles of unclaimed luggage in every corner. Regrettably, nothing of the sort happened. Das Gasthaus und Pension Schlumberger turned up trumps. By some quirk of organization our suitcases had arrived before us and had already been distributed to the appropriate bedrooms. The business of despatching us to the same destination was carried out with a quiet efficiency that horrified me. A sleek, rather supercilious young man checked our names, handed us a key and told us where our rooms were. I was half-way up to the fourth floor before the awful implications struck home. At the rate things were going, the owner of the powder blue suitcase was probably even now in the bridal suite shaking the confetti off her nightie. Another couple of seconds and she'd be finding my box of paper handkerchiefs and asking her virile young mate if they belonged to him. He'd say no and . . .

'By the right, these bloody stairs are a bit beyond a joke!'

I looked round to find you-know-who still dogging my footsteps.

'Mind you,' – he leaned panting against the banisters

– 'it'd help if tha' weren't charging along like a bloody steam train.'

And what did the speed of my ascent matter to him? Oh, no! I knew the answer but a power stronger than me made me put the question. 'We're not sharing a room, are we?'

The old man gave me a close-up of his gums and held out a wizened paw. 'Leslie Spalding,' he said, 'and I snore like the bloody clappers.'

I couldn't find the courage to match his smile. 'Edmund Brown,' I responded. 'I'm told I grind my teeth.'

'Tha's lucky to have teeth to grind, lad. Well, we'd best not hang about here. Supper's in ten minutes and we'll get nowt if we're late.'

A glimmer of hope flickered on the horizon. I thrust the key into Mr Spalding's hand. 'See you in the dining-room!' I shouted and sped back downstairs to the reception desk.

The suave young man regarded my overtures with suspicion. 'I regret that in no circumstances can rooms be changed, sir,' he announced in excellent English. 'Kindly address any complaint to the official courier of the Good-bye Tourist Agency.'

'No, no!' I sidled nearer to the desk. 'Everything's fine. Marvellous!' He looked justifiably surprised but I pressed on, having first glanced round to make sure that there were no eavesdroppers. 'No, I was just wondering if you could – er – well, help me. I feel a bit of a fool, actually,' – I gave him my little-boy-lost smile – 'but you look as though you're a man of the world and a good sport and . . .'

He reached under the counter and brought out a visiting card. 'Kindly be so good as to mention my name, sir.'

I read the card. It was brief and seemed to evade the point. '*Fräulein Elsa. Ungarische Massage. Wein 1, West-bahnhofstrasse 72. Englische Spooken.*'

The manager, or whoever he was, misunderstood my momentary loss of speech. 'Very clean,' he assured me in a discreet whisper. 'Highly recommended. Every satisfaction guaranteed. Miss Elsa has specialized for many years in accommodating the peculiar requirements of your countrymen.'

I pocketed my indignation (and the card because I might have an hour or two to spare after I'd dealt with my package). 'I'm afraid you've misunderstood me. My actual problem is a little more complex.' I looked him straight in the eye and dared him to disbelieve me. 'You know that young couple that are on their honeymoon?'

He nodded. So non-committal that it must have hurt.

'Well,' – my lips had gone all dry – 'we want to play a bit of a joke on them.'

'A joke, sir?'

'It's an old English custom,' I explained earnestly. 'They'll be most frightfully hurt if someone doesn't – well – sort of celebrate their first night for them. We always do it at home. In England. It's expected. Very traditional. Like rice and old shoes and kippers tied to the exhaust.'

'Kippers, sir?' These interpolations were not really questions. They were just perfectly expressionless echoes of my own words.

'So the rest of us on the tour got together and we decided we'd make them an apple-pie bed,' I gabbled, apparently under the impression that the quicker I spoke, the less fatuous it would sound.

'An apple-pie bed, sir?'

I looked at him anxiously. 'You know what an apple-pie bed is?'

'Oh, yes, sir. I know what an apple-pie bed is.'

'What a giggle, eh?' I said. 'On the first night of their honeymoon. There they are – all in love and everything – and they leap into bed and . . .' I didn't go much on the way he was staring at me. Bloody foreigner! I drew myself up stiffly. 'So, if you could just let me have your pass key or a spare key to their room, I'll nip up and make them an apple-pie bed while they're busy having supper in the dining-room. I'll let you have the key back right away, of course.'

He gave me what I can only describe as a pitying glance and became very interested in the contents of one of his ledgers. 'I am afraid that what you require is not possible, sir. I have a responsibility, you understand, and to let you have the key to another guest's room . . .' He shrugged his shoulders. 'I am sorry, sir.'

A middle-aged couple came up and asked for picture post-cards and stamps. I waited until he had finished serving them and we were once more alone. Only then did I get my wallet out.

When a few seconds later the cow bell went for supper, the spare key to the honeymooners' room was resting safely in my trouser pocket. I count myself second to none when it comes to the delicate art of persuasion.

The first clanks of the cow bell had barely died away before the flood gates opened and Foreign Frolic Tour No 571 stampeded to the trough. Down the stairs they thundered, shoving and pushing as though they hadn't seen a square meal for weeks. I joined them and together we burst through the dining-room doors like a tidal wave and surged over the long tables which had been set out for us.

We all seemed to be in a rollicking good humour as though we had just realized that we were supposed to be enjoying ourselves. We snatched up the free bread rolls, puzzled over the menu and admired the table decorations. So original of the management to think of Union Jacks and what matter that two were upside-down and one at half-mast.

The meal was served by a bevy of young ladies in dirndl skirts who scurried around with scared looks on their faces. At first I thought it was the Oberkellner they were frightened of but then I realized it was us. Shrieks of 'Ach, mein lieber Gott!' as the soup plates were dumped on the table and angry mutters of 'Englische Schweine!' were an eloquent commentary on what some of our more randy Frolickers were up to.

I was half-way through the goulash and gasping for breath when I remembered that I wasn't there for the food. I wiped my eyes, mopped the back of my neck and looked casually round.

I couldn't see hide nor hair of those blasted honeymooners anywhere.

Old Leslie Spalding – who else? – was sitting next to me. He'd finished his Weiner Schintzel and was already drawing a bead on a buxom miss who was advancing with a trayful of Apfelstrudel. I gave him a thump in the back to gain his attention.

He couldn't understand my anxiety and even, I felt, resented it as the buxom miss slipped past him unscathed. 'By heck,' he grumbled, ' tha's getting a bit kinky about them two, aren't tha'? I reckon they've decided to skip supper and, if I was in their shoes, I'd do t'bleeding same. A bird in t'hand, tha' knows! By the old Harry,' he added breathlessly as the buxom miss came swaying back with her empty tray, 'there's two there I wouldn't mind having in a bush, eh?'

I left him as he gave ample proof that lechery is apparently an instant cure for acute arthritis.

Three

Outside the nuptial chamber I paused to consider the situation. Should I, perhaps, knock? Would they open the door if I did? And then what the dickens was I going to say?

I wasted several minutes lamenting my fatal ingenuity. When – oh, when – was I going to stop doing things the hard way? There hadn't been the slightest trouble with the Customs and, if I hadn't been so damned clever, I'd have had that accursed box safe and sound now in my own suitcase.

Well, nothing ventured, nothing won. I pushed the six-language DO NOT DISTURB sign to one side and slipped the key into the lock. It turned smoothly and I felt the door ease open. Thank God they hadn't remembered to snap the inside catch down.

I took it all very, very slowly and carefully. Believe me! The curtains were drawn and the room was almost in darkness. I waited until my eyes got used to the light and, as I waited, I became aware of sounds coming from over to my left. Unmistakable sounds : male, female and creaking bed springs.

If I hadn't been in such a sweat to get Sir Maurice's package back, I'd have been completely overcome by the sheer embarrassment of it all. I mean, even in these enlightened days, some things are sacred, aren't they?

But this was no time to be faint-hearted and I pushed the door open another few inches. Judging by the sounds still coming from the bed, things were building up to a crescendo and it looked like being now or never for all three of us. I squeezed noiselessly into the room and pushed the door gingerly to behind me.

I could see quite well now and almost let out a whoop of joy as I spotted two suitcases standing unopened by the dressing-table. I was delighted that my profound knowledge of human nature had at last been rewarded. I'd known right from the start that those two bouncing around in the blankets weren't going to bother their heads with frothy nighties and such-like.

I had the powder-blue suitcase open in the twinkling of an eye. Once again I was knee deep in confetti but there was no time to worry about that now. I tipped the nightie out on to the floor and at long last got my hands securely on that box.

I didn't bother trying to tidy things up but, with the box tucked under my arm, began crawling on hands and knees for the door.

'Hey, you cheeky devil!'

I died a thousand deaths as the voice came loud, clear and hightly indignant from the bed. I collapsed on to a very dusty carpet and lay there trembling until long after it became obvious that the remark had not been addressed to me. The bed springs twanged alarmingly, the grunts increased in frequency and passion. It was more than time to go. With an effort I got enough strength back to make it to the door and, hooking my sweating fingers round the edge, I pulled it open. Once I was out in the corridor I leapt lightly to my feet, closed the door silently behind me and did a brief war dance.

Mission accomplished! Cum laude!

Going by the expression on the courier lady's face she had been watching me for some time before, on my third or fourth gyration, I caught sight of her. A lesser man might, forgivably, have been nonplussed at this encounter but I am nothing if not resourceful. I waved my box of paper handkerchiefs as though it were the most natural thing in the world.

'Just been borrowing a few of the old disposable nose-blowers, what!' I quipped as the confetti floated gently and abundantly to the floor.

She glared bleakly at me and then at the box, incredulity written in every crow's foot. Then she took a quick dekko up and down the landing to ascertain that there was nobody around but us chickens. When it was clear that it was going to be her word against mine in case of complaint, she approached to within a couple of centimetres.

'I'm going to get you, sonnie!' she hissed with such malevolence that I was quite taken aback. 'And, when I do, you are going to rue the day you were born!'

She waited politely while I wiped the spit from my eye before turning smartly on her heel and marching away.

Well, fine words butter no parsnips. Besides, in a fair fight I reckoned I could get the better of her any old day of the week. Easily. Not – thank God – that it would come to that because I'd be back safe and sound in England by lunch-time on the morrow.

Much reassured by the thought that I would soon be out of harm's way, I belted back to my room, determined to open the box and find out once and for all what was inside it. I realized that this action would constitute a breach of trust but I felt that, at a pinch, I could justify it. After all, it is well known that I am not the sort of man who ignores his instructions lightly and, if I was very careful, nobody need ever find out what I'd done anyhow.

I sat down on my bed and fished around in my pockets for a penknife. A quick glance at my watch to see how much time I'd got and . . . Oh, crikey, it was nearly half-past seven and Hundemuseumstrasse was simply miles away! The parcel, regrettably, would have to remain intact. Whatever happened, I mustn't be late.

Nor would I have been if Viennese taxi-drivers weren't a race of unmitigated, lily-livered cowards. The particular specimen I had the rotten luck to flag down drove at an un-steady twenty miles an hour, stopped for every red light and went pale whenever he caught sight of a traffic cop. In spite of all my encouragement and helpful advice, he dumped me in Hundemuseumstrasse exactly seven minutes after the witching hour. I grossly under-tipped the moron of course but that was small consolation.

Hundemuseumstrasse was an enormously long and some-what dilapidated street with a few small shops – all firmly shuttered up now – and far too many tall, gloomy houses. It might have been a respectable middle-class residential area once but that was a long time ago. Now the paint was peeling and the over-abundance of door bells indicated that the houses had been divided up into flats.

I pottered along past the unbroken line of parked cars until I came to No 574. I gave it a penetrating but unob-trusive glance as I walked slowly by. It looked exactly like all the other houses. I went on for fifty yards or so before I crossed the road and walked back on the other side until I was opposite the house again. Then I waited. For five minutes. For quarter of an hour. For half an hour.

At first I played it like we professionals always do. Cool and casual. I hovered about looking (a) as though I was wait-ing for my lady friend, (b) as though I was collecting car numbers as a hobby and (c) as though I was suffering from chronic amnesia. Before long, though, I had run through my entire repertoire and was reduced to simply standing there, shooting exasperated glances in the direction of No 574. Even that eventually became too much for me and I propped my weary bones up against the nearest lamp standard and sighed.

Really, it was too bad! I can't bear people who make appointments and then don't have the common courtesy to keep them.

My right foot went to sleep.

I woke it up.

My left foot went to sleep.

I woke it up and then – big deal – one of the lace curtains in the house moved. Somebody was taking a peep at me.

I squared my shoulders and shifted the box of paper hand-kerchiefs to a more prominent position and looked hopeful.

The edge of the curtain dropped back into place and not even my undoubted mental powers could get it to move again. There weren't many people knocking about but those that were gave me some odd looks. I felt that I was sticking out like a sore thumb and by a quarter to nine I had had it up to the back teeth. Sir Maurice had given me an emergency telephone number and, by golly, I was going to use it, as soon as I could remember it.

I had just got the first four figures and was groping confidently for the rest when the door of No 574 opened and three men came out. They stood for a second talking at the bottom of the steps and then one walked off to the right, another to the left while the third stepped off the pavement, crossed the road and came towards me.

'Got a match, mate?'

I was so busy admiring the subtlety of this opening gambit – the questioner was already puffing nervously at a lighted cigarette – that I didn't really notice that I had been addressed in English.

'I beg your pardon?'

'Got a match?'

He was an unsavoury looking man, small and thin. I put him somewhere in his middle twenties. He had a sharp little face, more cunning than intelligent, and a heavy five o'clock shadow whose greasy blackness found an appropriate echo in the colour of his nails. Nor was his appearance enhanced by his short and stubby haircut which was of the kind that only a really bad barber can give you.

I took my time about getting my lighter out so that he would have a chance to give the password.

His immediate response was to scowl unpleasantly, chuck away his lighted cigarette with considerable ill-grace and produce a comparatively unused one from the breast pocket of his jacket.

Had I got this bit of my instructions wrong? Was I the

one who was supposed to utter first? When the smoke which he had blown, accidentally no doubt, into my face had dissipated, I put my lighter back in my pocket and spoke.

'Rule Britannia, Britannia rules the wave!'

He looked at me as though I'd gone mad.

'Your turn,' I said, nodding encouragingly.

He spat a shred of tobacco out of his mouth and scratched his head.

I began to get impatient. 'Look, laddie,' I snapped, 'you've kept me kicking my heels out here long enough! Say your bit and let's get on with it, for the love of God!'

An expression of total incomprehension spread slowly across his face and I was just coming round to the idea that I'd made a mistake when something pointed and hard was jabbed into the small of my back.

The scruffy little chap in front of me relaxed. 'About bloody time!' he grumbled.

I sensed rather than saw that there were two men behind me.

'Quick march!' said a voice in my left ear.

I didn't give in without a struggle. 'Now, just a minute!' I began. 'What's supposed to be . . .'

Whatever was being pushed in my back was rammed home even further. 'Button it, big mouth! Burp, you lead the way! Now, you,' – I got another admonitory jab – 'follow him and don't try anything clever!'

Well, he could have been sticking me up with a fountain pen but I'd no intention of finding out the dangerous way. Although I couldn't see the joker who was issuing the orders, I could hear him and he sounded terribly like the sort of man who would carry a gun.

Burp, the little man with the cigarette, glanced up and down the street and then crossed over. He led the way towards No 574 with me and my two unseen companions following closely on his heels. We all walked at a fairly smart pace up the steps and through the double front door. Inside the dark hall, Burp opened the gates of an old-fashioned lift. Prompted by yet another poke in the back, I stepped into the cage and was on the point of turning round to face the front when an even more painful stab warned me that this would be unwise. I resigned myself to contemplating the tasteful wrought-iron work at the back of the lift.

We travelled upwards in an uncomfortable silence for half a minute. The lift ascended reluctantly and I guessed we must be on the top floor, or near it. As the gates were rattled open, my abductors removed their kid gloves. A hand was clapped over my mouth, my arms were wrenched crushingly behind my back and I was bundled out on to the landing. A moment later I was through the open door of a flat, down a short hall and standing blinking in the bright lights of a sitting-room.

Waiting for me in the middle of the room was yet another man and what he was pointing at me was definitely not a fountain pen.

The agonizing grip on my mouth and arms was released and I heard the door close behind me. Judging by the heavy breathing in the background, all three of the monsters who had shanghaied me had crowded into the room as well.

The man facing me with the gun frowned. 'Anybody see you?' he asked nervously. 'You sure? Well, all right, Burp – you get outside and keep your eyes open!'

'OK, boss!'

The door opened and closed again. Now we were four.

The boss spoke again. 'You searched him?'

'We didn't have time, did we?'

'Well, do it now!'

A pair of large hands began fumbling round my body. Usually I'm frightfully ticklish but on this occasion I couldn't even raise a ghost of a giggle.

'He's clean, Monkey.'

The man with the gun looked fractionally less nervous. 'You stay behind him, Cyril,' he ordered, 'and don't wait for him to move before you let him have it! Punchie, you go and stand over by the door!'

There was a grunt and the sound of heavy footsteps plodding across the carpet.

The man with the gun wiped the palm of his free hand on his jacket and addressed me direct. 'Well?'

'Well what?' I responded in a manner which came out cheekier than I had intended and earned me a thumping smack across the side of the head.

The man with the gun ran a finger round the inside of his collar. 'I'm warning you!' he blustered. 'We saw you hanging about outside. Who sent you?'

Not wishing to provoke more violence I became co-operative. 'S.O.D.,' I said.

That got me a vicious kick on the shins after a short pause for spelling it out.

'Oh, Sir Maurice Drom!' I said. Well, these rules and regulations about keeping your mouth shut are fine for heroes but what are we fully-paid-up, card-carrying cowards supposed to do? Personally, I'm all for speaking the truth and shaming the devil, especially when somebody's going to beat me into a pulp if I don't. Besides, I wanted to see if my revered lord and master's name rang any bells.

And – oh, boy! – didn't it just?

The face of the man with the gun crumpled and for a moment I thought he was going to burst into tears. With a petulant gesture he dropped the gun on a table and flung himself into an armchair. 'Oh, it's not fair!' he whined. 'I've taken every bloody precaution under the sun and it's still no good. How does he do it?'

I realized that the question was being directed at me. 'How does who do what?'

'There you are, you see!' he screamed reproachfully at his confederates. 'That's what I call loyalty. Put you under a bit of pressure and you'd break your necks spilling your guts! You want to learn a lesson from him. I'd like to see you lot keep your mouths shut if you was in his shoes.'

'I wouldn't let you down, Monkey,' came a hoarse voice from over by the door.

'Oh, wouldn't you?' muttered Monkey bitterly. 'You'd shop your own mother for a free pass on the buses.'

The man standing immediately behind me offered a quiet comment. 'West Hartlepool Joe pays well.' We were left to draw our own comparisons.

'Well, I pay well, don't I?' demanded Monkey furiously. 'We're on a packet on this job and you'll all get your fair share. You know that.'

'Fair share of what?' asked the man behind me. 'West Hartlepool Joe doesn't send one of his boys out all this way just for bloody peanuts.'

Monkey sighed miserably and turned his attention back to me. 'All right, what does he want?'

'West Hartlepool Joe?' I asked, being blessed with a quick mind.

'Who else?'

'I've never heard of him.'

'Oh, come off it, for Christ's sake!' Monkey stuck his bottom lip out like a spoilt child. 'I've been half expecting you to turn up. I know my bleeding luck. What's the angle?'

I shrugged my shoulders and, without thinking, changed my box of paper tissues from one hand to the other.

Monkey must have taken this movement as some sort of subtle hint and he held out his hand with another exasperated sigh. Not knowing quite what else I could do, I passed him the box. Monkey ripped the thin cardboard carton open and the contents spewed out over the floor.

I have never seen so much money in my life.

'Jesus!' gasped the man over by the door.

Monkey bent down and picked up the tightly bound wads of notes. He thumbed through one or two of them disconsolately. 'So that's the bleeding idea!' he said in pathetic disgust. 'What cut does he want?'

I was saved the embarrassment of answering by the man who had hitherto been breathing down my neck. He was drawn forward by the sight of the cash like a wasp heading for the jam pot. 'Twenty,' he mumbled, staring at the money. 'It's always twenty per cent he takes if he finances.'

'Twenty per cent?' moaned Monkey in horror.

'Plus his stake money back, of course. How much has he put up, Monkey?'

Monkey checked the bundles. 'Ten thousand!' he groaned. 'Who wants ten thousand at this stage? I've covered all our bleeding expenses. My God, Cyril, he's in this for real.'

Cyril licked his lips. 'West Hartlepool Joe usually is. Fancy having that sort of bread to chuck around!'

'Chuck around?' Monkey squeaked indignantly. 'All he's doing is betting on a one-horse race. Do you realise we're going to have to repay this loan with two hundred thousand pounds interest?'

Cyril goggled. 'It can't be that much!'

'It can. And it is.'

Cyril took a step forward. 'Look, let's forget about the job and just scarper with this lot.'

'And what about him?' Monkey jerked a greasy thumb at me.

Cyril hadn't overlooked me. 'Kill him. Dump his body somewhere where it won't be found and beat it. With this much lolly we could disappear for years.'

Monkey was tempted. You could see that. But, after a few moments' painful thought, he shook his head. 'West Hartlepool Joe'd move heaven and earth to get us. And he would. He's got contacts everywhere.'

'He'd have our guts for garters,' said the third man sadly from his station by the door. 'Remember what he did to Harry Young. And he'd only nicked fifty nicker.'

Monkey nodded and, stacking the money in a neat pile on the table, told me I could sit down. The atmosphere became easier and I was offered a cigarette.

'No hard feelings?' Monkey said with a gallant attempt at a smile.

'None.'

'Actually, we're very grateful for West Hartlepool Joe's interest, really. This job's costing a packet to set up so – all contributions gratefully received, eh? We're very grateful, aren't we, Cyril?'

'Delighted,' said Cyril with a scowl.

'And you'll tell West Hartlepool Joe that?'

'It'll be a pleasure,' I said smoothly, jollying the boys along.

'I suppose you're to stop with us until the job's done?' It was obvious that Monkey knew the answer and was just making polite conversation.

'That's right,' I said.

'And we're to pay West Hartlepool Joe's cut to you?'

I nearly nodded my greedy little head off as life suddenly took on quite a rosy glow. How much of the green stuff had been mentioned? Two hundred thousand pounds? With that sort of a handout I could eke out my declining years in modest comfort and all I had to do to get it, apparently, was box clever and not shove my blooming foot in it. For one with my flair it was a piece of gâteau.

Meanwhile Monkey had been chattering on.

'I beg your pardon?'

Monkey repeated his remarks a trifle sharply. 'I said, you'll have to lend a hand. There's no room for dead wood on this job.'

Well, in my state of euphoria, the dear little chap could have had my back teeth if he'd wanted them. What was a bit of co-operation where two hundred thousand buckshee quid were concerned? 'You can count on me!' I assured him from the bottom of my heart. 'What are we going to do, eh? Rob a bank?' You'll notice that I had at least realized that I had fallen amongst thieves.

Monkey slumped back disgustedly in his chair. 'A comedian, yet!' he spat. 'Look, smart boy, do us a favour! Cut out the humour. You know as well as I do what the bloody job is or you wouldn't be here.'

That was one slip it behoved me to retrieve quickly. 'Of course!' I agreed, laughing heartily. 'Just having my tiny joke, what? Mind you,' – becoming very business-like – 'I only know the broad outlines. You'll have to fill me in on the finer details.'

This process was duly carried out over the supper table, with me not caring to mention that I had already eaten. First of all I was introduced, somewhat cursorily, to the members of the gang. There were just the four of them. The leader – the thin, anxious-looking man – went under the name of Monkey Tom. His chief lieutenant was the one who had casually proposed that I should be bumped off. I didn't like him much and his soubriquet – Cyril the Shiv – suited him very well. The other two men were much smaller fry and obviously came right at the bottom of the pecking order. The one who had asked me for a light out in the street was called Burp and the other – a stupid-looking hulk of a man – went under the name of Punchie Lewis. By and large they were a pretty plebeian quartet and, if it hadn't been for the money and various other reasons, I would have preferred not to associate with them. I think the feeling was, possibly, mutual.

Supper was one of those meals that sort out the men from the boys. It was prepared in a frying pan by Punchie Lewis and tasted even more greasy and repulsive than it looked. The liquid refreshment was just as uninspiring. Monkey Tom was on warm milk because of his ulcer and Punchie Lewis never drank anything except fizzy lemonade as he was in perpetual training for what he claimed was his imminent return to the boxing ring. Cyril the Shiv was teetotal, too, informing me with a sneer that he respected *his* body. I ignored the implication and, drawing in my tum, turned hopefully to Burp who had his own personal bottle of wine. On closer inspection this proved to be a well-known brand of iron tonic but, since the label said it was guaranteed to be five per cent alcohol I consented to share it.

'Well, Eddie,' began Monkey, unhappily poking his sausages round in a sea of fat, 'as you know, we're going to kidnap Sir Maurice Drom's daughter, Muriel, and hold her to ransom.'

My mouthful of iron tonic went straight down the wrong way.

Four

Punchie Lewis's well-meant ministrations left me with a cleared windpipe and three crushed vertebrae. I took as long as I could to get my breath back so that I could have time to think. The revelation that these crummy villains were plotting to kidnap Muriel Drom had been something of a shock but it didn't take me long, of course, to get the whole thing in perspective. Well, it was obvious, wasn't it? Sir Maurice had set me up for this. He knew (none better) that if he'd told me the whole story they wouldn't have got me out to Vienna without a strait-jacket. So, he feeds me some rubbish about a simple courier job and topples me in at the deep end. To sink or swim? Where his own daughter was concerned?

Maybe he didn't like the girl?

I stifled these defeatist thoughts before they could undermine what was left of my self-confidence. Sir Maurice was relying on me, I told myself stoutly, for one very good reason: he knew that whatever happened I wouldn't let him down.

Punchie Lewis stopped pummelling me in the back and I found myself feeling a lot better. On reflection I was rather touched by Sir Maurice's faith in my abilities and vastly relieved that I hadn't, after all, got my instructions muddled up. It wasn't so long ago that I'd almost begun thinking that I might have been waiting outside the wrong house in Hundemuseumstrasse.

44

Burp kindly filled up my glass with another helping of his iron tonic and I twinkled endearingly at Monkey over the rim. 'Actually,' I said innocently, 'I was wondering about that. I mean, why pick on Sir Maurice Drom? He's not a millionaire, is he?'

''Course not!' Cyril the Shiv chipped in scornfully. 'He's just a lousy, stinking civil servant.'

'So?'

'You know what job he does at the Board of Trade, don't you?' asked Monkey.

Well, did I or didn't I? I hedged. 'Not exactly.'

'He's the big white chief of the Special Overseas Directorate. And you know what they do, don't you?'

I took a tentative bite of sausage and said nothing.

'They're spies!'

Rather meanly I denied Monkey the blank astonishment to which I'm sure he felt he was entitled. 'Oh, yes,' I said indifferently, 'I knew *that*.'

'But that's the whole point. Don't you see? If we kidnap his daughter, they're all going to think there's something political in it, like all these other snatches. They'll be expecting a demand for half the bloody cons on the Moor to be set free. Then, when the ransom note arrives and they find that all we want is a lousy million quid, they'll be so relieved they'll cough up without a murmur.'

'Who's they?' I asked, carefully mulling all this over.

'The bloody government!' explained Monkey excitedly. 'What's a million pounds to them? It's only the tax-payer's money and they'll pay it over and be glad to.'

'Especially,' added Cyril with a most unpleasant grin, 'when we threaten to sell her to the Russians if they don't. Or the Chinese. That'd ginger 'em up a bit, wouldn't it?'

Well, of course, the whole thing was simply ludicrous. No government in its right mind was going to shell out that amount of cash just to restore some chit of a girl to the bosom of her family. Governments simply don't succumb to threats of that nature. Or do they?

But the more I thought about this crazy kidnapping scheme, the more I began to realize how jolly clever it was. Monkey Tom and his chums were going to hit at any country's most sensitive point: its security. With his daughter in alien hands, Sir Maurice would be wide open to pressures which no loving father could be expected to withstand. And of how many state secrets was he the depository? He'd been mixed up in spying of one sort or another for over thirty years. He must know a packet. If he chose to talk, he could rip our security organization clean open from top to bottom. What was a million pounds against a disaster of that magnitude?

I began to regard Monkey with new respect. Why did I never come up with bright ideas like that? 'They'll leave no stone unturned to get you,' I warned him.

'They wouldn't dare!' he retorted confidently. 'We shall make it clear in our ransom note that we'll turn the girl over to the Russkies at the first sign of any attempt to rescue her. You think they'd risk calling that bluff?'

'But – after the girl's safely back home?'

Monkey grinned. 'With a million quid in your pocket, you can disappear without a trace. Look at them Great Train Robbers! They gave the cops a good run for their money and we shan't make the mistakes they did. There's ways and means. You know that as well as I do.'

I felt it was time that we got down to a few brass tacks especially if I was going to nip this merry little jape in the bud. 'When are you planning to make the snatch?' I asked.

'Tomorrow,' said Monkey Tom blithely and gave me my second near coronary in ten minutes. 'Well, that's when we leave for Marjendorf to spy out the land. I dare say it'll be another two or three days before we're ready to pull the actual job.'

'Where's Marjendorf?'

Cyril the Shiv shot me an old fashioned look. 'You don't know much, do you? I thought West Hartlepool Joe was supposed to have tabs on everything.'

'He has!' I said shortly.

'He doesn't seem to have told you much!' Cyril pulled out his flick knife and began paring his nails. 'Makes me wonder exactly how you come to find us so easy.'

Luckily I was saved from further embarrassment not by the bell but by Monkey Tom's amour propre. He was touchy about his position as leader of the gang and kept a jealous eye on the obviously ambitious Cyril. The fact that Cyril disliked me was almost enough to make Monkey my friend for life.

'Marjendorf is a little village up in the hills above Linz,' he said, reverting to the question I'd forgotten in the heat of trying to outwit Cyril. 'That's where the girl is.'

'I thought she was in Vienna,' I said.

'She was, but now she's gone off to this dump for a couple of weeks on some sort of foreign language course.'

'Russian,' said Cyril, determined not to be left out of the act.

Monkey scowled at him. 'The people who run the course more or less take over the whole village. It's only a tiny little place, seemingly. We'll probably have to put up somewhere in the neighbourhood. It's not going to be too easy, though, hanging around Marjendorf without' – he glanced dubiously at his fellow crooks – 'arousing suspicion.'

I could see exactly what he meant. That bunch would have stuck out like a fistful of sore thumbs in the rush-hour at Charing Cross. Without any effort on my part, my big mouth started flapping. 'Well, why doesn't one of you actually join the course as a student? They usually run classes for complete beginners and I'll bet they've still got some vacancies left. That way you'd have somebody right in the village with no questions asked.'

Which is why, the next morning, I found myself speeding through the Austrian countryside, a potential late entry to the 19th Russisches Sprachseminar. As Cyril said sneeringly – better one volunteer . . .

Monkey Tom had a copy of the brochure issued by the organizers of the course and I studied as best I could as

Burp hurtled us along in a comfortable but elderly Mercedes which the gang had acquired for the occasion.

Monkey had got the jitters in a big way and my erratic wanderings through the maze of German subordinate clauses were not helped by his endless chattering. There was no point in regurgitating everything over and over again. The arrangements we had already agreed upon were simple to the point of puerility and repeating them didn't make them sound one whit better. After five weary hours our collective brain had come up with the following: I was to join the course; I was to get pally with Miss Drom; under the pretext of romance, I was to lure her to some secluded spot whereupon the boys would arrive in force and the kidnapping would take place.

Oh, there were a few gaps, of course. We all realized that. And it was these that Monkey Tom was trying to plug. He rattled on about our communications problems while I, deep in the cultural delights that lay before me, answered him from time to time with a few ill-natured grunts.

I skipped nimbly over conversation, dictation, translation and grammar and paused only briefly at the optional extras of Russian history, Russian geography, Russian literature, Technical translation and Russian shorthand and typing, before turning to the page with the recreations on it. Swimming, table tennis, horse riding (which had to be booked in advance) and country walks. Dear God!

I looked up to find Monkey Tom chewing distractedly at his nails. 'What was that you said about a towel?'

'I thought you could hang a towel up in your bedroom window as a signal.'

'As a signal for what?'

Monkey's brow creased with the strain of it all. 'Well, I haven't worked that out yet but we could think of something.'

I was firm but kind. 'No towel.'

Monkey heaved a deep sigh.

'By the way,' I said, putting aside the prospectus until I felt stronger, 'what are you going to do with Miss Drom once we have her in our clutches? Take her back to Hunde-museumstrasse?'

'That's none of your bloody business!' snarled Cyril who was sharing the back seat with us.

'That's right!' Monkey chimed in quickly. 'We've got it all arranged, don't you worry. You'll be told when the time comes.'

Well, it was nice to know that they'd got something fixed up.

'You sound as though you don't trust me,' I laughed.

There was an awkward silence. Cyril the Shiv sneered out of the window and Monkey suddenly became very occupied with his maps on the grounds that Burp had missed the road. Considering that we were on an autobahn of such straightforwardness that not even Burp could lose himself, the grounds rang hollow.

The knowledge that I was not completely persona grata with the gang had been troubling me for some time. So far they had refused to let me out of their sight for one single moment. All my ideas about getting to a telephone, ringing Sir Maurice's emergency number and shouting for help had come to naught. They hadn't even let me go to the loo without an escort. Over breakfast (stale buns, margarine and instant coffee) I had made a determined effort to break away on the grounds that I had some shopping to do. I could hardly present myself at the 19th Russisches Sprachseminar in no-thing but the clothes I stood up in. Monkey, a bit of a snappy dresser himself, was sympathetic. He agreed that it might be unwise for me to return to my hotel and, as soon as the shops were open, despatched Cyril to make the necessary purchases on my behalf. Apart from making a few objections, which were fully justified, about Cyril's sartorial tastes, there was nothing much I could do about it and any hopes I'd had about using the telephone in the flat were scotched when Monkey Tom himself spent the best part of an hour on it fixing up for me to join the course.

Insult was added to injury when I heard Monkey describing me as a complete beginner. As a matter of fact I speak the language with an ease and fluency denied to most natives of that enigmatic land. Indeed, if it hadn't been for my complete mastery of the tongue of Pushkin and Tolstoy, I should never have become a member of the Special Overseas Directorate or got myself into the messes like the one I was in now. I was tempted to put Monkey in the picture as to my linguistic prowess but discretion proved stronger than pride. It was extremely unlikely that any of West Hartlepool Joe's minions were capable of stringing so much as a grammatical sentence together even in their own language.

I was more satisfied when I heard Monkey insisting that I should be given a bedroom to myself. Accommodation in the village was rather short but, in the end, I was allocated to one of the cottages which turned a meagre penny by putting us students up. Monkey expressed complete satisfaction with this arrangement on being assured that my temporary shelter would be primitive but clean.

No sooner had these telephonic arrangements been concluded than Cyril the Shiv was back with my shopping and it was time for us to set out for Marjendorf.

In view of what happened later, I have wondered if perhaps I should have behaved differently at any point. After deep and prolonged consideration I can only place my hand on my heart and say – no. I put it to you, dear reader – what choice had I? The gang had mistaken me for the emissary of West Hartlepool Joe, as big a villain presumably as they were themselves. If I had been so foolish as to point out their error to them, I should have been killed. And what good would that have done anybody, including me? No, once having assumed the mantle of West Hartlepool Joe's messenger boy, I had to go on with it.

Mind you, I'd have liked to have known a bit more about West Hartlepool Joe himself though it was pretty obvious that he was some big-time operator who went in for financing the illegal escapades of lesser fry like Monkey Tom. And financing them, moreover, whether they wanted his help or not. He sounded a most delightful character but I was safe as long as I was presumed to be under his protection. So – on with the charade!

Burp swung the Mercedes off the autobahn and drove without stopping through Linz. Then we were heading north, up into the hills. This was real country and well away from the usual tourist haunts. The roads were steep and narrow and frequently crawled their way through small villages. Monkey Tom writhed miserably on the back seat. The terrain was apparently most unsuitable for a quick getaway.

'You'll have to give us a good start,' he told me fretfully. 'A couple of hours at least. If the hue and cry goes up any sooner, we'll be done for.' He looked out of the window. 'These roads'll be pure hell in the dark.'

'Aw, quit worrying, boss!' said Burp from the driving seat. 'I could do seventy down this lot with my eyes closed.' And, to prove that here was no idle boast, he took the next hairpin on two wheels.

Monkey and I unwound ourselves from a loving embrace.

Marjendorf, when we finally got there, looked to me even less promising from a kidnapping point of view than the approach roads had done. It was a tiny little place, dozing peacefully round a sun-baked square. There was a Gasthof, a church, two or three shops and some thirty houses. Our arrival did not go unnoticed. A large fat dog, laid out on a doorstep, opened one eye and looked at us.

I got my suitcase and extricated myself from the car.

'We'll not hang about,' muttered Monkey, shooting anxious glances in every available direction and speaking out of the side of his mouth. 'Remember, if anybody asks you, we were just casual acquaintances who happened to give you a lift.'

'Right,' I said.

Monkey put a hand out to stop me closing the door. 'And we'll ring you at this pub place tonight to let you know where you can get in touch with us. We'll phone dead on nine so see that you're there waiting.'

'OK,' I said.

Monkey just couldn't leave it alone. 'When you phone through your reports, be careful what you say,' he warned me. 'You never know who's listening. Did I tell you I'd be calling myself Robinson?'

'At least six times,' I said.

Luckily Cyril the Shiv had had enough, too, and under his impatient goading Monkey Tom was persuaded to let me off the leash. I watched the Mercedes zoom off and, with a sigh of relief, began to hump my new suitcase over to the hotel.

The hotel possessed a small concrete veranda which was furnished with an assortment of battered iron tables and chairs and decorated with an impressive array of the flags of all nations, hanging limply on their poles. I deduced, correctly as it turned out, that we Russian language students were going to form a motley crew. I went across the veranda and pushed my way into the dark, cool interior of the hotel. Like the grave. I coughed tentatively and shuffled about with my feet. Not a sound. Everybody must be enjoying their mid-afternoon siesta. Well, hard luck!

I poked around and eventually found the kitchen. I woke the cook who was fast asleep on a chair, his head resting comfortably on his folded arms. He woke the maid-of-all-work who was kipping in a corner on a sack of potatoes. She slouched off to pass the buck further up the line. After about ten minutes the proprietor himself appeared, fastening his trousers as he came. None of them was exactly glad to see me but the hotel made a lot out of the language students and the proprietor, at last, accepted my untimely arrival with sleepy philosophy.

'Ah, yes!' he told me through a mighty and uninhibited yawn. 'You are staying with Frau Bubisch. I'll take you along there now and you can get yourself settled in.'

'Shouldn't I report to the Herr Direktor first?' I asked.

He shook his head and scratched lethargically under his armpits. 'They're all down at the school. You don't want to walk all that way in this heat. They'll be back up here in about an hour and you can see him then. Is that all the luggage you've got?'

Mine host conducted me through the village at a leisurely pace and eventually we came to a row of cottages perched on the very edge of the hill. He pushed open the door of the first one.

'This is Frau Bubisch's,' he said and led me into a sparsely furnished room on the ground floor. 'Make yourself at home. The toilet is down at the end of that passage. You know you have all your meals at the hotel?'

Thanks to the brochure, I did, and the inn-keeper ambled contentedly off and left me to my own devices.

I'm a town boy myself and I found the peace and quiet of Marjendorf more than a little eerie. Still, I trotted bravely down to the little room at the end of the corridor and then treated myself to a cat-lick in the surprisingly cold water out of the jug on the bamboo washstand. The bed was hard and narrow with an unusual upwards curve at one end. On closer inspection I decided it was really an examination couch from some long deceased doctor's consulting room and I rejoiced that I wasn't going to have to spend more than a night or two on it.

I strolled back to the Gasthof. Now that the sun was passing over the yard-arm, things were becoming quite animated. Two small boys were fighting in the dust in front of the church and a solitary woman came dejectedly out of the grocer's. Yes, Marjendorf was really humming! Things were jumping back at the hotel, too, as the students – their day's work over – came straggling up the hill. Some went straight to their lodgings but most of them crowded on to the concrete veranda where they slumped exhausted onto the iron chairs and ordered coffee and Coca-Cola from the maid-of-all-work.

I passed rather self-consciously through their midst and went through into the bar. There I found Herr Doktor Klimenko, Direktor und Geschäftsfuhrer, who graciously permitted me to ply him with white wine while we settled our business. He was a big man, about sixty, with a luxuriant crop of white hair and a stubby white moustache liberally stained at the edges with nicotine. A few minutes' conversation revealed that he was supremely uninterested in anything except money and, as long as his students paid their fees, he didn't care if he never saw them at all. It was an attitude which, in the circumstances, I couldn't help but applaud. Old Klimenko wouldn't lose much sleep – much less bestir himself to call in the cops – if a couple of his pupils vanished into thin air.

Very desultorily we discussed to which of the four or five available classes I should be assigned. I claimed to know a little Russian already but modestly refused to define exactly how much so as to leave myself room for manoeuvre. As soon as I found out how much Russian Miss Drom knew, I was going to achieve the same standard and join her class.

The good doctor unexpectedly made things easier for me.

'You'd better join Frau Woodcock's group,' he said, glancing at his watch as though he felt I had already had more than my fair share of his attention. 'She usually gets landed with the foreigners.' He got to his feet. 'A charming woman and an excellent linguist. You'll like her.'

I decided I could risk it. 'Is Miss Drom in Frau Woodcock's class?'

'Miss Drom? Oh, the Engländerin. Hm, yes, I think so.'

'Well, I imagine that'll do me fine, then.'

'Good, good!' He looked hopefully towards the door. 'Well, you can let me know tomorrow which optional subjects you want to take. And now – if you'll excuse me . . .'

I watched him depart with considerable satisfaction. Things were moving along nicely and my optional subjects were going to present no problem as I should be taking precisely those which Miss Drom had selected.

I treated myself to another glass of the Gasthof's excellent white wine and prepared to think about what I ought to do next.

The bar was gradually filling up as more people came filtering through into the gloom. The high backs to the benches made it rather difficult to get a proper look at them all so I wandered over to the bar counter to buy some cigarettes. From this vantage point I glanced casually round. Most of the students looked terribly young and disgustingly healthy. Nearly all the boys sported beards and wore their shirts open to the navel. The girls, naturally, were more interesting and my attention was riveted by a handsome, long-legged filly who had been toasted to a warm brown all over.

My hopes rose.

And fell again as she burst into a stream of fluent, colloquial and obviously native German. This was not Miss Drom and I was a looney for ever thinking it might be.

Just then the door from the veranda opened again and two more females came in. One look was enough to pigeonhole this pair. They were so English that they might as well have had Union Jacks sticking out of their ears. In marked contrast to the Continental popsies, my compatriots were the colour of unripe Stilton with mousy brown hair and sullen faces. One of them wore a cotton frock covered in hideous pink and yellow flowers while the other sported a heavily smocked peasant-type blouse tucked into a pleated tartan skirt. Both of them had their bony shoulders draped in woolly cardigans.

What price swinging Britain now?

'Oh, it's much cooler here, Elphie,' declared the one in the Hunting Stewart. 'And quieter.' She looked about her with the air of a duchess paying a duty call in the slums. 'Where shall we sit?'

Elphie squinted down her nose. 'That looks the cleanest, don't you think?' She led the way to the far end of the room where the pair of them fastidiously removed some dirty crockery to another table. Having carefully dusted the benches with their handkerchiefs they sat down and ordered two coffees in loud clear voices from the maid-of-all-work who had already learned not to keep the two English misses waiting.

I lit a cigarette and told myself I just couldn't be that unlucky.

They were opening their text books now and studying them with great concentration and total bewilderment. After

55

a few moments' silence, Elphie looked up with a frown.

'I haven't really got the hang of these dreadful numerals, have you, Muriel, dear? They're frightfully complicated.'

Muriel dear shook her head and agreed that she, too, had lamentably failed to master this particular problem and my heart zoomed right down into my boots.

Where it stayed for some considerable time.

Five

Nothing ventured, nothing won. I told myself that three times before I found the will power to cross the room. Some of the young entry at the other tables gave me an odd look or two – and who's to blame them?

I decided in my wisdom on a hail-fellow-well-met approach. 'Well, hello, there!' I trilled. 'Jolly glad to find somebody who speaks the same lingo, what?'

For one awful second I thought I'd come out without my trousers or sprouted two heads or something. Then the ladies averted their eyes and tried to pretend I hadn't happened.

Well, if I let myself get discouraged as easily as that by the fair sex, I'd be a permanent fixture on the psychiatrist's couch by now. I insinuated myself on to the bench next to Miss Drom, thus causing her to shoot up to the far end. When she had unplastered herself from the wall and was sitting comfortably, I resumed.

'Yes, we Britishers must hang together when we find ourselves in furrin' parts, mustn't we? Otherwise we may find ourselves hanging separately – ha, ha, ha! By the way,' – I held out a hand that was sweating freely – 'Eddie Brown's my monicker.'

I paused to see if this revelation had any effect upon Miss Drom but it left her cold. Her pal was less fastidious. She brushed my fingertips with her own, blushed and said, 'Pleased to meet you.'

'Likewise,' I responded gallantly just as the waitress arrived with the coffee. 'Aha,' I trumpeted, smoothing assuming the role of big spender, 'permit me! Wie viel, Fräulein?'

The maid-of-all-work looked at me as though I'd gone stark-staring verrückt. 'Neun Schillings, bitte.'

I dropped ten Schillings with a flourish on her tray. 'Keep the change!' I said grandly.

She pocketed her fourpence with a resigned 'schön'.

'And bring me a coffee, too, will you?'

'With biscuits, mein Herr?'

What a question. Couldn't she see that in my present mood no expense was being spared?

I confirmed the biscuit order and turned back to Miss Drom and her friend who were cowering in their cardigans. 'You haven't told me your names,' I twitted them.

'Miss Drom,' said Miss Drom.

'Miss Elphick,' said her friend and both of them got their handkerchiefs out and wiped their coffee spoons.

From then on I made light conversation with the sort of determination that has taken lesser men from rags to riches in six months. Les girls didn't yield an inch. Either they ignored my gambits entirely or doled out monosyllabic replies which dripped unwillingly from the extreme end of their lips.

I tried the weather.

Much too hot.

I tried Marjendorf itself.

Quaint but not quite so hygienic as one might have wished.

The Russian language course?

It promised to be most instructive.

The teachers?

All very kind and conscientious.

'Maybe I could give you a hand with your homework?' I addressed my offer pointedly to Miss Drom.

That would be cheating.

'Oh, I don't mean doing it all for you,' I explained. 'I

was thinking more in the lines of a bit of private tuition.'

Did I accompany this remark with a leer? Miss Drom and Miss Elphick both reacted as though I did. They exchanged warning glances, drank their coffee up to just above the dregs and rose to their feet.

'It's time we were going,' said Miss Elphick.

I stood up to allow Miss Drom to slide out. 'How about going for a walk?' I asked getting desperate. 'It said in the brochure that there were lots of nice . . .'

'We like to do a full hour's work before supper,' Miss Drom told me over her shoulder as she followed her chum out of the door. 'After all, we aren't here to enjoy ourselves, are we?'

Monkey Tom when he phoned me that evening at nine, uncharacteristically refused to be daunted by my lack of progress.

'She's just playing hard to get,' he assured me.

'She's not, you know.'

'Ah, these dolly birds are all the same. They like to give a chap the run around.'

'Miss Drom is no dolly bird,' I pointed out sourly, 'and the evident repugnance with which she counters my every advance is not, I give you my word, a display of coyness.'

Monkey sighed heavily down the receiver. 'Flattery,' he suggested.

'You must be joking.'

'God damn it, man, she can't be as bad as all that!'

'Want a bet?'

He sighed again. 'Have you tried throwing your money around? If there's one thing women can't stand, you know, it's a tightwad.'

I scowled out through the glass windows of the call box into the darkened hall as bitter memories came flooding back. 'I bought her and her friend a cup of coffee each this afternoon. Since then the opportunities for lavish expenditure have been limited. All our meals have been paid for in advance and Miss Drom does not drink, smoke or eat foreign chocolates.

So, if you have any thoughts about me plying the po-faced bitch with oysters and champagne, forget it!'

'Her friend?' Monkey was full of bright ideas this evening. 'Now, there's an angle! Why don't you make a big play for the other girl and make the Drom judy jealous? Then, you switch your attention to her and she drops into your arms like a ripe peach.'

Monkey had been seeing too many of those old Hollywood movies on the telly. I tucked the telephone receiver under my ear, lit a cigarette and brooded over the dread possibility of courting Miss Elphick in cold blood.

I had turned up earlier for supper in the Gasthof still under the delusion that I couldn't be as repulsive to any member of the opposite sex as all that. Miss Drom wasn't the type to be suffering from a surfeit of suitors and, sooner or later, she was bound to succumb to the old Brown charisma. Women a damned sight more attractive than she was had hauled up the white flag when I'd hoved into view.

Or heaved.

The entire complement of the Russian course, teachers and pupils, fed in a large back room, well isolated from the rest of the pub's clientele and at tables for eight or nine. We grouped ourselves fairly haphazardly, by age or nationality or what-have-you. There was nothing rigid about it. I deliberately entered the dining-room a little on the late side as I knew there was faint hope that the Misses Drom and Elphick would join me. I should have to join them.

I saw at once that I wasn't going to be trampled to death in any rush. The ladies had installed themselves at a table at the far end of the room. The only other occupant was a very frail old emigrée who, I found out later, gave the lectures on Russian geography. She had a kindly, benevolent expression on her face which was quite remarkable when you consider that Miss Drom and Miss Elphick were bombarding her with a stream of halting small talk in the most execrable Russian I have ever heard. It was only when I took a seat next to them that I understood the old dear's equanimity: she had switched her hearing aid off.

Miss Elphick celebrated my arrival by breaking off in mid-sentence and adjusting the position of a large nobbly walking stick which, for some reason, she had brought with her into the dining-room. Her eyes glinted with satisfaction as she saw that I had seen that I was no longer dealing with a couple of defenceless women.

As supper progressed, however, Miss Drom at any rate became fractionally more sociable. I was able to help her out from time to time as she wallowed in her laborious monologue with the old lady and eventually she herself got fed up with the whole business and condescended to chat to me a bit.

Miss Elphick didn't like this. 'Come along, Muriel, eat up!' she said brusquely when we were only half way through the pudding course. 'We shall be late for the lecture.'

'What lecture's that?' I asked.

'Nizhny Novgorod,' said Miss Drom, gulping down her pears and custard. 'With coloured slides.' She glanced up at me. 'Are you going?'

There are some things above and beyond the call of duty. And a magic lantern show on Nizhny Novgorod is one of them. I shook my head. 'I'm expecting a phone call,' I said.

Which brings us back very neatly to me in the telephone kiosk with Monkey Tom still rabbiting away at the other end of the wire.

'What did you say?' I demanded.

'God!' moaned Monkey, who seemed to have got back to normal. 'Why don't you listen? I said you'd have to get cracking. We've got to make the snatch as soon as possible.'

'No, before that.'

'I said the boys were getting restless. They don't go much on being stuck out here in the backwoods with damn all to do.'

'Oh, hard cheese!' I commented bitterly.

'No, well, you know how it is – this dump we're in is a bit short on feminine company. There's nothing but a few old peasant women with figures like potato sacks.' He sniggered most unpleasantly. 'That's why the boys are anxious to meet the Drom dolly – see? We're going to draw lots for her.'

'Draw lots for her?'

Monkey appreciated my surprise. 'Well, I did think I should have had first tumble, me being the boss and everything, but you can pull your rank too often in my experience. After all, this is only a sort of side-issue, really. It doesn't affect my authority and standing, if you see what I mean, so I agreed we'd settle it by the turn of a card.'

I gazed at the phone in shocked silence.

'Don't worry, though!' Monkey's voice came through tinnily but blithely. 'We're going to cut you in as well. It's all going to be done fair, square and above board. You'll get your turn.'

As soon as he rang off I tried to get through to that emergency number in Vienna, being of the opinion that the sooner I dropped this little lot in somebody else's lap the better. Things were beginning to get rather nasty. The kidnapping of Sir Maurice's daughter was a dastardly enough conception in itself but that the likes of Monkey Tom, Cyril the Shiv, Burp and Punchie Lewis should be gambling for the poor girl's favours was too much. Was nothing sacred these days?

Now, I don't want to criticize the Austrian telephone service. I'm sure they did their best, such as it was. Suffice it to say that an hour's increasingly bad-tempered effort on both sides achieved nothing except two wrong numbers, one in Linz and the other, oddly enough, in Kanselhöne-Annenheim. It was after some very frank speaking by the subscriber in Kanselhöne-Annenheim that the long distance operator suggested tearfully that I should try again for the number I wanted the following day.

Tight-lipped, I agreed and left the telephone box more or less committed to playing along with the kidnapping lark for a bit longer. After all, I wasn't too keen to start crossing swords with the Monkey Tom consortium until I had something more than just my own strong right arm to defend me.

I didn't sleep at all well that night and it wasn't just that my couch had been stuffed with bricks, either.

In the morning I pursued Miss Drom with undiminished ardour. I latched on to her at the breakfast table and even succeeded in getting her to let me carry her books on the long dusty walk to the village school which we had appropriated for our classes. Upper Austria was sweltering in a heat wave and the morning was already uncomfortably warm. Miss Drom had compensated for her total ignorance of the Russian language by stocking up on an excessive supply of linguistic aids. In answer to my seemingly humorous enquiry as to what the hell she'd got in her briefcase, I discovered that I was toting three large dictionaries, two elementary grammars and a learned tome on irregular verbs which the stupid nit had borrowed, God knows why, from the library.

Thanks to my self-sacrifice, Miss Drom arrived at the school looking cool and calm with her little white cotton gloves unsullied. Oh, yes, she was wearing white cotton gloves. And white cotton ankle socks, too, but I prefer not to think about them.

I can't say that closer acquaintance with Miss Drom made her appear any more enticing. She didn't, if I may so phrase it, grow on one. Indeed, one would have brushed her off pretty damned quick if she had. No, on the contrary, the harsh light of day revealed facets of her personality which had been mercifully concealed in the poorly-lit interior of the Gasthof. She was very flat-chested for such a large girl. She was knock-kneed and thick around the ankles. Her eyes were close set, her brow was low and she habitually looked as though she had just downed a couple of pints of best vinegar. Believe me, being seen around in her company was doing my reputation as a man of fashion and discernment no good at all.

The morning passed, oh, so slowly. I was worn out, anyway, by my sleepless night and the boredom of the Russian lessons was excruciating. I yawned and fidgeted through the dictation class set at the cat-on-the-mat level and felt the school bench biting into my bones as we ploughed haltingly through the first declension of masculine nouns.

The mid-morning coffee break brought little relief and no rest as I queued up to buy the coffee for all three of us. Miss Drom and Miss Elphick, their lips loosened by caffeine, became quite talkative and for a quarter of an hour regaled me with spiteful comments on the other (and younger) members of the course. They paused every now and again to ask if I didn't agree that the dress, appearance, speech and manners of our juniors were not perfectly deplorable. Of course I agreed and hastened to explain that the feverish glances I had been bestowing on some of the bronzed beauties milling around were motivated solely by disgust.

After coffee, the conversation class. The theme was the iniquities of Stalin's forcible collectivization of the peasants and, as a topic for conversation, it died the death well before Miss Elphick had worked out what it meant. The final class was a bit better and I slept sweetly through a lecture on Lermontov, as did almost everybody else.

Carrying Miss Drom's load of books back to the Gasthof, I was as keen to get on with the kidnapping as even Monkey Tom could have wished. Whatever the future held, it would have to be an improvement.

Faint glimmerings of a possible plan that might keep Monkey happy for a bit came when Miss Elphick mentioned a forthcoming attraction. A Russian film, it appeared, was to be laid on for us the following evening after supper. I didn't really start getting worked up about this until I learned where the venue was to be: a converted barn right on the outskirts of the village which was used for occasional cinematograph performances.

'We must remember to take a torch with us,' said Miss Elphick with that air of brisk competence which was perhaps her most nauseating characteristic. 'It'll be pitch dark by the time we come out.'

A whole series of clever ideas went skittering through my mind. 'What's the film?' I asked.

'Gobbledegook,' said Miss Drom, her inability to pronounce any Russian word of more than one syllable letting her down again.

'What?'

Eventually we worked it out that it was Tolstoy's *Resurrection* in a mammoth Soviet production which would last six hours. Mercifully we were to endure it in two parts, one this week and one next.

'I say,' I said with that fatuous heartiness for which I was rapidly become notorious, 'we ought to get up a little theatre party, what?'

Miss Drom was uncivilly blunt. 'Why?'

'Well, just to celebrate the occasion, don't you know. And besides I wouldn't dream of letting you girls trail back late at night unescorted right through the village. Heaven only knows what might happen!'

'I shall have my walking stick,' Miss Elphick assured me grimly. 'Muriel and I are well able to look after ourselves.'

'It'll be my treat,' I said, and that clinched it as the tickets were going to cost twenty-five Austrian Schillings a head and neither Miss Drom nor Miss Elphick exactly chucked their money around.

Having got this far I must confess I rather let my ingenuity run away with me. It was the challenge, I suppose. I mean, it's not every day you get the opportunity of planning the perfect kidnapping, is it? Anyhow, I spent the rest of the day sizing up the potential of the other males on the course. It was unlikely that any of them would rush at the chance to make up a foursome and I guessed that I should have to resort to some kind of inducement. But first I had to select my man. Not too young – which eliminated three-quarters of the students – and not too old – which ruled out the entire male teaching staff. Eventually I found a likely candidate in the bar. It was late afternoon and he was reading a copy of *Last Exit to Brooklyn*, in English, over a cup of coffee. He was a sallow-complexioned chap, about my age but nothing like as well preserved. There was a rather scruffy, down-at-heel air about him but that was all to the good as he'd probably be grateful for the opportunity to earn an honest penny.

I got myself a glass of wine and joined him at his table. 'I say, do you speak English?'

He pushed his spectacles back on his nose. 'Of course.'

That was one hurdle that had to be surmounted because neither Miss Drom nor Miss Elphick possessed more than a couple of grunts in German.

I made my approach delicately. 'Can I offer you a glass of wine?'

He was surprised and slightly suspicious but he accepted. I ordered the wine. 'Cheers!'

'To your health!'

'Would you – er – like to earn some money?'

He considered the question carefully. 'How much and for what?'

'Five pounds?' I suggested.

He took another sip of wine and did his mental arithmetic. 'So – let us say four hundred Austrian Schillings. Continue, please.'

There were no flies on this Bube.

I explained about the film which was to be shown the following night. 'I'll pay for your ticket, of course,' I added, seeing no reason to economise with the ill-gotten gains Monkey had given me for expenses.

He looked pleased. 'Good, I wanted to see that picture but I could not afford the price. But you have not told me what it is you wish me to do.'

I explained about my little theatre party. 'Now, all I want you to do is to make up the fourth, see? We'll have supper together here – with a bottle of wine, perhaps – and then go to the cinema. When we get there, you will assist me to ensure that I sit next to Miss Drom.'

He frowned. 'Miss Drom?'

I sighed. ' The one in the tartan skirt with the white ankle socks.'

He rolled his eyes up so that the whites glowed milkily in

the dimness of the bar. 'Lieber Gott!' he breathed.

I didn't care much for his attitude but I wasn't in any position to get shirty about it. I consoled myself with a few unkind thoughts about bloody foreigners and went doggedly on. 'When we leave the cinema, we shall split up into two mixed couples. This may not be as easy as it sounds but it will be your duty to get Miss Elphick' – I answered his raised eyebrows – 'the one with the walking stick – away so as to leave me and Miss Drom alone for at least an hour.'

'You wish me to make love to Fräulein Elphick?'

'If you like.'

He looked so groggy that I ordered another couple of glasses of wine. When they came, he'd made up his mind.

'No!' he said.

I was not unprepared for the setback. 'Eight hundred Austrian Schillings,' I said. 'Four hundred now and four hundred on the successful completion of your duty.'

I was intending to do the decent by him, cross my heart. I was going to leave the second four hundred in an envelope with the proprietor of the Gasthaus but the lousy Kraut cut his own throat.

'How do I know you are to be trusted?'

That insolent remark lost him four hundred Schillings. 'An Englishman's word is his bond,' I replied haughtily.

He shrugged his shoulders. 'I will believe you.'

We solemnly shook hands and then, as his hand remained palm-upwards in front of me, I got my wallet out and paid over the first instalment.

'Now,' I said as he carefully counted the money and checked each note, 'you'll get the balance at breakfast the day after tomorrow, provided you give me a full hour alone with Miss Drom. More, if you can.'

He eyed me greedily. 'How about an extra fifty for every hour over the first one?'

Why not? It wasn't going to cost me anything. We shook hands again and, since our glasses were empty, I ordered more wine.

Hans – we had now slipped easily into first names – with three glasses of free wine slopping around inside him, got quite forthcoming. 'You are truly wishing to seduce Fräulein Drom?' he asked, still not really believing me.

It seemed easier to say yes.

'But, why? Even at your age you could surely do better.' He leaned forward. 'Perhaps I could arrange something for you? Some of the young ladies here . . .'

'I happen to be interested in Miss Drom,' I said firmly.

'But, why? She has' – he flapped his hands about as he sought for the mot juste – ' pimples.'

Pimples? Now, that was really a gross slander! Miss Drom's complexion, while nothing to write home about, was free of all such blemishes and I told Hans so.

'No, no, not on the face!' he explained impatiently. 'Here,' – he thumped himself vigorously on the chest – 'instead of bosoms!'

Six

Monkey was delighted when I reported my progress to him
and between us we finalized the arrangements. I had already
reconnoitred the village and decided that the bottom corner
of the village cemetery would be a nice quiet spot. Monkey
promised he would be there waiting with the car and the rest
of the gang at midnight.

'No, better make it half-past eleven,' I said. 'We come out
of the cinema about a quarter past and I don't know if I can
detain her for more than fifteen minutes or so without arousing
her suspicions.'

This perfectly straightforward observation inspired Monkey
to suggest several ways, all of them lewd, in which Miss Drom
and I might occupy our time. I brought the conversation to a
close.

When I'd got rid of Monkey Tom and his disgusting mind,
I rang that Viennese number again. This time the operator
assured me that she'd got through, but there was no reply. I
waited half an hour and tried once more. Same result.

This was worrying. It was one thing to plan the kidnapping
of Miss Drom as a sort of academic exercise to keep Monkey
from slitting my throat but quite another to be confronted
with the prospect of having to carry it out. I did consider
doing a speedy bunk but, apart from a lively apprehension
that Monkey would make it a point of honour to catch up

with me, I did feel under some obligation to Sir Maurice. Not much, but some. If his only child was about to be abducted, the least I could do was keep an eye on things.

Still it was no good crying over unobtainable telephone numbers and I could always try yet again later on. After supper. I don't like missing my meals.

Not that the food dished up by the Gasthof scaled any gastronomic heights. Or maybe it was the company I was forced to keep that took the edge off my appetite. Whilst the other tables were all centres of mirth and innocent merriment, ours was distinguished only by the sullen speed with which we wolfed down our food. Conversation with Miss Drom and Miss Elphick was never exactly sparkling and the old geography teacher only raised her head from her plate to give us a vague smile from time to time.

During this – did she but know it – her penultimate evening meal in Marjendorf, Miss Drom stuffed her face with a book propped up on the empty flower vase in front of her. She had been given a role in the play which the students were to present as part of a varied entertainment in the Church Hall at the end of the course. Herr Doktor Klimenko, the director, personally selected the cast on a diplomatic rather than an artistic basis. Even so he had not felt able to give Miss Drom more than the smallest possible part and ever since she had been mumbling her two lines over and over in an effort to memorize them. Miss Elphick, a mere member of the choir which was to render no less than three Ukranian folk songs for our edification and delight at the same entertainment was apt to be a mite scathing about her Thespian chum.

'I can't think what you're making such a fuss about, Muriel, dear,' she observed as we waited for our helpings of flannelled veal. 'You've got nearly a fortnight.'

Muriel dear merely scowled and mumbled away to herself harder than ever.

Miss Elphick couldn't leave well alone. 'Anyhow, I'm sure you're getting the pronunciation all wrong.'

It was Miss Drom's turn to come the old acid. 'Well, if

I am, dear, I'm sure you'd be the last to know. Count Dudintsev said only yesterday that you had no ear at all.'

Count Dudintsev was the unfortunate octogenarian whose job it was to instil in us a love of Russian poetry. He went around the village with a permanently pained expression and had an unfortunate habit of ducking into doorways whenever he saw any member of his class approaching.

Miss Elphick gave one of those humourless laughs. 'I don't think one needs an ear, darling,' she cackled. 'One look at Mr Brown's face is enough.'

Which left me with the difficult task of assuring a fuming Miss Drom that, in fact, I considered the pronunciation of every one of her six words to be quite beyond reproach. Such an assurance went against the grain but I couldn't afford any rifts in the lute which might affect my plans for the following night.

I had just about managed to placate the pair of them when Hans slouched past. We exchanged a comradely wave.

The old geography teacher suddenly came to life. She leaned across Miss Drom and poked me in the chest with her table knife. 'That one is a spy!' she announced loudly and clearly in Russian. 'For which side is, unfortunately, unknown.'

Miss Drom, Miss Elphick and I gazed at the old dear in astonishment as she licked her knife delicately and continued with her meal.

'What did she say?' demanded Miss Elphick.

It was no time for honesty. I don't like people, however gaga, talking about spies. It makes me nervous. Especially when I have just entered into a quasi-business relationship with one of them. 'She was merely remarking what a nice fellow Hans is,' I said.

'Of course,' cooed Miss Drom with a superior smile at her friend. 'Didn't you understand, Elphie, darling?'

After supper I renounced an exhibition, by three of our hairier young gentlemen, of Cossack dancing, and repaired once more to the telephone kiosk. Here, since my memory is not quite of the photographic variety, I tried a new wheeze.

To the despair of the operator, I began asking for variations on the original number. Well, you've got to try everything, haven't you?'

I expect some clever devil has already worked out how many variations you can get with a six-figure number. I've no doubt it's astronomical. It wasn't long before I had exhausted both the telephone operator and my supply of loose change. Oh, to hell with it, I thought, and went to bed.

I will draw a veil over the exquisite tedium I endured the next day. The only bright spot was that Miss Drom, while still not liking me all that much, was beginning to get used to me. It helped that she and Miss Elphick were going through one of those minor crises which dear friends tend to experience every now and again, and were passing the time having well bred little spats at each other. In order to pull a fast one on her chum, Miss Drom was now willing to accept my surreptitious help with her at-sight translation and staggered everybody by her instant fluency.

I played truant after lunch and had another session on the telephone, trying the Viennese number and as many variants as I had time for. The answer was still a lemon.

I went back to my lodgings and tried to work out what I ought to do next. If I told Miss Drom the whole story, would she believe me? Should I throw myself on the mercy of the Austrian police? Should I try and ring up Sir Maurice in London and ask him what to do. Should I just quietly disappear by myself and let the chips fall where they may? Should I . . .

The afternoon was terribly hot and that doctor's couch can't have been as uncomfortable as I'd thought. It was after half-past four when I woke up. My subconscious, unlike what they tell you in books, hadn't solved a damned thing and now time had run out on me as well. I should have to go through with the kidnapping and play it by ear from there. I even managed to kid myself that this was the most sensible course of action that I could take, that – really – this was what Sir Maurice had always intended I should do.

Not feeling one bit better now that I had come to a decision, I began to prepare for my departure from Marjendorf. Not that there was much I could do. I stowed away as many of my belongings as I could into my pockets. Everything else would have to be left behind. I seemed to be leaving a trail of lost property across the length and breadth of Austria. My passport and wallet got top priority, followed closely by a toothbrush and a cheap little safety razor that Cyril the Shiv had bought for me. A clean pair of socks went into one jacket pocket and a couple of new handkerchiefs into the other. I could carry my raincoat over my arm and perhaps conceal a spare pair of shoes in . . . In the end I did so well that my landlady was only going to get a cheap plastic suitcase out of me. With two shirts and a sweater on, I was as hot as hell and looked like Fatty of the Fourth but, at least I was cutting down on the number of clues I should be leaving behind for the police. We secret agents have to think of these things.

And as soon as I had thought of them I began to wish I hadn't. Right now I could do without visions of slavering alsatians, man-hunts and the insides of stinking Continental jails. In some American states, I recalled in spite of myself, they sent you to the chair for kidnapping. I trusted that the Austrians had a more civilized approach. What with Freud and everything they probably only gave you psychiatric treatment for eighty years. Or ninety, when they heard the cock-eyed yarn I was going to be spinning. Would they be sophisticated enough to appreciate that in helping to kidnap Miss Drom I was really only protecting her?

By the time I'd finished defending myself before a row of boot-faced Austrian judges (and reducing them to tears by my eloquence) I was late for supper. When I arrived in the dining-room everybody had got his or her feet well in the trough. There was quite a gay atmosphere. People were talking excitedly and laughing a lot and making silly jokes in pidgin Russian. How I envied their carefree innocence! Our table, of course, was the exception to the rule. The old geography

C*

teacher was still there at the head, smiling contentedly as the maid-of-all-work gave her an extra-large helping. Miss Elphick was on one side of her, tucking in without relish. Miss Drom was on the other, casting the odd pearl into deaf ears.

It would be worth soiling my hands with a kidnapping to get away from this lot.

Hans, I noted grimly, was not there. I sat down next to Miss Drom and then had a look around the room for my wandering boy. I soon spotted the rat, sitting at another table and having one whale of a time with a flaxen-haired floosie whose above-the-table assets were such as to make strong men go weak at the knees.

I lost no time in putting a stop to *that*. Hans caught my glowering eye and, whispering something screamingly funny in his girl friend's ear, brought his half-empty plate across to our table. Miss Elphick's eyebrows all but did a vertical take-off when she found him slipping into the seat next to her. Hans felt that some greeting was necessary. 'Hello, you lovely strumpet!' he said, pronouncing each syllable with Teutonic precision.

With a start like that to the evening, who needs disasters?

Sticky, that's the word which best describes my little dinner party. Miss Drom and Miss Elphick gathered their skirts around them as though they were being beset by lepers and Hans withdrew into a sulky silence. The old geography teacher didn't do much to lighten the atmosphere by continually crossing herself and making mystic signs at Hans to ward off the evil eye.

When, eventually, we set off for the cinema, it is hardly to be wondered at that the two girls went on ahead, clinging to each other for protection, while Hans and I slouched after them with faces as black as thunder.

It was, weather-wise, a beautiful evening. Dusk was falling and the villagers looked kindly and benevolent as they stood in their doorways, gossiping and watching almost the entire Russian course troop past. Every now and again one or other of the students would catch sight of his landlady and call out a cheery greeting to her. All around young, happy voices came wafting through the soft warm air. It was a night to reconcile man with his creation.

Our sullen quartet plodded on. When we reached the hall in which the film was to be shown, Hans and the girls stood smartly back to give me a clear passage to the cashier. I damned them all to the living fires of hell and bought the tickets.

Inside the hall the sight of row upon row of hard kitchen chairs did nothing to improve our morale. We found four vacant places and I shoved Hans first into the row with such vehemence that he all but fell flat on his face. Miss Elphick, complete with her trusted shillelagh and pocket torch, went next, assisted by a slightly more courteous push in the back. I myself had intended to sit between Miss Elphick and Miss Drom but the girls were determined not to be parted. Miss Drom, with a gasp of terror, ducked under my arm and flung herself into the chair next to her friend. I sighed and resigned myself to taking the only remaining seat. All was not completely lost. I had got Miss Drom next to me, even though I should have to share favours with the redoubtable Miss Elphick.

When we'd been waiting there for more than quarter of an hour I felt like kicking myself. All my plans had been based on the assumption that the show would start on time. How could I have been such an idiot? Fancy me of all people imagining that anything organized by Russians would be even vaguely punctual. Too late I remembered those soirées which my old Russian teachers had been forever getting up; tearful Armenian folk songs, ill-executed balalaika solos and heavily prompted recitals of Pushkin and Lermontov. The contents of the entertainments had varied but the timing arrangements were always the same. The shows were invariably advertised as starting at 7.30 in the hope that the audience would be there by eight so that the performance could begin, as it had always been intended that it should, at half-past eight. The public regrettably, was always one jump ahead and the first rendition was always fought against the apologetic whispers and embarrassed giggles of the late-comers.

'I wonder,' said Miss Drom frostily, holding me responsible for the delay, 'how much longer we are going to have to wait.'

I indicated the entwined couple on the seats in front of us. 'They don't seem to be very worried!' I laughed.

Her face crinkled up into a pretty good imitation of a prune. 'I think that,' she said, 'is positively disgusting!'

Whereupon I resolved to stifle my baser instincts until the lights went down, which they eventually did to a chorus of mocking cat-calls. After only a couple of false starts we were off! 'Gold Mining in Siberia'. A boring, twenty-five minute short that was full of the usual Soviet Workers all laughing their happy heads off. I think I must have dozed off somewhere along the line – I had had a very strenuous and worrying day – because the next thing I remember is that we were well into the big film. And the heroine, Maslova, was a right smashing bit of crackling! Before long I was drooling over her and all but hissing every time the cad-hero appeared on the screen.

Indeed, I got so carried away by the celluloid drama that it was only when they put the lights on for a five-minute interval that I remembered (a) how damned hard those chairs were and (b) Miss Drom.

'It's very good, isn't it?' she ventured, not, poor moron, having understood a word.

I licked my dry lips. 'Yes!' I croaked so passionately that Miss Drom spent the rest of the interval gabbling anxiously with Miss Elphick.

The second half started with a long tedious chunk in which the delectable Maslova did not appear so I was able to devote myself to thoughts of duty.

A crack, comparable with that of a rifle shot, rang out as I hitched my chair nearer to Miss Drom and attempted with suave casualness to drape my arm across the back of her chair. One or two nosey parkers peered round to see what was going on.

Those with salacious minds must have been bitterly disappointed. Miss Drom sat bolt upright, as though somebody had shoved a poker down her spine, and quivered.

'Excellent film, don't you think?' I murmured as I bent forward and took her hand.

For a second everything hung in the balance.

Then . . .

'Ugh!' shuddered Miss Drom fastidiously. 'Your hand is all flabby and *damp*!' She pushed me away and got her handkerchief out to wipe her palm. Then she retrieved her gloves, put them back on and folded her arms resolutely across her chest.

I went back to watching the film and for the rest of the performance I kept my greasy paws to myself.

When the show was over, though, just before midnight, my restraint got its reward. In the general stampede for the exits, Miss Drom and I got separated from Hans and Miss Elphick. Miss Drom, being such a refined sort of girl, shrank from the struggling and brawling going on around us to such an extent that we were almost the last couple to leave the hall.

Outside it was pitch black as the village didn't possess any street lighting and the moon had not yet risen. I stood politely aside so that Miss Drom could encounter any hidden hazards which might lie before us.

'Oh, dear!' she squeaked. 'I do think Elphie might have waited! She knows she's got the only torch.'

We stumbled out onto the road now so I could afford to be generous. 'Never mind, we'll manage. Here, you take my arm!'

Miss Drom weighed the unknown horrors of the night against the devil she knew and I'm delighted to be able to tell you that I won.

From then on all should have been smooth sailing as, arm-in-arm and nicely isolated from our companions, we picked our way through the inky blackness to where Monkey Tom and his gang were waiting. Unfortunately Miss Drom's night vision proved to be several degrees better than mine, as was her sense of direction and her knowledge of the twisting village streets. We hadn't gone a hundred yards before I was bloody well lost. Miss Drom, on the other hand, was supremely sure of her bearings and dragged me along at an alarming rate. If I didn't do something quickly, I could see us arriving back safe and sound at her lodgings and Monkey coming after me with a meat cleaver.

'Now, just a minute!' I protested, slamming on the brakes and jerking Miss Drom to a halt. 'Are you sure we're going in the right direction?'

'Of course I'm sure!' Miss Drom didn't take criticism too well. 'And do try to get a move on, Mr Brown! I'm getting a bit sick of you dragging back at every step.'

'I still think we're heading in the wrong direction,' I insisted stubbornly. 'I think you're taking us straight toward the cemetery.'

'Of course I'm not, you fool!' At times Miss Drom did so remind one of her dear father. 'The cemetery's down that road there to the right. This road leads straight into the village square. The petrol station's just ahead of us on the right and this building here is the abattoir. Now, stop arguing and come along! I know perfectly well exactly where we are.'

And so – now – did I. Oh, I'm not just a pretty face.

Actually, things in general were beginning to look a little less black than they had done since even my failing eyes had got used to the darkness and, here and there, windows were lighting up as people reached their lodgings.

Having found which road led to the bone-yard, I was left with the task of enticing Miss Drom down it. It was a task which might have daunted a lesser man, but I've been blessed with an imaginative mind.

I clutched Miss Drom round the neck. 'Good God!' I choked. 'Did you see that?'

'See what?' She tried to unhook my fingers.

'*That!*' I gasped, gesticulating wildly so that she couldn't be sure where I was pointing. 'It was Miss Elphick wasn't it,?'

'Elphie?' Miss Drom peered at me through the darkness. 'How could it have been Miss Elphick? She'll have been home for ages by now.' She sniffed the air suspiciously. 'You've not been drinking, have you?'

I went on with my Laurence Olivier act and pointed a trembling finger down the road which led to the cemetery. 'There it is again!' I hissed. 'And who's that leaning over her? Is it Hans?'

I don't honestly think Miss Drom believed a word I was saying but, determined not to stand for any nonsense, she set off at a brisk march towards the cemetery. I skipped gleefully along in her wake.

Before we had got half-way along the uneven surface of the lane, I caught sight of the waiting Mercedes. It was parked without lights close up against the cemetery wall and a casual passer-by might have thought was empty, if it hadn't been for the polka dots of four fiercely burning cigarettes coming from inside.

Miss Drom had seen the car, too. 'There's a car there,' she said, as though it was my fault.

'Oh, never mind that!' I snapped. 'What about poor Miss Elphick and that black villain, Hans?'

Miss Drom began to slow down. 'You didn't really see them, did you?' she asked doubtfully. 'I mean, I know Elphie. She'd never come down here alone with a . . .'

We were level now with the Mercedes and the time had come for direct action. I clasped Miss Drom in my arms. 'You are being kidnapped,' I informed her with, all things considered, admirable sang-froid. 'Come along quietly and no harm will befall you.'

I doubt if the stupid bitch even heard me. At the first physical contact she had just erupted and, for so puny a girl, was inflicting a deal too much damage. Her nails ripped a couple of times down my face before I managed to get her flailing arms clamped down to her sides. Then she lashed out at me with her well-shod feet. All my entreaties for calm and co-operation proved unavailing and when she bit the hand I had placed over her mouth to stifle the screams I considered I had done my fair share and more.

'Well, come on!' I bawled at the hitherto unresponsive bulk of the Mercedes. 'Don't just sit there, you damned fools! Get out and give me a hand!'

Miss Drom chose this moment when my attention was partly diverted by the need to summon assistance to deal me a most foul and unladylike blow slightly below the bread basket. My screams mingled with hers.

I heard the clicks as the doors of the Mercedes swung open and the whole scene was suddenly illuminated as the interior courtesy light came on. Miss Drom twisted in my grasp like a demented eel as she turned to confront this new threat. Cyril the Shiv was the first to fling himself into the fray with his flick knife clenched between his teeth. It was a terrifying spectacle and, much to my gratification, Miss Drom fainted clean away.

I let her drop to the ground and hastened to examine my own injuries. Monkey Tom, Cyril, Burp and Punchie Lewis gathered silently round the prostrate body of Miss Drom and somebody switched on a pocket torch. The beam played on Miss Drom's face and the silence became heavier.

It was little Burp who spoke first and succinctly summed up the gang's reaction to the first sight of their victim. 'Jesus Christ!' he said.

Cyril the Shiv, usually quite a loquacious fellow, contented himself with an eloquent expectoration and strolled disgustedly back to the car.

Monkey, as leader, obviously felt that something more constructive was expected of him. He scratched his head and then shook it disbelievingly. 'She looks like Marty Feldman!'

Well, it was an interesting idea and one I would have liked to pursue further but time was pressing. The village around us was quiet but we had been making the mother and father of a row and in these enlightened days you couldn't rely on the superstition of the peasants attributing it all to ghosts. I hoisted up my trousers while Burp and Punchie Lewis lifted Miss Drom up and got her with some difficulty into the back of the car. Monkey retrieved her handbag and looked around generally to see if we'd left any clues. Not, as I reflected glumly, that the cops were going to need any stray hairs or muddy footprints to get on *my* trail.

Everybody tumbled into the car and Burp took off with a tyre scream you could have heard in Salzburg. We were well clear of the village and racing headlong down a precipice before those of us in the back of the Mercedes got ourselves sorted out. I eventually managed to heave myself on to one of the tip-up seats and this left Miss Drom, half-sitting, half-lying, on the back seat between Cyril and Monkey. Her eyes were closed and her mouth was open.

'Phase One successfully completed!' announced Monkey proudly. 'Though I must say, Eddie, I thought you were never coming.' He sniggered. 'Cyril, here, reckoned you'd double-crossed us and you should have heard what he was going to do to you when he caught you.'

Miss Drom who'd been playing possum, lunged for the door. Cyril the Shiv yanked her back by the hair.

'Help!' screamed Miss Drom, achieving a fine top C with no apparent effort. 'Au secours! Police! Fire! Murder! Rape!'

'Who does she think she's kidding?' muttered Monkey peevishly as he fumbled in one of his back pockets. 'Here, Cyril, shove some of this down her gob and let's have a bit of peace and quiet.' Unscrewing the top, he handed Cyril a hip flask.

Cyril, who was a remarkably strong chap, managed to pin Miss Drom down against the back of the seat. Her piercing screams ceased as she saw the flask approaching and she clamped her lips shut. Cyril didn't mess about. He seized Miss Drom's nose tightly between his finger and thumb and waited with commendable patience until her mouth sagged open. Then in went the neck of the flask and a considerable quantity of its contents.

Miss Drom, the tears springing into her eyes, choked and coughed and spluttered.

'That should shut her up for a bit,' observed Monkey sourly.

I felt I could do with a snorter myself and I took the flask out of Cyril's hand.

'Here,' shouted Monkey, 'don't . . .'

He was too late. A good four fluid ounces of a rather inferior brandy went searing down my gullet before he'd time to snatch the flask away from me.

Seven

Which is why I can't give you a first-hand account of how we crossed the frontier.

Monkey Tom, that Napoleon of the underworld, had thought of everything. Including a cheap brandy laced with enough knock-out drops to fell a rogue elephant.

When I recovered consciousness it was broad daylight and I was lying on the floor of the car, partly covered by a rug and with somebody's dirty boots planted solidly on my chest. I felt like death warmed up. My eyes were burning, my throat was parched, my stomach . . .

'Where am I?' I groaned.

Monkey raised his feet a couple of inches and peered down at me. 'Oh, shut up!' he said, obviously in a miff about something.

I lay and suffered in silence for a few minutes before painfully dragging myself up into a sitting position. I was surprised to find that I was no longer in the Mercedes. Somewhere along the line I had been transferred into a somewhat smaller, newer car. A Fiat, I found out later. Burp was driving it and Monkey occupied the rear seat in solitary state.

'Where's Miss Drom?' I asked.

'In the boot.'

With many a piteous groan I joined Monkey on the back seat. 'And where are Cyril and Punchie?'

'Driving diversionary cars, of course. Where the hell do you think?'

'I see,' I said closing my eyes against the dazzling light which was thundering in through the window.

'We split up before the frontier,' grunted Monkey.

I thought perhaps he wanted to talk. 'And we've got rid of the Mercedes?'

'You didn't think we were going to drive all the way to the hideout in the same bloody car we did the snatch in, did you? This is the third bus we've used. And lugging you and the girl in and out every time was no bleeding picnic, believe me. What the hell you had to go and grab that bloody flask for . . .'

I hoisted myself up a bit straighter. Oh, my aching bones! 'Where are we?' I wound my window down and let a comparatively cool stream of air play over my face.

'Nearly there.'

'Where's there?'

Monkey didn't get chance to tell me, even if he was going to, because at that precise moment Burp ripped the car off the main road and charged up a goat track into the mountains. For the next twenty minutes conversation was out of the question. As we bumped, rattled and skidded upwards, Burp managed to keep one hand free of the spinning steering wheel to operate the horn. I didn't know which was going to explode first: my head or my stomach. But I had my suspicions. What was happening to poor Miss Drom in the boot didn't bear thinking about. There was, however, one blessed respite when we hurtled round a corner (with a five hundred foot drop on my side) and found ourselves bonnet to bonnet with a truck coming down the hill. The encounter was resolved with the utmost good humour by Burp zipping into reverse and obligingly hanging half the car over the ravine while the truck squeezed past. The truck driver was all gratitude and showered us with buon giornos and grazie tantos.

'Hoho!' I said in the brief interval before Burp took off again. 'We're in Italy.'

Monkey Tom scowled and I wondered, once again, if I wasn't in danger of being a bit too clever. After all, would West Hartlepool Joe be likely to have a henchman in his employ with my obvious cultural attainments? Still, it was no time to bother about moot points like this and I concentrated on preparing myself to make a good death.

We tore in a cloud of dust and chickens through three villages but, when we reached the fourth – and, by the feel of it, the top of a mountain – Burp turned us off on to a side track and we bumped more slowly along this for perhaps a quarter of a mile. I noted that the houses we were now passing were different from the mouldering peasant hovels we'd seen in the villages. Here were much more elegant and sophisticated structures, with brightly painted shutters and charmingly laid out gardens. Such a conspicuous display of wealth could only mean that we were in the quarter of the tourists and the week-enders.

Burp drew up in front of one of the less attractive villas and got out to open the double gates. The car rolled through and, once we were safely behind the high white-washed walls, Monkey mopped his brow.

'Thank God!' he said reverently before turning round on me. 'Come on, you! We've got to get this girl into the house. Burp!'

'Yes, Monkey?'

'Get this car into the garage and fix it! Fast as you can. You can bring the bags and things in later.'

'OK, boss!'

Miss Drom flopped about like a rag doll but Monkey and I got her out of the boot and carted her inside without too much fuss and palaver.

'Dump her on the sofa!' instructed Monkey, who was beginning to behave like a shrunken Charles Laughton on the quarterdeck of the *Bounty*. 'And now, Eddie, you and me's going to have a large whisky.'

'I thought you didn't drink,' I said as I arranged Miss Drom's limp body in a more decorous position.

'I don't but, by God, I'm going to have one now!'

A sentiment with which I heartily concurred.

The room we were in had a small bar in one corner and it was the work of a moment to find a nice unopened bottle of the hard stuff. Monkey and I settled down in a couple of armchairs to kill it and before long we were chattering away together as though we were the oldest and dearest of friends. Monkey, of course – now that the whole thing was over – just couldn't help blowing his own trumpet.

In the greatest detail he insisted on explaining to me precisely how the getaway had been planned and executed. My head was buzzing as cars and number plates were changed, frontiers crossed in all directions, diversionary sorties made into Czechoslovakia, Yugoslavia and Germany, endless permutations rung on the original group of five men and a girl for which the police might be looking. Though I would have died rather than admit it, it did look as though the gang had done a pretty efficient job. The authorities were going to have more than their work cut out to untangle Monkey's elaborate web of deception.

'Have you sent off the ransom note?' I asked, hitting the whisky good and hard while I had the chance.

Monkey placed his hand politely over his mouth to stifle a belch. 'Pardon,' he said. 'Yes, we've arranged to have it posted in Hungary. It'll be on its way by now.' His face slipped back into its normal harassed look. 'And I didn't get that fixed up for free, either. Ask somebody to do a little job for you these days and they charge you the bloody earth. I daren't tell you what this house is costing me – and the fellow's supposed to be an old pal of mine.'

'Never mind,' I comforted him. 'At least you've got West Hartlepool Joe's contribution.'

'You must be joking! That's the sort of hand-out it'd be a pleasure to do without. I just hope Sir Maurice coughs up quick, that's all. If he doesn't I'll be bloody well bankrupt.'

'You don't think he may take it as some sort of practical joke?'

Monkey sagged in his chair. 'Do us a favour, mate!' he begged. 'Maybe I ought to send him a lump of her hair, just to be on the safe side. Or an ear or something.'

I turned to look at the subject of our conversation. She was not there.

'Jesus!' howled Monkey and flung himself out of the room, yelling for Burp.

I went over to the window, just to show willing. If Miss Drom had managed to get away, nobody would be more relieved than me. She'd probably been conscious for quite some time and had just lain there quietly until Monkey and I had got absorbed in our conversation. And good luck to her! One glance was enough to show me that she hadn't gone out of the window. Or, if she had, I'd soon be getting my black tie out of the mothballs. I hadn't appreciated just how high up we were. Yawning in front of me was a sheer drop with at the bottom – miles and miles away – the glinting blue waters of a lake. I shot out a hand to steady myself on the edge of the window. These dizzy heights not being at all my cup of tea.

There was a commotion behind me. Burp, scarlet in the face, was frog-marching Miss Drom back into the room. Behind them came Monkey, flapping and squawking and clucking like an old hen. He vented some of his relieved anxiety on me.

'Well, don't just stand there!' he screamed. 'Give Burp a hand with the bitch! Shove her in that chair!'

Rather diffidently I placed my hand on Miss Drom's shoulder. Whereupon she twisted her head round and bit me quite severely on the thumb. This naturally put me temporarily hors de combat and by the time I'd finished trying to erase her teeth marks from my skin, Miss Drom was securely tied with several miles of rope to her chair.

'That'll fix the cow!' snarled Monkey, and Burp, after giving his knots one last check, went outside again.

'All's well that ends well,' I quipped.

Monkey scowled at me. 'No thanks to you,' he grumbled.

'Where the hell were you? If it hadn't been for Burp grabbing her, she'd have got clean away and we'd have been right up the bloody creek. Well,' – he wiped his forehead with a trembling hand – 'she's had her chance. She'll not get another.'

Miss Drom meanwhile had recovered her own breath. She caught sight of me. 'Judas goat!' she spat. 'Stool pigeon! Filthy scum!'

'If you want to gag her,' said Monkey, turning away indifferently, 'you can bloody well do it yourself.'

Miss Drom now directed her venom at him. 'You won't get away with this! My father happens to be a very influential man and he'll have every police force in Europe hunting you down. I don't know what you expect to gain by seizing me like this. Even you can't be stupid enough to think that anybody's going to pay a miserable collection of cheap thugs like you any ransom money. Why, I don't doubt that the police are already on your trail and, when they catch up with you, you'll get twenty years in prison at the very least. If I were in your shoes, I'd clear off now – before it's too late. My goodness, I wouldn't want to spend the rest of my life rotting away in a cell. And your confederates – are you sure you can trust them? There'll be a huge reward for my safe recovery, you know. Huge! I . . .'

Miss Drom's voice rose shriller and shriller until Monkey's frayed nerves could stand it no longer.

'Holymarymotherofgod!' he groaned. 'Doesn't she ever bloody well belt up?' He jerked his head at me. 'Come on, Eddie! You and me'll go out on the patio and leave her to it.'

Only too thankfully I gathered up the whisky and the glasses and followed him out of the room. Monkey carefully locked the door behind us and pocketed the key.

Outside on the patio with the sun blazing down, life became more bearable. Even Miss Drom's nattering – losing her audience hadn't stilled her tongue – was reduced to a mere irritating murmur in the background. I unfolded a striped canvas chair and spent the rest of the day dozing gently and getting myself a tan. Before it grew dark both Cyril the Shiv and Punchie Lewis turned up and reported that everything had gone off according to plan as far as they were concerned. Monkey received the news without actually throwing his cap over the hill. Indeed, both he and Cyril were extremely restless and nervous, possibly because, unlike Burp and Punchie Lewis, they were bright enough to know the risks they were running. The enterprise wasn't out of the wood yet and there's many a slip between kidnapping your victim and collecting a million quid.

Monkey alternated between gloomily chewing his nails in silence and fretfully going over and over everything that had happened. Was Punchie Lewis sure that nobody had seen him nick that car in Munich? Was Cyril absolutely certain that he'd dropped Miss Drom's gloves near the Austrian customs post on the Czech frontier? Could somebody called Ferdie really be relied upon to phone the police in Copenhagen about having seen five men dragging a protesting girl into a car?

'For Christ's sake,' snapped Cyril, 'of course he can! You know Ferdie.'

'But did you give him an accurate description of Miss Drom?' asked Monkey, wringing his hands in agony of apprehension. 'It'll be no damned good if the cops don't think it's her.'

'I know it'll be no damned good!' yelled Cyril, jumping to his feet. 'Why don't you stop picking at it? If something's gone crook, it's gone crook, hasn't it? All the blabbering in the world won't alter that.'

An anguished Monkey gazed up at him. 'Oh, God, Cyril, you don't think anything really has gone crook, do you?'

'No, I don't!' Cyril looked round for something he could vent his temper on and found me. 'What the hell are you looking so bloody pleased about?' he demanded.

I handled it quite well, I thought. Turning the other cheek trying to calm him down, treating the thing as a joke. He drew his knife on me. Luckily the others grabbed him before he could carve his initials on my bare chest and, after an exciting little scuffle, we all eventually simmered down.

'How about some grub?' asked Burp, neatly turning our attention to more mundane matters. 'I haven't had a decent scoff for twenty-four hours.'

Monkey latched on to this eagerly. 'Good idea!' he said. 'Who's going to do the cooking? Punchie?'

Not if he could help it. 'Aw, heck, boss,' he rumbled, 'you know I can't work all them gadgets in the kitchen.'

'How about you, Burp?'

'I've got a few more jobs to do on the car, boss,' said Burp, already on his feet and moving. 'I was going to leave 'em till morning but maybe . . .' Exit Burp.

I knew Monkey wouldn't dare ask Cyril so I volunteered. I'd had enough sun bathing for one day, anyhow. I put my shirt on. Cyril, however had other ideas.

'Why don't you get the tart to do it?' he asked. 'Cooking's women's work, isn't it?'

Monkey hesitated. 'Suppose she refuses?'

'Suppose she does?' Cyril smirked unpleasantly.

Monkey shot him a worried glance. 'Steady on, Cyril! We don't want any rough stuff.'

'Who says there's going to be any rough stuff? Give me ten minutes with her and I promise you I won't lay a finger on her.' The smirk widened. 'She'll cook us some grub though.'

Cyril was a sadistic, slimy bastard and the last thing I wanted to do was get at outs with him. On the other hand I could hardly stand idly by while he shredded Miss Drom into tiny pieces. I began walking firmly in the direction of the kitchen.

'Save your strength,' I advised him. 'She's the world's worst cook. She told me so in Marjendorf.'

Cyril, not fooled for one moment, leaned back in his chair. 'Well, hark at little Sir Galahad!' he sneered. 'Do you know what, Monkey? I reckon he's taken a fancy to the bird.'

'He's welcome!' said Monkey bitterly. 'Me, I wouldn't have her, not if they were giving her away with Green Shield stamps. Imagine having that yack-yacking at you all bleeding night! Blimey, I've come across some lousy old scrubbers in my time but she takes the bloody biscuit. You can leave my name out of the hat.'

'Mine, too,' grunted Punchie Lewis. 'And Burp's not keen, neither. He reckons there's a couple of Eyetie girls in village that'll do us.'

'Well, well!' Cyril was still gazing speculatively at me. 'Everybody's getting cold feet all of a sudden, aren't they?' He turned away and stared out blankly over the abyss. 'I think I've lost interest, too.'

'Now, hang on a minute!' I began but Cyril waved my protests aside.

'She's all yours, Eddie, boy! Tonight and every night! And may all your troubles be little ones.'

If there'd been any ground glass amongst the pile of provisions in the kitchen, I'd have used it on the lot of them – Miss Drom included. Why was it always me that was left holding the baby? Not that Miss Drom was any baby and not that I had the slightest intention of holding her, but you know what I mean. I must be one of nature's fall guys.

However, by the time I'd got half way through whipping up my culinary speciality – fried egg and chips – I was kidding myself that everything was really for the best. Sooner or later I had to have a heart-to-heart tête-à-tête with Miss Drom and it might be as well to have it sooner. Our spending the night together wouldn't arouse the suspicions of the gang though I should continue protesting out of sheer pride. Cyril the Shiv might start putting two and two together if I didn't.

Miss Drom spurned my egg and chips, which was her privilege of course, but there was no need to draw everyone's attention to the fact that they were swimming in fat. She should have seen Punchie Lewis's cooking. Monkey took one look at his plate, heaved and declared that it was more than his ulcer could stand. I fetched him a couple of dry biscuits and a glass of soda water. Everybody else, though, was too hungry to care and the egg and chips disappeared in record time. Which left us with nothing much else to do but go to bed.

The sleeping arrangements at the hideaway were somewhat peculiar, not to say inconvenient, but they had their advantages from the kidnappers' point of view. There were three bedrooms: one at the back and two overlooking the staggering view down to the lake. The trouble with the two front rooms was that the only way you could get into the second was by going through the first. Maybe this second room was originally intended to be a boxroom or a dressing-room or a nursery or something. Whatever the explanation, it certainly made a nice secure little prison for me and Miss Drom, especially when Monkey Tom and Cyril installed themselves in the outer room.

Miss Drom and I were conducted to our chamber with all the bawdy comment and rollicking good humour that supposedly accompanied the bedding of newly married couples in the Middle Ages. The gang guffawed themselves sick and every saucy quip was capped by another even saucier. I maintained an aloof, dignified silence but Miss Drom, not really understanding what was going on, attempted to give back as good as she got. Unfortunately, she had neither the vocabulary nor the imagination to compete with a foursome of blackguards like Monkey and his boys. It was only when the two of us were alone in our room and she saw me wedging a chair under the door handle that her vituperative powers came into their own and we got what she thought about me played with full orchestra.

I tried to calm her down.

She started screaming blue murder and made a rush for the window. When she saw the fate that awaited her out there, she drew back and decided to sell her honour dearly where she stood. It was lucky for me that the bedroom was extremely sparsely furnished, containing nothing more lethal than a narrow bed and an old dressing-table. If it hadn't been, Miss Drom would have made short work of me. Even with the limited implements at her disposal she managed to split my head open with a shrewd and savage blow. I hadn't envisaged anybody using a dressing-table drawer as a weapon.

'For the love of God,' I said as I tried to staunch the river of blood pouring down my neck, 'calm down, can't you? I'm not going to touch you, honest injun!'

'Filthy pig!' she spat. 'Gutter rat! You keep away from me!'

There was nothing I would have liked better. My head had shattered the drawer into several pieces and Miss Drom now selected the largest piece. She began jabbing its splintery end viciously at my face. I could see that if I didn't watch it I'd be greeting the dawn with at least one eye missing. I approached as near as I dared and reduced my voice to a level which, I hoped, wouldn't carry through to the room next door where Cyril was most probably glued to the key hole.

'Listen,' I hissed, 'I'm on your side!'

'Barbarian!' bellowed Miss Drom. 'Lecher! Seducer of young girls! Snake in the grass!'

I side-stepped a well-directed swipe during which a rusty nail I'd not noticed before missed my throat by no more than a whisker. I tried again. 'Your father sent me! Sir Maurice! I work for him. I'm a member of S.O.D.'

Without relaxing her guard Miss Drom considered this. 'Liar!'

'Oh, be reasonable, woman! Why should I lie about it?'

'I don't know,' said Miss Drom haughtily. 'You're probably an habitual liar and this is some kind of trick.'

'My name is Edmund Brown. Hasn't your father ever mentioned me?' My unthinking effort to get close to Miss Drom produced another flourish with the splintered wood. 'Oh, come on! I ask you, do I look like a kidnapper?'

'Yes,' said Miss Drom.

I acknowledge that I asked for that one. 'Now, listen! I don't know all the details but obviously your father knew somehow about this plot to kidnap you and he sent me out to protect you.'

'And a fine job you've made of it!' sneered Miss Drom.

'There have been difficulties,' I retorted stiffly. 'Sir Maurice, as it happens, didn't give me a very good briefing. Still, it's no time to bother about that now. The important thing is that I'm here.'

'What's the name of Daddie's secretary?' demanded Miss Drom cunningly.

'Ross. Miss Ross. And she's known you ever since you were a babe-in-arms. You send her a picture postcard every time you go on holiday. See? Now, would I know all that if I weren't what I say I am?'

'You might.' Miss Drom's tone was as surly as ever but I could tell that her heart wasn't in it. She lowered her piece of wood a fraction of an inch. 'What exactly had you got in mind?'

'To get you out of here, of course.'

'How?'

'That's what we've got to discuss.' I looked back at the door leading out to the other bedroom. 'You'll have to let me come a bit nearer. If they overhear us out there, it'll be curtains for both of us. Now, why don't we both just sit down quietly on the bed and . . .'

Miss Drom was two jumps ahead of where she thought I was going. 'We can talk just as well with you sitting on the floor. And, remember, I'm watching you!'

Eight

Miss Drom heard me out without interrupting me more than once every thirty-five seconds.

'So I think,' I concluded, 'that something must have gone wrong with that emergency telephone number in Vienna. If only there'd been an answer from them, we wouldn't be in the mess we're in now.'

Miss Drom eyed me sceptically. 'Are you sure Daddie knew I was going to be kidnapped?'

'What else? I mean, all this business about delivering a packet to his contacts in Vienna was obviously just a load of old codswallop.'

'You're quite certain you didn't make any mistake in the address?'

Now, that was going too far! 'Of course I'm certain!' I replied angrily. 'What do you take me for? A moron or something?'

'It's just that, if Daddie knew the danger I was in, I can't understand why he didn't make proper arrangements.'

Well, if it came to that, neither could I. 'Your father knew he could rely on me using my initiative,' I said modestly.

Miss Drom sniffed. 'Why didn't you go to the police?'

Talk about an interrogation! 'I didn't get a chance, did I? I told you, once Monkey Tom had told me what his plans

95

were, he took damned good care not to let me out of his sight for a second. They wouldn't even let me go and do my own shopping.'

'But what about all the time you were in Marjendorf?' Give her her due, Miss Drom didn't only look like a bulldog. 'You'd every opportunity then to do something constructive. If you couldn't get an answer from the Viennese number, why didn't you ring Daddie in London? Or you could have reported the whole business to the Austrian police. Good heavens, you could have even gone to Vienna to the British Embassy and taken me with you. We should both have been perfectly safe there. As it is, you did absolutely nothing – except make every possible effort you could to assist these dreadful men.'

'Look,' I said, 'if your father had wanted the police or the Embassy involved, he could have told them himself, couldn't he?'

Miss Drom shook her head. 'I'm afraid that doesn't excuse you, Mr Brown. Frankly, I find your behaviour and your attitude quite incomprehensible and I shall certainly inform Daddie all about it when I get home. Believe me, he'll want a better explanation than any you have produced so far. And who' – she switched topics without any discernible pause for either breath or thought – 'is this West Hartlepool Joe supposed to be?'

'I don't know,' I said crossly. 'I imagine he's one of these master-mind criminals you read about. You know – he never pulls any jobs himself but just finances the lesser criminals and then takes a hefty cut out of their loot. The small fry have to lay out quite a lot of money before they commit a really profitable crime and they can hardly apply to their bank managers for a loan, can they?'

'You're sure you're not making all this up?' demanded Miss Drom, looking at me severely. 'You must admit, West Hartlepool Joe sounds a most unlikely soubriquet.'

'It's no worse than Monkey Tom. And, anyhow,' – I shifted about uncomfortably on the floor – 'it's no good our bothering our heads about all that now. We've got to decide what we're going to do next.'

Miss Drom had no doubts on that score. 'You've got to get me out of here, and without delay. There's no question about that, is there? I presume my safety is the paramount consideration.'

'Oh, of course.' I hoped I sounded convincing. Actually I was just wondering if it might be possible to combine Miss Drom's safety with my profit. I hadn't, you see, been entirely frank with Miss Drom. I'd told her all about the Hundemuseumstrasse business and how Monkey Tom had mistaken me for the emissary of the unlikely West Hartlepool Joe and about the hefty sum of money I had handed over. What I hadn't mentioned was the even heftier sum I was due to collect once the ransom had been paid. Well, I couldn't hand it over to West Hartlepool Joe even if I wanted to, could I? Two hundred thousand pounds is a lot of money and I've got my old age to think of. The beauty of it was that, as far as I could see, there wouldn't be any comeback. Even if Monkey Tom swore black and blue that he'd given me the cash, nobody was going to believe a lousy punk like him. West Hartlepool Joe didn't know me from Adam and who cares about stealing from the government? Mind you, I wasn't daft enough to imagine that Miss Drom would take a sympathetic view of my dreams so I didn't bother telling her. 'I was wondering,' I resumed carefully, 'if we wouldn't do better to wait.'

Miss Drom contented herself with giving me a glare full of suspicion.

'Once the ransom money is paid over,' I said, 'these boys are going to drop their guard. That's the time we should make a run for it. While they're still waiting for the money they're going to be watching you like a flock of hawks.'

'What a perfectly ridiculous idea!' Miss Drom's vehemence was such that I had to beg her to keep her voice down. 'Oh, all right,' she hissed, 'but, really, you are enough to try the patience of a saint! If the ransom money is paid over, there won't be any need for me to escape, will there, you fool? They'll just let me go.'

I might have known it wasn't going to work. 'Well, that's one way of looking at it,' I admitted, stifling my disappointment and fury.

'It's the only way of looking at it! That's what kidnapping is all about. I should have thought even you would know that.'

'All right, what do you suggest?'

'I've told you! You must get me out of here immediately.'

I chewed at my bottom lip resentfully. 'I hope you realize that we'll have to be successful at the first attempt. If we fail, Monkey and the others will know that I'm an impostor.'

'You're supposed to be the expert,' observed Miss Drom sarcastically. 'You'll just have to see that we don't fail.'

God, those floor boards were hard. There wasn't even a bit of mat to soften the contact.

'Well,' said Miss Drom, 'what – for the fiftieth time – do you intend doing?'

'Oh, how the hell do I know?' I stood up before complete petrification set in.

'You must have some idea. We shall have to make our way to Rome, of course.'

'Why Rome?'

'Because that's where the Embassy is! Do try to concentrate, Mr Brown! We shall have to slip away from this house and get to Rome as quickly as possible. Where are we exactly, by the way?'

I shrugged my shoulders. 'Somewhere in the north of Italy, I suppose.'

'Don't you know what lake that is down there?'

'No, I don't.' Miss Drom was a chip off the old block, all right. 'I hope you realize how difficult this is all going to be.'

'I have never,' said Miss Drom, 'been deterred by mere difficulties.'

'Now, listen,' – I got so carried away by the necessity of

knocking some sense into her head that, without thinking, I began to sit down on the bed. Miss Drom used her feet to fend me off. 'Oh, sorry!' I collapsed on to the floor again. 'First of all, have you got any money – Italian money?'

'Of course not.'

'Do you speak Italian?'

'Well no. But I'm sure lots of them speak English.'

'I congratulate you on your optimism!'

Miss Drom wasn't so thick that she coudn't see what I was driving at. It was going to be no joke, searching for an English-speaking Italian with Monkey thundering down the mountainside in pursuit of us. Being without money wasn't going to help, either. I was glad to see that Miss Drom was beginning to look as daunted as I felt.

'All right,' she conceded, 'perhaps Rome is a little too ambitious. We'll just have to make for the nearest police station.' It had been a long, tough day and I was too tired to argue. I took the coward's way out, crossed my fingers and agreed that this was precisely what we would do, should the opportunity arise.

'We must make our own opportunities, Mr Brown,' came the smug reply. 'I shall give you until six o'clock tomorrow evening.'

'You'll give me until six o'clock tomorrow evening for what?' I spluttered.

'To get me out of the clutches of these dreadful men,' said Miss Drom calmly. 'If you haven't succeeded by then I shall have no choice but to unmask you.'

'But what bloody good will that do?' I felt most indignant.

Miss Drom smiled a thin little smile. 'It won't do any good at all, Mr Brown,' she admitted frankly. 'but I don't see why I should be the only one to suffer. Do you?'

After that there was nothing left but to settle down and try and get some sleep although I would dearly have liked to punch the living daylights out of the sanctimonious bitch.

Miss Drom sank back in a mass of soft pillows and warm blankets. 'I shan't sleep a wink,' she said.

I tried to set her mind at rest by assuring her that she had nothing – but *nothing* – to fear from me. 'I hope,' I added, to clinch matters, 'that I know the respect due to Sir Maurice's daughter.'

Miss Drom hoped so, too.

'Well, then,' I said, rising stiffly to my feet and measuring the bed with a completely chaste eye, 'I think if we fitted ourselves head to tail . . . You can have the pillows, of course, and I'll just screw up my jacket and . . .'

Miss Drom merely shook her head.

'You can't expect me to spend the night on the floor!'

Miss Drom picked up her piece of wood. 'You can't, Mr Brown, be more dissatisfied with the sleeping arrangements than I am myself. I am quite certain, of course, that you will behave like a gentleman but I don't think we should take any unnecessary risks. We both have our crosses to bear and I can only recommend you to bear yours with the fortitude that I am bearing mine.'

I wouldn't have resented lying on that damned floor so much if it had been in the least bit necessary. Miss Drom aroused no animal passions in me, except a perfectly natural desire to strangle her as she settled down into a loud, steady snore.

It was an endless night.

However, morning came at last and Miss Drom and I were let out with an excess of lewd giggles and knowing winks. Nobody, not even clever-devil Cyril, had any doubt but that Miss Drom and I were now on terms of the utmost intimacy. Punchie Lewis and Burp, avid for a blow-by-blow account, crowded into the kitchen while I got breakfast for six ready.

Punchie was all but dribbling. 'What was she like, Eddie? Was you the first, eh? How many times did you . . .?'

'You deserve a ruddy medal!' said Burp admiringly. 'Honest, I don't know how you could. I know looks aren't everything but that judy . . .' He gave me a slap on the back. 'You look right bushed, mate.'

'Yeah,' agreed Punchie Lewis, 'proper shagged.'

I dropped another egg viciously in the frying pan. 'Burp,' I said loftily, 'I wonder if you would mind helping Punchie lay the table?'

I must have put it too subtly because neither of them budged.

'Did she put up a fight?' asked Punchie. 'I thought she'd have scratched your eyes out soon as . . .'

I seized a handful of cutlery out of the drawer and all but chucked it at him. 'The table!' I repeated.

'Huh?'

'The breakfast table! Go and lay it!'

'Oh, all right, if that's what you want.'

'And you, Burp, shove these egg shells and things in the dustbin outside. If there's one thing I can't stand it's an untidy kitchen.'

That got the pair of them out from under my feet but the relief was short lived. Burp was back again.

'Here, Eddie,' he said, holding out an envelope towards me, 'look what I found shoved under the back door.'

I turned an egg over and read the inscription at the same time. 'It's addressed to Monkey Tom.'

'Yeah,' agreed Burp uncertainly, 'but how did it get here?'

'Well, since it hasn't got a stamp on it, it was obviously delivered by hand.'

'Yeah, but nobody knows we're here.' Burp was looking at the envelope as though he thought it would explode. 'This place is supposed to be top secret.'

'What about the chap you rented it from? He must know.'

Burp shook his head. 'He knows somebody's here but he don't know who. This business was all fixed up very careful. Monkey's name was never mentioned. We used three or four go-betweens. Nobody could possibly know he was here.'

'Well, somebody does,' I said impatiently. 'Why don't you give it to Monkey and he can open it and find out who?'

'Yeah,' said Burp, still standing there like a lemon. 'I

don't like the sound of this, Eddie. Somebody's bloody well slipped up somewhere. Monkey's going to blow his bleeding top.'

Monkey did blow his bleeding top. You could hear the screams all over the house as accusations and recriminations fell around like leaves in an autumn breeze. Even I came in for my share of the rough side of his tongue although, as I kept pointing out, I could hardly betray what I didn't even know.

'Well, somebody's opened their big fat mouth!' yowled Monkey, clutching his stomach as his ulcer took its revenge. 'One of you's blabbed!'

We all reiterated our protests of innocence while Miss Drom sat waiting for her breakfast with one of those superior, I-told-you-so smiles on her lips. Luckily she had enough sense to keep her mouth shut because I don't think Monkey could have stood much more without running amuck.

'It's the ingratitude that hurts,' he whimpered. 'Where would you lot be if it hadn't been for me? Wallowing in the gutter, that's where, you useless slobs! You owe everything to me, everything. And the only way you can find of repaying me' – his voice broke with emotion – 'is to go around shooting your mouths off.' He sank down at the breakfast table and buried his head in his hands while the rest of us stood sheepishly around.

Only Punchie Lewis ventured to put his feelings into words. 'Aw, boss!' he pleaded and shuffled his feet.

Monkey nobly pulled himself together and was about to launch forth at us again when Cyril leaned forward and calmly took the still unopened envelope out of his leader's palsied fingers. Monkey's jaw dropped but by then Cyril had already slit the envelope open with his flick knife and was taking out a sheet of paper.

We waited in silence while he read the note. And we went on waiting while he read it a second time.

'Well,' he said at last as he handed the single sheet to Monkey, 'I'll be buggered!'

Monkey's reaction, when he in turn had perused the missive, was even less revealing. All our master mind could do was sit there, opening and shutting his mouth like a stranded cod fish.

'What is it, boss?' croaked Burp.

Monkey shook his head slowly from side to side and was just about to pass the blasted letter to Burp when I broke in. If I hadn't we'd have been mucking about like that all day.

'What's happened?' I barked.

It was Cyril who answered. A Cyril, incidentally, who was now grinning like a Cheshire cat that's swallowed the canary. 'We've been offered a million and a half for Little Miss Loud Mouth here,' he said. 'A million and a half – cash.'

Even Punchie Lewis got the gist of that in double-quick time and, after a short shocked pause while everybody worked out his cut, the shouting all started at once.

Monkey, taking good care that Cyril shouldn't steal his thunder again, eventually restored order and, flourishing the letter in our faces, consented to tell us a bit more about it. What he said made my blood run cold.

The highly attractive bid for Miss Drom had been made by the Russians!

'I don't believe it!' I gasped. I could see that the Russians might be delighted to get their hands on Sir Maurice Drom's only daughter but I couldn't believe that they would go about it so openly. I have had a fair amount of contact with the KGB and other under-cover Soviet organizations and, in my experience, they are cagey to the point of obsession. It was incredible that they should have revealed their identity so frankly at the very beginning of negotiations. I said so, at some length.

Cyril pounced on me. 'How come you know so much about the Russkies?' he demanded.

'I work for West Hartlepool Joe, don't I?' I retorted, thinking with the speed of light.

'So?'

'So – who do you think sprung George Blake?'

That pulled him up short in his tracks. 'George Blake the spy? You don't mean that West Hartlepool Joe . . .'

I examined my nails with easy nonchalance. 'He made the arrangements. You don't want to believe all that rubbish you read in the newspapers, you know. Actually, Joe's fixed up quite a number of jobs for the Russkies. They pay very well.'

'You're telling me!' gurgled Burp who was happily spelling out the words of the note for himself.

Monkey's face had got some of its colour back. 'But you don't think this has come from the Russians?' he asked, turning hag-ridden eyes on me.

I shrugged my shoulders. 'Well, I think it's suspect. Suppose you published this note? The Soviet Union would be completely discredited, wouldn't they? They're pretty sensitive about their public image, you know.'

Monkey took the note back from Burp and studied it gloomily. 'I can't see us giving this note to the newspapers,' he objected. 'We'd be cutting our own bloody throats.'

'Of course we would!' Cyril chimed in. 'They know that. They're not fools. Besides, all they'd have to do is say it was a forgery. No, if you ask me, they'd no choice but to tell us that this is an official Russian offer.'

'Oh?' I said. 'And how do you make that out?'

'Because, if they hadn't, we'd never have believed it was genuine for a minute, would we? Look, we're not rabbiting about chicken feed. We're talking about one million five hundred thousand quid. Now, who's got that sort of money to chuck around these days? Governments, that's who. I mean, look at her! Nobody else'd cough up fourpence to get her back.'

'It could be a joke,' I said.

Monkey managed a strangled sarcastic sort of laugh. 'A joke?' he echoed. 'I wouldn't have treated it as a joke if it had come from the man in the bloody moon.'

'Too true, boss!' murmured Burp, who was doing elaborate

sums on a bit of scrap paper. 'Here, how many bloody noughts is there in five hundred thousand?'

'Never mind that, you dumb ox!' roared Monkey. He snatched the paper out of Burp's hand and ripped it into tiny pieces. 'Don't you see what this means? Russians or bloody Martians – we've been blown! You're all that damned busy thinking about the money that you can't see the danger we're in. Somebody knows exactly where we are and that we've got the girl with us. We've got to get out of here!'

From the look of him, he was on the point of making a run for it there and then but Cyril grabbed hold of him and shoved him back in his chair. 'Oh, use your loaf, Monkey! How far do you think we'd get? They'll have been watching this place ever since we arrived, you can bet your boots on that. We've got to decide now what we're going to do. We've got – what?' – he glanced at his watch – 'five hours before they're going to turn up. All right – well – we sit down quietly and have some breakfast. Then we'll feel more like discussing things. Now, where's that letter?'

For one hilarious moment it looked as though between us we'd lost it but then Cyril noticed that Miss Drom was busy reading it. He snatched it back. It is some indication of how wrought up even he was that he didn't give her a good slap round the ears for her presumption.

The idea that we should all settle down and have breakfast didn't really work. Monkey Tom in particular was constitutionally incapable of putting his troubles on one side even for five minutes. He sat, gnawing at a piece of toast and bemoaning his fate. The rest of us weren't much better. One and a half million does rather tend to stick in one's throat.

'How much room will it take up?' asked Burp.

'Oh, shut up!' said Monkey wearily.

Burp looked hurt. 'Well, I was only asking. We've got to be prepared, haven't we? Do we want a suitcase or a bleeding lorry?'

Monkey scowled blackly at him and then turned to Cyril. 'What are we going to do?'

Cyril hunched his shoulders. 'They haven't left us much choice.'

'You think we ought to see them?'

'What else? They've said they're coming at two o'clock, haven't they? OK – they'll come. Then what are you going to do about it? Shut your bloody eyes?'

'Jesus,' sighed Monkey Tom, 'this I could have done without! Do you reckon we can trust 'em, Cyril?'

Cyril hunched his shoulders again.

It was obviously time for me to step in and spread a little sweetness and light. 'They'll probably pay you off in dud notes,' I warned.

Monkey looked at me as though I'd crawled out from under a stone. 'You must think we was born yesterday!'

'You're not seriously thinking of accepting this offer, are you?' I asked anxiously.

'Why shouldn't I?'

'Well . . .' I tried to think of some convincing reason for turning down all those noughts. A reason that would convince me, never mind Monkey. Patriotism? 'They're communists,' I said.

'Who cares?' That was Cyril with his cynical outlook. 'If I was sure we'd really get the money I'd not be sweating. What's bugging me is them pulling the old double-cross. What's to stop them moving in here with a couple of bloody bazookas and just taking the girl?'

'West Hartlepool Joe hasn't any scruples about dealing with commies, has he?' demanded Monkey Tom. 'What's England ever done for me?'

I preferred to address myself to Cyril, who seemed to be asking the more pertinent questions. 'The Russians aren't fools,' I said. 'They're operating in a foreign country and the last thing they'll want is to call attention to themselves. An all-out attack on this place would have the Italian police swarming around like flies. No, I think the Russians will play it one of two ways. Either they'll pay you off with phoney money or they'll get in here all nice and quiet for a discussion of policy and then you'll find yourselves looking down the wrong end of a gun. There'll be no fireworks or killing or anything if they can help it. That'd only lead eventually to some very embarrassing questions. I reckon they'll just tie you lot up, take the girl and vanish. What can you do about it? You can hardly go screaming to the cops that you've been robbed, can you?'

'The lousy sods!' moaned Monkey, taking the whole thing personally. 'The rotten stinking bastards! Honest to God, they're all on the bloody make these days. It's getting so's you can't trust nobody. Well,' – he looked around at his associates – 'anybody got any ideas?'

Burp scratched his head. 'Looks as though we're due to get the thick end of it whatever we do, boss.'

'Bloody Reds!' said Punchie Lewis sadly.

'I vote we give 'em a taste of their own medicine,' said Cyril. 'We've got ammo and a couple of Sten guns in the basement.'

'That'd only bring the cops down on our necks,' objected Monkey. 'I think we ought to make a run for it now.'

Cyril shivered. 'And get caught out in the open? No bloody thank you!'

Meanwhile yours truly had been stirring up his old grey cells. 'Listen,' I said, 'I've got an idea.'

They all turned to me hopefully, including Miss Drom who was making elaborate efforts to catch my eye. Wondering if she by some miracle might have something constructive to contribute to the discussion, I nodded encouragingly at her.

'Do you think I could have another cup of tea, Eddie?' she asked.

Nine

Well, frankly, I should have seen the writing on the wall there and then but I'd more important things to worry about than Miss Drom addressing me by my Christian name. Or I thought I had. I told her, rather sharply, to help herself and then began expounding my plan to the boys. It was devilish cunning.

'Now, listen,' I began, 'we've got more than two choices. It isn't just a matter of staying here and meeting the Russians or running away. There's a third way out. We can do both!'

The trouble with trying to build up to a dramatic climax in real life is that the audience participation is so lousy. On this occasion Monkey Tom blinked, Cyril sneered, while Punchie Lewis and Burp looked blank. Only Miss Drom hung flatteringly on my every word. I pressed on.

'You stay here all right and parley with the Russians but you get Miss Drom away somewhere, out of the house. That way, if the Russkies try to pull a fast one, they'll find the bird has flown.'

Monkey's face brightened. 'That's not a bad idea,' he said. 'Yes, I think we've got something here. We only tell 'em where the judy is when we've got the cash. Yes, that's clever.'

'Clever – hell!' scoffed Cyril. 'I've told you – they'll be watching this place for sure. How do we get her away?'

'Ah,' I said, rather patronizingly, 'I've thought of that. Now, as I see it, they can't be keeping too close a watch on this place. I mean, we haven't got 'em standing out there in the garden or anything. I think they'll be watching somewhere down the road because it's the only way out of here unless we're going to chuck ourselves over the cliff and get down to the lake the quick way.'

I laughed when I said this. I'm a great one for introducing the odd touch of humour.

Cyril's glacier-cold eyes narrowed. 'Why the hell don't you get on with it?' he asked.

'All right – the Russians are watching the road so, if we send a car out, they'll see it. They'll even be able to see who's in it but they'll never dare risk stopping and searching it.'

'You hope,' said Monkey.

'Well, my suggestion is that we send a car out. What could be more natural than that Burp here should pop down to the nearest town to do some shopping? With' – and I let them have the punch-line straight between the eyes – 'me and Miss Drom hidden in the boot.'

Cyril laughed very nastily. 'Jesus, that wouldn't fool a kid of two!'

'Of course it wouldn't!' I agreed. 'But the Russians aren't kids of two. They'll never be expecting us to pull something as simple as this. That's the main virtue of the scheme.'

'Then what?' asked Monkey, making a meal off his bottom lip.

'That little town down by the lake, the one you can see from the windows – it's a holiday resort, isn't it? All right, Burp parks the car somewhere near the beach. Then, when he's sure the coast is clear, he lets me and Miss Drom out and we slip away and mingle with the tourists. Who'd ever think of looking for us there? And, if they did, how would they ever find us? We'd look just like everybody else in floppy hats and sun-glasses and all the rest of the gear. When Burp has done his shopping or whatever, he drives the car back up here. The Russians are perfectly happy. One man in one car went out, one man in a car has come back again. Once you've had your talk with the Russians, you send Burp back down the hill again to pick us up.'

Cyril shook his head. 'It'll never work, not in a thousand years. For one thing, how are you going to stop that tart screaming blue murder once she's in the town?'

'Well, you'll have to lend me a gun, of course,' I said craftily. 'She won't open her trap if she knows it's going to mean a bullet through the guts. Besides, for all she knows, screams might bring the Russians before the cops. Oh, and you'll have to let me have some money, too. Then we can go wandering round the shops like the other holiday makers and buy the odd ice-cream. Look, I'm telling you – this is the only way to play it.'

'Hm.' Monkey rubbed his jaw dubiously. I could see that he wasn't exactly sold on my idea but he badly wanted Cyril cut down to size. 'Well, you might have something there, Eddie.'

'Balls!' said Cyril.

'You got a better idea?'

'Hundreds,' said Cyril sulkily. 'You want your head examining, Monkey, if you go for this.'

'Oh, there'll have to be a few modifications but the general outline's not bad.'

'Modifications?' I didn't care much for the sound of this.

Monkey grinned spitefully at me. 'You didn't think I was going to let you take the girl off on your ownsome, did you, Eddie? I'm not that wet round the ears. Cyril's going with you, just to keep an eye on things.'

'Oh, no!' Cyril shook his head. He'd no intention of letting Monkey get within spitting distance of a million and a half pounds without being there to provide some comradely support. 'Punchie can go.'

'But that's going to leave you a bit thin on the ground here, isn't it?' I objected.

'First things first,' said Cyril. 'The tart's the most important thing. Without her we don't get a brass farthing from nobody. Anyhow, if we ship you three off soon enough, Burp'll

be back in time to lend a hand with the Russians. In fact' –
he slapped his hands together in triumph – 'I know what he
can go shopping for! A couple of bottles of vodka! That'll
look perfectly natural if anybody follows him.'

'Oh, fine,' I said. 'But you're going to have a bit of a job
concealing three of us in the car, aren't you?'

Monkey was quick to provide a solution. 'No. You and
the girl go in the boot and Punchie can go on the floor under
the dashboard. We can shove a rug over him. Now, what
about clothes?'

'Clothes?'

'You were the one who was talking about mingling with
the tourists. OK – so you'll have to be dressed like them.
There's a pile of old swim suits in one of the bedrooms.
We'll have you in a pair of briefs and the judy in a bikini
and you can spend the afternoon sunbathing down by the
lake. Now, the Russkies are due here at two o'clock. You leave
here with Burp at half-past one. No – better make it a quarter
past. That'll give him time to get back here and help us.
How long do you think they'll take, Cyril?'

Cyril pursed his lips. 'Not long. An hour at the very
most. I don't suppose they'll want to hang around.'

'Well, we'll say two to be on the safe side. Eddie, you can
give us till four o'clock and then telephone us here. If everything's OK, we'll send Burp down to pick you up. If it isn't we
can make other arrangements. Now, any questions, anybody?'

I would like to have asked how on earth Miss Drom and I
were going to disappear hand-in-hand into the sunset now but,
of course, I didn't. The unwelcome presence of Punchie Lewis
was going to complicate things though I tried to console myself with the thought that the situation could be worse. At
least Miss Drom and I were going to be much nearer to outside help down in the town than we were stuck up here on this
bloody mountain. And the gang, though wary of me, weren't
really suspicious. When the time came I should have the
element of surprise on my side. My natural optimism began
to get the better of me. Well, Punchie Lewis wasn't exactly

the brightest intellectual star in the firmament. If I couldn't outwit him with one hand tied behind me . . .

All in all I trotted off quite cheerfully to help Burp sort out some suitable beach wear for us from the pile of old clothes which earlier lessees of the villa had apparently left behind them. I soon unearthed a pair of swimming trunks for myself in a rather fetching navy blue, but suiting Miss Drom proved more of a problem. Not that there weren't plenty of ladies' models. Indeed, even discounting those that the moths had got at, we were left with four very shapely confections. Not, unfortunately, Miss Drom's shape.

Burp was a simple soul. 'Praps,' he said, holding up a top half in imitation tiger skin that made the imagination boggle, 'she could sort of pad herself out with cotton wool or old socks or something?'

I shook my head. 'A couple of ankle-length overcoats wouldn't do it!' I rummaged through the heap again and came up with a grey and pink bottom half that didn't look quite so voluptuous as the rest. 'Can you find the bra that goes with this?'

'Maybe she'd like to go topless!' sniggered Burp. 'Here, is this it?' He held out a thin strip of cloth in the appropriate colours which was obviously intended to be tied in a bow at the back.

'That'll do!' I said. 'Miss Drom will merely have to reef it in a bit more than most. Now, what about Punchie? Won't he need something?'

'No, Punchie'll have to wear his ordinary clobber,' said Burp as he began stuffing the unwanted clothes back in the cupboard. 'He's got the gun, you see.'

I was all ears. 'The gun?'

'Well, he can't walk about with it shoved down a pair of them skimpy pants, can he?' asked Burp reasonably.

I agreed he couldn't. It was disappointing to learn that Punchie was going to be armed. I had hoped that, with two of us to guard Miss Drom, weapons would have been considered superfluous.

Burp shut the cupboard door quickly before all the things inside had time to fall out again. 'You want to watch out for Punchie, Eddie,' he said.

'Oh?'

'He's not a bad old bugger, really, but he gets a bit trigger happy sometimes. Jumpy, you know. Monkey don't usually let him have a gun.'

'Doesn't he?' I said thoughtfully.

'His reflexes have all gone to pieces. He sort of shoots first and ask questions afterwards, poor old sod. Except that he's too dumb to think up any questions to ask. I shouldn't make any sudden movements, if I was you. Otherwise you'll have him blazing off like a box of bleeding fireworks.'

'Thanks for the warning.' I followed Burp out of the bedroom. 'Good shot, is he?' I asked casually.

'The pip out of a playing card at forty paces,' Burp assured me earnestly. 'Funny, isn't it? He could name his own price you know, if only he could just control his reflexes. Pity, really.'

'Yes,' I agreed. 'Poor old Punchie.'

We had an early lunch – sardine and chips – which I cooked. They could say what they liked but this mob was going to miss me when I'd gone. After everybody had left their fill, Miss Drom and I retired in turns to our bedroom and changed into our swimming suits. Then we went out to the garage where the rest of the gang were too preoccupied with their own worries to bother about what we looked like. Punchie Lewis was standing by the car, an unsightly bulge spoiling the hang of his blue serge jacket. Cyril jerked his head impatiently at the open boot of the Fiat. All the tools and the spare wheel had been cleared out but it still wasn't exactly spacious accommodation.

For a minute I thought Miss Drom was going to object, and I was right. She protested loud and long. Since the proposed proximity of our two near-naked bodies wasn't exactly sending me ecstatic either, I ventured to join my voice to hers with such persuasive effect that Monkey actually drew a gun on us.

'Get in!' he screamed. 'Get in and, for God's sake, shut up!'

I took my life in my mouth and asked, very meekly, if we might borrow a spare travelling rug. Monkey considered blasting me where I stood but the thought of West Hartlepool Joe's possible displeasure restrained him and he nodded curtly at Cyril. Cyril had to be awkward, of course, and he fetched out a piece of old sacking which, to the intense amusement of everybody except Monkey, I wrapped solicitously round Miss Drom before assisting her into the boot. Not having a drawn sword, it was the best I could do.

When Miss Drom was finally installed I squeezed in on top, beside and all round her. It was a very tight fit. Cyril grabbed the odd arms and legs which were still dangling outside and and shoved them in. I had just raised my head to enquire if there was going to be enough air to sustain life when the boot lid caught me a stunning crack on the cranium as it was slammed down.

Before I had time to apologize to Miss Drom for the thoughtless word I had used, there were more slams and then a quite unbearable roar as the car engine burst into life. I felt the bumps and swings as we took off down the driveway and hit the rough road outside. If Miss Drom and I hadn't been wedged so intimately together, we should have had every bone in our bodies smashed to smithereens. The brakes squealed a mere inch or so under my ear, another sickening lurch and we were out of the village and hurtling down the mountain road. As rides go, it was fractionally smoother but the endless twists and turns were excruciating and the stink of exhaust fumes was getting stronger every second.

Inside the boot Miss Drom and I fought for oxygen and lebensraum as best we could. Here, at least, there was complete equality of the sexes. I bit and clawed Miss Drom just as fervently as she gouged and scratched at me. The journey couldn't have lasted more than ten minutes at the most but it felt like a life sentence. I never even noticed when we came off the mountain road and proceeded at a gentler pace through the town and it took several seconds to realize that the vicious jolt which just failed to fracture my back was merely Burp's final assault on the brake pedal.

I tried to get one hand free to batter on the lid of the boot for succour but Miss Drom seemed to be everywhere. We were entwined like some carnal Chinese puzzle. I thrashed about desperately. One arm moved slightly. I thrust it forward until an outraged gasp from Miss Drom warned me whither that was leading us. I desisted and sank back in hopeless exhaustion. Death by suffocation is a horrible prospect but what I say is – if you gotta go, you've gotta go. I just hoped that I was going to take that Drom bitch with me.

The boot lid opened.

'Come on!' hissed Burp. 'Show a bloody leg!'

Only too conscious that Miss Drom and I were showing much more than our nether limbs, I dragged myself up painfully towards the light. With Burp's help I got out of the boot and hobbled away to examine my wounds. I was black and blue all over. Punchie Lewis came lumbering up with an armful of straw hats, dark glasses and brightly coloured towels.

'Got any embrocation?' I snarled.

'Huh?'

'Oh, never mind!' My head had stopped spinning now and I accepted my share of the paraphernalia that Punchie was carrying. With sun-glasses on – why do they always make you feel invisible? – I felt I could risk having a good look round. We were parked in a line of cars on a road which ran parallel to the beach. There were plenty of other people strolling aimlessly about, more interested in photographing each other and stuffing themselves with ice-cream than in paying the slightest attention to us. It was terribly hot and the sun was blinding. I looked and looked but, of course, there wasn't a rappresentante della legge anywhere in sight.

'Anybody following us?' I asked Punchie.

He wiped his forehead with his handkerchief and shook his

head. 'Burp reckons not but they'd do it careful-like, wouldn't they?' He nodded back in the direction from which we'd come. 'I've been watching the road. There's only one car come along after us and that had five kids in it. All Eyeties. I think we're clear at the moment.'

'Suffering Christ!' Burp came bustling up, pushing a reluctant Miss Drom ahead of him. 'Get moving can't you?' He locked the car doors. 'I'm going off to get the booze now and then I'm driving straight back. I'll see you lot later.'

Miss Drom, Punchie and I walked slowly across the road and down the little flight of wooden steps on to the beach. The surface of the lake danced in the heat as we picked our way gingerly over the pebbles and round the recumbent bodies and the gaudy umbrellas. The spiaggia wasn't very big and it had a fair number of people on it but eventually we found a vacant spot not too far from the water's edge and spread our towels out.

'Anybody seen a gabinetto?' I asked, smoothly introducing the first word I learn in any foreign language.

Punchie registered his normal lack of comprehension. 'Huh?'

'The bog,' I explained. 'I just thought I'd . . .'

'You should have thought of that before,' said Punchie, very self-righteous. 'I did. Monkey give me strict instructions. We all stay together all the time.'

I'm sure the way his hand strayed to his jacket pocket didn't imply any kind of a threat but I sat down just the same.

Miss Drom, sandwiched between Punchie and me, tugged hopefully at her bikini but it still wouldn't cover more than the six square inches it had been designed for. She sighed deeply and only just caught the top half in time. 'I wish we had one of those umbrellas,' she whined. 'The sun is so hot and I burn terribly easily. I . . .'

'Can it!' said Punchie, and I took my hat off to him.

'If I get sun stroke,' Miss Drom warned him, 'I shall be sick, really sick.'

'Lady,' grunted Punchie as he tried to staunch the rivers of sweat running down his neck. 'I believe you. Now, belt up!'

For the time being there was obviously nothing to be done except string quietly along. I settled myself face down on my towel and spent the next five minutes endeavouring to re-arrange the pebbles under my chest into a more comfortable pattern. Miss Drom, muttering and grumbling to herself, eventually assumed the same posture. Only Punchie, I noted sourly, remained sitting bolt upright, suffering but still obedient to Monkey Tom's orders.

With the sun beating down on my back I closed my eyes and began working out my next moves. The little waves on the lake lapped gently and soporifically only a few feet away from my head and the voices of the other people on the beach gradually sank into an unobtrusive murmur. I snuggled down. Well, whichever way the cookie crumbled, I was going to emerge from this business with a lovely sun tan. I began to picture myself – bronzed, bright-eyed, athletic, the muscles rippling under the warm brown skin of my arms and shoulders. Panther-like, with lithe sinewy legs and a pancake-flat stomach, I set my lantern-jaw and flung myself on poor old flabby Punchie Lewis. He was no match for me. He reached for his gun but I was too quick. With wrists of steel I twisted . . .

Miss Drom sank her fingernails into my spare tyre and I sprang to my knees with a howl that had half the beach sitting up and staring at us.

'What's up with you?' asked Punchie, his hand dropping away from his pocket as he saw that I was as bewildered by my outburst as he was.

I licked my lips. They felt all dry and parched. I had a funny taste in my mouth too. 'I don't know,' I said stupidly, though not too bemused to bestow a glance of pure hatred on Miss Drom. 'I must have dozed off and had a nightmare or something.'

'Dozed off?' chuckled Punchie. 'You've been snoring like a pig for the last bloody hour.'

'You certainly have!' agreed Miss Drom at her most acid.

'Nonsense!' I looked at my watch. As I had expected, the hour was a gross exaggeration by at least six and a quarter minutes.

'Oh, I'm so *hot*!' complained Miss Drom. 'Couldn't we go and have an ice-cream or a lemonade or something?'

'That'd only make you hotter,' explained Punchie earnestly. 'What you really want to cool you down is a nice, scalding cup of tea.'

'All right!' snapped Miss Drom, her temper showing again. 'Well, can we go for a nice, scalding cup of tea?'

'No,' said Punchie placidly.

So the three of us went on sitting there, sweltering and – as far as Miss Drom and I were concerned – sulky. I hugged my knees and tried to think. If we made a run for it, would Punchie Lewis shoot? If he shot, which one of us would he fire at first? I knew for sure that it would be me so I didn't pursue that line of thought any further. Was I man enough to grapple with Punchie while Miss Drom made her escape and went for help? Was Miss Drom man enough to tackle Punchie while I got clear? I looked at the ex-boxer with as impartial an eye as I could manage. He'd gone to seed all right, but more in the head than in the body. If it came to a showdown, he'd make mincemeat of the pair of us. So – strong-arm tactics were out. I should have to resort to guile.

I looked at my watch again. Blimey! In half-an-hour or so Burp would be back with the car and then, whichever way the conference with the Russians had gone, we were sunk.

I saw Miss Drom eyeing me. Very cautiously I put my watch on half-an-hour and indicated that she should do the same. Then I leaned across her and addressed Punchie.

'Isn't it about time you were giving Monkey Tom and Cyril a ring?'

Punchie duly consulted his time-piece. 'Naw! Monkey said to ring at four. It's only just gone half-past three.'

'Really?' I sounded suitably surprised. 'I make it a couple of minutes after four. You sure your watch is right?'

'I think so.' Punchie turned to Miss Drom. 'What time do you make it, love?'

Miss Drom's watch agreed with mine.

Punchie Lewis began to look worried.

'I'll go and ask those people over there,' I offered generously. 'I mean, Monkey may be relying on you. We don't know what's been happening up there at the house, do we? Those Russians might be up to anything.' I turned my back on him and began to put my sandals on. And there, right under my foot and staring me in the face, was the answer to all my problems. Why bother with guile when you've got a good heavy stone to hand? I couldn't imagine why I hadn't thought of that before.

'No,' said Punchie, meaning that he didn't relish the idea of my asking any of our neighbours what time it was. 'We'll go and telephone now. It can't do any harm if we're a bit early.'

'All of us?' I asked, prising my stone loose with an idle toe.

'Yeah! Monkey said as how we'd all got to stick together all the time. You're to phone and me and the girl'll wait outside the box.' Punchie struggled to his feet and began to brush the sand off his trousers.

'Good!' I said. 'Well, let's go! I've had more than enough sun for one day.' I rolled off my towel and on to my knees, still keeping my back towards Punchie. I picked the towel up, shook it and carefully folded it up with the big round stone in the middle. Then I stood up.

Punchie Lewis was just bending down to pick his own towel up when I swung and caught him a resounding blow across the back of the head.

He pitched forward with a grunt on to his face. I caught a momentary glimpse of startled faces and gaping mouths as the people nearby gradually realized what I'd done. Miss Drom was still lolling on her towel. I seized her arm and yanked her to her feet.

'Come on, you stupid cow!' I screamed. '*Come on!*'

Ten

We had several acrimonious discussions about it later but —
she can say what she likes — I still think it was Miss Drom
who directed our flying feet towards the water's edge. Not that
I hadn't seen the float pulled up there and not that I hadn't
realized that the casual witnesses of my assault on Punchie
might well think that I was the criminal and attempt to detain
me, but I definitely did not pull Miss Drom towards the lake.
She pulled me. Once there, I admit I seized the initiative and
launched both the float and Miss Drom onto the bosom of the
deep with an irresistible determination born of pure panic.
Panic because, out of the corner of my eye, I had seen that
though Punchie Lewis was down he was not out. Even as I
was assisting Miss Drom to her feet, Punchie had already
begun his agonized struggle to beat the count. No doubt he'd
made many similar efforts during the course of his pugilistic
career, being too stupid to know when he was beaten.

Be that as it may, by the time my heart beats had dropped
to only double their normal rate, Miss Drom and I had
paddled ourselves a good fifty yards from the shore. I risked
a glance back over my shoulder.

Punchie Lewis was staggering about like a drunk at
chucking-out time and clutching the back of his head. He was
surrounded by quite a crowd of near-naked sympathizers whose
offers of help and advice were so overwhelming that the poor

old bastard couldn't free himself to reach his gun. Which was an agreeable sight.

More disturbing was the presence of an irate little group who were gesticulating wildly in our direction. Foreigners, of course. It struck me that these must be the people to whom our float belonged. If so, they were making a devil of a fuss over a few lousy bits of wood stuck together with glue. Good heavens – one of them, a tough-looking hombre, was actually entering the water! He was going to swim after us!

'Faster! Faster!' I yelled at Miss Drom who was just wasting time by turning round to see why she was having to do all the work. 'Put your back into it!'

We were lucky that the two double-bladed paddles with which the float was furnished had not fallen off in our scramble to get water borne. Perched somewhat damply on the narrow cross pieces that served as seats, Miss Drom and I flailed away. It was unrewarding work as these craft were not built for speed. Still, the thought of what lay behind us lent power to our arms and gradually we moved further and further out into the centre of the lake. The lone pursuer packed it in and swam back to the shore.

With Miss Drom still going enthusiastically in front of me I took another short breather and looked back to see how things were developing on dry land. I was surprised to see how far away we were. Miss Drom must be stronger than she looked. I screwed my eyes up. Those two distant figures striding purposefully across the beach? Policemen? Well, that should cramp Punchie Lewis's style more than somewhat and I began to fret less about bullets plummeting into my naked back. I peered up and down the shore-line. For once the area seemed to be free of those noisy, buzzing little speed boats which, if requisitioned to form a posse, would have soon cooked our goose for us.

I got my paddle going again just as Miss Drom twisted round again to see what I was up to. She was beginning to look a bit tired and I immediately realized that one of us ought to preserve his strength for the rigours to come. I dipped my paddle gently in and out of the water in time with Miss Drom's more thrustful strokes.

It was much cooler out in the middle of the lake and indeed, now I came to think of it, my bottom was not only damp – it was quite chilly as well.

Miss Drom rested abruptly on her paddle. 'How wide is Lake Garda?' she panted.

'Search me! Who says it's Lake Garda, anyhow?'

'I saw a signpost for Brescia when we got out of the car. Thirty-five kilometres. So this must be Lake Garda.'

Quite the bloody little detective! Not that it mattered whether it was Lake Garda or Loch Lomond – we still had to get across it.

'It looks an awfully long way,' complained Miss Drom, trying to rub the unsightly goose pimples off her arms and shoulders. 'I rather think Lake Garda is the biggest of the Italian lakes.'

Well, wouldn't you just know it!

'Distances over water are very deceptive,' I said, wondering if they were and, if so, which way.

'We can't turn back,' said Miss Drom. She shaded her eyes with her hand and stared longingly at the far horizon.

I endeavoured to boost her morale. 'I told you I'd get you away, didn't I?'

'Out of the frying pan!' came the sullen rejoinder. 'And, I must say, you took your time about it. I thought you were going to sit there like a stuffed mummy all day.'

'One has to wait for the psychological moment,' I pointed out icily. 'And now, if you've quite finished your rest, I think we should continue.'

Miss Drom picked up her paddle. 'It's getting frightfully cold. You don't think we're going to have a storm, do you?'

'A storm? Don't be ridiculous!' I retorted – or I would have done if a deafening clap of thunder hadn't drowned the concluding words.

And these blooming foreigners have the cheek to talk about *our* weather!

After the thunder we had a few flashes of lightning. Then more thunder, each peal sounding nearer than the last. A few minutes later a stiffish breeze blew up. It began to rain. Heavily.

Miss Drom and I paddled miserably on. There was nothing else we could do. It was only a matter of seconds before we were soaked to the skin and frozen to the marrow. The shore ahead of us disappeared in the driving rain and overhead the sky thickened with black, lowering clouds. Cold, cruel waves slopped up over our legs and feet as we were tossed sickeningly around. The goose pimples on Miss Drom's back acquired a strange greenish tinge.

My thoughts wandered nostalgically back to our hideaway up in the mountains. With all its drawbacks it had at least been warm and dry. I couldn't help reflecting that, if it hadn't been for Miss Drom, I might still have been up there instead of being rocked about so frighteningly down here in the cradle of the deep. The company was better, too, and . . . whoops!

A particularly large wave nearly capsized us. Miss Drom and I both let out shrieks, which was perfectly understandable in the circumstances, but she – the silly bitch – let her paddle drop as she clutched for the sides of the float. By the time we had got back on an even keel, the paddle had sunk forever into a watery grave.

'Perhaps,' I twitted her, 'you would like to borrow mine?' Miss Drom did her celebrated imitation of Queen Victoria being unamused.

The storm cleared as suddenly as it had arrived. One minute it was all howling gales and pouring rain and the next we had the lake as smooth as glass and the sun burning into our backs again.

'We must be travelling from west to east,' said Miss Drom brightly as she reclined at her ease while I slaved away with our only paddle. 'The sun is sinking behind us, you see, and that means . . .'

'Look,' I snarled, 'skip the geography lesson and have a

look at that float, there by your left foot. It's not split, is it?'

Miss Drom had a look. 'Yes, it is,' she said. 'Oh dear, we're not going to sink, are we? There seems to be rather a lot of water pouring in.'

'Well, find something to stuff in the crack!'

'What?' wailed Miss Drom, waving a helpless hand about her. 'We haven't got anything.'

'A bit of seaweed or something might do.'

'This is a *lake*, Eddie! You don't get seaweed in a lake.'

'Well, shove your hand over it, then! Look, if you don't do something we shall ship so much water that this damn thing will go clean over and we'll sink.'

I'll bet that Dutch kid at the dyke didn't make half the fuss. And I'll bet he did a better job. Under Miss Drom's ministrations we sank lower and lower in the water until the float gently abandoned us and went to the bottom. Afer that it was a case of swim for the shore, boys.

Terra firma was only a hundred yards away so we made it without too much difficulty.

Miss Drom, arms akimbo, watched me struggle ashore. 'Well? What now?'

I collapsed face down at her feet and let a couple of litres of vintage lake water dribble out of my mouth. 'Give us a chance!' I choked.

'For one of Daddie's operatives, you're not very fit, are you?'

'Oh, go rot in hell!' I mumbled.

Miss Drom sat down beside me. We had landed in a small sandy inlet. Behind us was a barrier of ragged cliffs. Admittedly it was only about six feet high but from where I lay it put Everest to shame. Once we had surmounted this precipice, though, I calculated that things wouldn't be too bad. There was bound to be a road running along the lake and I thought I had enough Italian to persuade a passing motorist to take us to the nearest police station. Now that we hadn't got Monkey Tom and the rest of them thundering after us, I should be able to take my time over the explanations. And, who knows, we might even strike lucky and thumb a lift from an English-speaking car.

'Are you going to lie there all day, Eddie?'

They should have had her overseeing the building of the pyramids.

By the time I'd got to my feet, Miss Drom was already up and away, masterfully surveying the cliff face we had to climb. Two seconds and she'd got it all worked out.

'There's not much in the way of footholes,' she announced as though challenging the rocks to contradict her, 'and it's far too steep to try scaling it at the run. We'll have to use a stirrup double-handed assisted lift.'

'A what?' I asked weakly.

'It's quite simple. We used to do it in the Girl Guides. Now, you stand with your back right up against the cliff. Oh – do come *along*, Eddie! That's right! Now, feet wide apart and cup your hands in front of you! Fingers laced. Good. Now, I . . .'

'Wait a minute!' I said, dropping everything as she came towards me at a gallop. 'What are you going to do?'

'I'm simply going to place my right foot in your cupped hands. You heave me up and my left foot goes on your shoulder, my right foot on your head and – there I am – over the obstacle! It's as easy as pie if you do it all quickly. Then, when I'm up, I'll give you a hand from the top.'

I had been wondering about that.

'It sounds a bit tricky,' I said.

'Nonsense! I've seen quite small girls do it.'

'Well, in that case,' I said smartly, 'I'll climb up on you! I mean, you'll never be strong enough to pull me up from the top.'

And, at the second attempt and when I'd removed my sandals, that's how we did it. Miss Drom buckled under my weight but – stout girl – she didn't break. All that remained then was to hoist her up beside me.

I lay down on my stomach and trailed a helping hand over the cliff face. Miss Drom came like the Charge of the Heavy

Brigade. She jumped and missed, scraping herself agonizingly against the rocks as she slithered down them.

'You moved your hand!' she shouted when she'd picked herself up and dug a stone or two out of her face.

'As if I would!' I called back.

At her second attempt she made no mistake. Her fingers closed like a vice on my hand and my arm was dragged several inches out of its socket. I had the choice of heaving her up or joining her on the beach below. I heaved. Between us we started a major landslide but Miss Drom wasn't the girl to be put off by a few rocks bouncing off her head. She scrambled up beside me and still had enough breath left to tell me I was supposed to be pulling and not leaving all the work to her.

There's no future in arguing with women. I tried to divert her attention to less controversial subjects. 'What,' I asked, 'have you done to your foot?'

It was a good thing I mentioned it, otherwise she might have bled to death. A sizeable pool of blood was already seeping down through the patchy grass.

Miss Drom looked down and went as white as a sheet. 'I must have cut myself,' she said in a frightened voice. 'Oh, dear!'

I grabbed her before she could faint and lowered her to the ground. 'Let me have a look!'

It wasn't, as far as I could see, a particularly bad cut but Miss Drom was certainly bleeding like a stuck pig.

'Oughtn't you to stop it?' she asked.

I nodded. I'd had a pocket diary once with a lot of First Aid hints in the front. I was almost sure that you were supposed to stop heavy bleeding as soon as possible. 'What we really need,' I said, 'is a good tight bandage.'

Miss Drom, assuming from my confident tone that she was in the hands of a qualified practitioner, relaxed while I looked around hopefully for a good tight bandage. There wasn't one in sight. To the west of us was the wide, blue and – thank goodness – empty expanse of the lake. To the north and south stretched acre upon acre of coarse grass land and scrub. To the east, across more grass and scrub, I could just see what I presumed must be the road. There was no traffic on it and it was, I guessed, at least a mile away.

Miss Drom caught my returning eye. The blood was still coming cheerfully out of her foot in little spurts. I supposed that, given time, it would congeal. I looked at Miss Drom and then I looked at myself. We were somewhat inadequately equipped for dealing with emergencies.

'I suppose,' I said, 'you don't happen to have a handkerchief on you?'

She didn't.

'It's a pity,' I observed, 'that we didn't bring one of the towels with us. Or even,' I added with another glance at her foot, 'two.'

Miss Drom's face crumpled and the tears were not far away. 'Why don't you do something?' she whimpered. 'It hurts.'

I squatted down beside her and spoke softly to cushion the shock. 'Miss Drom, I am afraid I shall have to ask you to remove your bra.'

'*What?*'

That took her mind off her bleeding foot all right.

She clutched herself as though I was going to strip her there and then by brute force.

'The top half of your bathing costume,' I explained patiently. 'I shall have to use it to bandage your foot.'

Another thousandth of an inch and her eyes would have popped clean out of her head. 'How dare you?' she bellowed.

'We've got to stop the bleeding. What else can we use?'

'You shameless brute!' she screamed. 'You sadist! You ... you! Just wait till I tell Daddie!'

'Miss Drom, look around you! Water, grass, shrubs and sand. That's all. Between us, we have precisely three pieces of cloth. You have two and I have one. Right? Now, it is a matter of supreme indifference to me which piece, or even pieces, we use. I merely thought that your – er – top half would be the least of the three evils, but suit yourself.'

Miss Drom choked back her tears and sniffingly added two and two together. It still made three substitute bandages. 'I'll never forgive you for this!' she informed me bitterly. 'Never!'

'Damn it all, woman, it's not my fault! If you want to go on bleeding like a stuck pig while I go and get help, that's fine by me. With luck, I might be back in a couple of hours and . . .'

'You'll have to turn your back and keep your eyes closed!'

And they talk about the permissive society! I took up a kneeling position and faced away from Miss Drom. After a second or two there was a tap on my shoulder and I held my hand out behind me to receive the pink and grey bra from fingers that were as cold as chastity.

I don't claim it was the best bit of bandaging in the world but it tight and it looked as though it might do the trick.

'Well,' I said, gazing resolutely out across the lake, 'that's the best we can do for the moment. Now, you'd better hang on here while I go and try and get some help. I'll be as quick as I can.'

'You're not proposing to leave me here alone?'

'What else?'

'Like *this*?'

What a fuss about nothing.

I tried to keep my voice reasonable. 'I don't think it would be very advisable to walk on that foot.'

'But suppose somebody – an Italian – should come along and see me? What on earth would they think? Or suppose that terrible Monkey man and those others came searching for us? I should be completely at their mercy.'

'Well, what do you suggest? That we should both sit here until the United States cavalry gallops up to the rescue?'

'There is no need,' said Miss Drom, very hoity-toity, 'to descend to cheap sarcasm.'

'What else do you expect, for God's sake?'

'Nor is there any need for foul language.'

I relieved my feelings by beating my fists on the innocent

ground. 'It'll be dark in an hour or two and I'm getting cold. Now, whether you like it or not, I am going over to that road to try and find some help. I don't see what alternative we have.'

'You'll have to carry me,' said Miss Drom calmly.

Now, I don't want you to think I'm one of your seven stone weaklings. Nor that Miss Drom was either. As a matter of fact, her weight doubled every fifty yards though actually carrying the stupid cow was the least of my difficulties. Well, have you ever tried picking up a half-naked girl with your eyes closed? Believe me, we had our moments.

Eventually, however, and in spite of Miss Drom's militant modesty, I got her slung over my shoulder in what may or may not be known as the fireman's lift. I held her legs steady with my left hand and let the rest of her anatomy take care of itself. As positions go it wasn't a very comfortable one for either of us but the proprieties were scrupulously observed. From where I was, and when I'd opened my eyes again, you couldn't see anything that would have stirred the blood of the most rabid sex maniac.

Before long Miss Drom was complaining again. My shoulder was cutting her in two and having her head hanging down like that was making her feel sick.

Well, I was more than ready for a rest. I lowered Miss Drom to the ground, whereupon she let out a shriek like a wounded banshee and clamped her arms crosswise over her chest. I averted my eyes.

Then we tried it again with Miss Drom supported by both my arms while she used hers to protect her naked bosom from my lascivious gaze. That was murder and after a few agonizing steps my knees buckled and we sank together once again onto the grassy sward.

'Look,' I puffed, 'you'll just have to put your arms round my neck. Otherwise you're just a dead weight and I can't manage.'

By now even Miss Drom had been forced to recognize my limitations. She bit her lip. 'You promise not to look?'

'Cross my heart and hope to die,' I promised wearily and, closing my eyes once more as a gesture of good faith, I stretched out my arms for her.

We did better this time, once Miss Drom had got a series of girlish squeaks and wriggles out of her system. Every now and again her left bosom snuggled confidingly against my jaw and, at first, we both flinched fastidiously away from the contact. After a while, though, I began to find it increasingly difficult to turn my head. Miss Drom's once shrinking clasp had shrunk into a positive stranglehold.

I kept my eyes glued on the far horizon. 'You're strangling me,' I pointed out and laughed, though – God knows – I didn't think it was very funny.

'Sorry!' cooed Miss Drom, skilfully adjusting her position so that, however meagre her frontal assault, I could hardly fail but know it was there.

I went hot and cold all over.

I tried to keep the panic out of my voice. 'Soon be there now!' I assured her heartily. 'Then your ordeal will be over, eh?'

'Ordeal?' echoed Miss Drom, pressing even closer. 'Oh, I don't think it's quite as bad as that, Eddie, do you? I mean it's little adventures like that that make a sort of bond between people. Are you getting tired? We could stop and have another rest if you like.'

Perish the thought but – could Miss Drom possibly be a student of Confucius? You know – the bit about relaxing and enjoying the inevitable. Inspired by the dread of what might happen if we stopped, I struggled grimly on. Fear put the steel back in my aching sinews. The road ahead became the symbol of my salvation. There lay civilization, safety and other people. I was going to make it there or bust.

And, talking about busts . . .

No! I was not even going to *think* about busts.

I swallowed hard. 'Is you foot still hurting?' I asked.

Eleven

We pushed our way through a crumbling fence and out on to the dusty, deserted road. I dropped Miss Drom like a hot brick and stared hopefully in both directions. We might have been on the moon.

Miss Drom had sunk into a decorous, if bedraggled, huddle and I addressed myself to her back. 'I'll give it ten minutes,' I announced. 'Then, if nothing comes along, I'm going to start walking.'

The shadows were getting longer and the chalky surface of the road didn't look as though it had been disturbed for generations.

'That's a car, isn't it?' asked she of the bat-like ears.

I jumped out into the middle of the road. 'Where? Where?'

A cloud of dust surged up in the distance and began moving leisurely towards me. I slicked my hair down and made myself as presentable as possible. It would be too heartbreaking if the occupants of the car took fright and drove past without stopping. Even as I was considering this dire possibility, the car suddenly put a spurt on. In spite of the dust I could see it quite clearly now. It was a snazzy white coupé job. A one-off Alfa Romeo, if my eyes didn't deceive me. The top was down, revealing the delicate mauve upholstery and a woman alone behind the steering wheel.

Now, was she going to pull up for a near-naked man on a

lonely road or was she not? I wondered if I ought to fetch Miss Drom out. The sight of her would surely convince even the most timid motorist that we had been struck by a genuine disaster.

The woman in the car had now definitely seen us. I waved. She waved back. I mimed that she should slow down and, marvellously, she swung the car round through a hundred and eighty degrees and brought it to rest right beside me.

I had my little speech all ready. '*Per favore, parla inglese? No? Multo difficile! Mi porti alla policia, pronto! Ha capito?*' That was if I was obliged to converse in the language of Dante, of course. Should our rescuer speak English, I counted on producing something a bit more polished and persuasive.

The woman in the car didn't give me chance to open my mouth. 'Why, you poor things!' she said in one of those deep throaty voices that always set me a-tingle right down to the soles of my feet. 'Do get in!' She leaned across and invitingly opened the passenger door.

Miss Drom, crouching in the gutter, hesitated.

The woman in the car twinkled an amused, almost conspiratorial smile at me and reached behind her on to the back seat. 'Perhaps your companion is liking to borrow the rug?'

I nodded my head and accepted the rug in something of a daze. The driver of the car was one of the most beautiful women I have ever seen in my life. Not young. In her middle thirties, I should guess, but not a whit the worse for that. Her smooth dark hair was drawn back in an elegant bun that nestled in the nape of a long slender neck. Her eyes were huge and smoky coloured. Her nose was a trifle on the big side but that merely added a piquant note of patrician distinction to her face. Her wide smiling lips were drawn back over the exquisite pearls of her teeth and her chin . . .

'*Eddie!*' came the familiar whine from behind me.

I twinkled an amused smile back to our benefactress, sketched her a sophisticated bow and walked over to the miserable drab cowering under the hedgerow. 'Here you are!' I growled, tossing the rug at her.

We put Miss Drom in the back seat – out of sight, out of mind – while I slid gracefully into the front next to honey-bunch. I closed the door with one of those soft plonks that only money can buy and there we were – purring softly away.

'I wonder,' I said after clearing my throat once or twice, 'if you would mind dropping us at the nearest police station?'

Helen of Troy, Mona Lisa and the young Garbo smilingly shook that charming head. 'First I must take you to my house and attend to your needs. It is impossible for you to go to the police station like that. We Italians are strange people. The policemen would not understand. Besides,' – she raised the loveliest pair of eyebrows this side of the Rockies at me – 'there is no urgency, is there?'

'Not the least in the world!' I assured her hoarsely.

Conversation lapsed after that. Well as far as I was concerned, everything had already been said.

She drove very fast but very well, which was no more than one would expect. I was too fascinated by the sight of her slim gloved hands on the steering wheel and the occasional glimpses I snatched of her profile to bother much about where we were going. With a bobby-dazzler like that next to you, who watches the scenery? I'm not even sure how long we were driving. It could have been five minutes or it could have been an eternity.

Open cars, however opulent, do tend to be a mite breezy though, and in my scantily-clad condition I was rather relieved when our speed dropped to a comfortable twenty miles an hour or so. I tore my eyes away from the object of my desires and had a look round. We were climbing up another blooming mountain. For one ridiculous moment I thought we were being driven back to Monkey Tom's eyrie again but then I remembered that these hills were on the other side of the lake and miles and miles away.

I turned back to contemplate my gorgeous chauffeuse. She – oh, happy day! – was looking at me.

'By the way,' she said, and again I thrilled to the marrow,

'we have not introduced ourselves. My name is Elena – Elena di Tonarelli di Muccio.'

'Signora?' I queried, daringly.

Those lips parted in that smile. 'Marchesa,' she murmured apologetically.

Wow!

'I'm Eddie Brown,' I responded, making it into as much of a declaration of undying devotion as I could. 'That,' I added as an afterthought with a nod towards the back seat, 'is Miss Muriel Drom.'

And, dismissing this jarring note from my mind, I slipped back into the most delicious reveries.

'Would you be so kind as to open the gates for me, Mr Brown?'

For a second I couldn't understand what Marchesa Elena Tonarelli di Muccio was doing with all her clothes on but then reality came flooding back and I tumbled out of the car to fulfil my beloved's demands. En passant I paused to advance our relationship a step or two further. 'Not Mr Brown, gracious lady,' I corrected her seductively, '– Eddie.'

I pushed the stiff, wrought-iron gates open as though they were hung on well-oiled hinges and weighed no more than a feather. There's nothing like having a handsome female watching you to lend strength to your arm. The car rolled through and I closed the gates again behind it. I wasn't quite so besotted that I didn't, albeit a little late in the day, have a quick glance round. We had, presumably, now reached our destination. It was one worthy of the Marchesa.

From the wrought-iron gates a wide, curving drive swept for a good half mile through rolling parkland. At the far end it swung round in front of a large white villa which was surrounded by terraced gardens ablaze with the colours of high summer. I had only time to notice that the whole estate was surrounded by a high stone wall before I was leaping off, gazelle like, for the car which had stopped and was waiting for me.

As we drew nearer the house I found that my first impressions had been somewhat flattering. There were unmistakable signs of neglect and decay. Paint was peeling and the flower beds had an under-carpet of weeds. Tufts of coarse grass were pushing up here and there in the drive. The small squares of lawn hadn't seen a mower recently and some of the clumps of azaleas or bougainvillaeas or whatever looked decidedly tatty.

We drew up beside a flight of marble steps. They were cracked and chipped but, really, this slight but pervasive air of decadence was not without its charm. Probably, like most aristocrats, the Tonarelli di Muccio family was just not quite as well-heeled as they used to be.

We got out of the car and I escorted the Marchesa up the steps past a series of noble statues. Behind us, Miss Drom, still swathed in her car rug, limped along in our wake looking about as appetizing as a mobile Scottish wigwam.

The Marchesa graciously permitted me to open the door for her and, since she had suddenly put a spurt on, Miss Drom had to be allowed in ahead of me, too. We found ourselves in an enormous entrance hall that looked like something out of a film set. Three double doors, their white paint picked out in gold, opened off at the sides while in the middle of the chessboard marble floor was a fountain with real water coming out of a fish's mouth. Beyond the fountain a wide staircase rose majestically to the first floor.

The sheer size and magnificence of all this left Miss Drom and me speechless.

'Now,' said the Marchesa, carelessly dropping her driving gloves on an ormolu table, 'I think the first thing we must do is provide you with some clothes. Will you both come this way?'

Miss Drom and I pattered up the ceremonial staircase and were shown into a couple of bedrooms.

'You will find plenty of my husband's clothes in the wardrobe,' the Marchesa told me. 'Please help yourself to anything you require. I am sure you will find something that will fit you. If you wish to wash, the bathroom is through there. Meanwhile, I will see if I can find some clothes of mine to fit Miss – er – Drom.'

'There's not,' I responded gallantly, casting a connoisseur's eye over the Marchesa's curvaceous form, 'much chance of that, I'm afraid.'

The Marchesa gave me a reproving tap on the arm. 'Naughty boy!' she giggled.

And left me swooning.

I had a marvellous time hunting through the Marquis's clothing and he certainly had plenty for me to hunt through. He seemed to be a bit wider in the shoulders than me so I rejected the tails and the dinner jackets and the formal suits and settled for casual wear. Showered, shaved and with my hair smoothed down with the Marquis's own silver-backed brushes, I dressed in a pair of cream-coloured slacks and a matching turtle-necked sweater in heavy silk. A last dab of his Lordship's after-shave and I was raring to go.

The Marchesa was standing in one of the double doors when I came down into the hall. She had changed, too. Into a sort of shimmery gold trouser suit that flashed and sparkled every time she breathed.

Maybe I should have made that shower a cold one.

'I hope you drink martinis,' said the Marchesa as she beckoned me into a large drawing-room which was catching the last rays of the setting sun.

Smoothly assuring her that I would happily drink dish water were it but poured out for me by her sweet hand, I accepted the thin-stemmed glass and knocked back the contents in one gulp, holding the Marchesa's eyes with mine as I did so.

She looked a little surprised but poured me out another drink without comment.

'To us!' I breathed and drained it to the dregs.

The Marchesa sank down on to a silken divan. 'Help yourself,' she said weakly.

I did, and joined her amongst the cushions.

'Your fiancée will be down in a minute,' she said as she moved slightly so that I wouldn't land in her lap.

I mopped the martini off her knees with her husband's handkerchief. 'My *what*?'

'Your fiancée. Did I misunderstand Miss Drom? I thought she gave me the impression that you were engaged to be married.'

'We are certainly not engaged to be married!' I said firmly, not wishing to have any misapprehensions on that score. 'Our relationship is less than platonic. We are not even good friends.'

'Oh?' said the Marchesa. 'Well, she is a very sweet girl, I think.'

I took the Marchesa's glass and put it, with mine, on the table. 'Let's not,' I said, 'waste time talking about Miss Drom. Let's talk about us!'

You could see that the Marchesa was interested, really, but she wasn't the woman to be rushed. 'I must warn you that things are a little disorganized here,' she said hurriedly. 'Actually, the villa is closed. It is only an accident that I have come down here for a couple of days. There are no servants so you will have to eat whatever I can find in the ice-box.'

'Food,' I said, taking her little hand in mine, 'is the last thing I am thinking about at the moment.' I turned her hand over and kissed the inside of her wrist. Passionately.

There was a sharp intake of breath from the Marchesa but, since she didn't actually plant a bunch of fives in my face, I reckoned I was getting the old green light. I moved closer and slipped my arms round her. 'Elena!' I breathed masterfully.

I got my technique from Charles Boyer and it usually goes down a treat.

This time, however, the lady fended me off. 'Not now!' she whispered. 'Miss Drom is coming.'

'But later?' I insisted, determined not to release my hold without some hope for the future.

The Marchesa gave me her most brilliant smile. 'But, of course, carissimo! Later.'

'When, for example?'

The smile grew even more enticing. 'Tonight, perhaps! My room is next to yours.'

'Whacko!' I said, and let go of her.

My actual words may strike you as being pretty banal but there is a language of the eyes, too, you know, and I was communicating most eloquently with mine.

The Marchesa stood up to greet Miss Drom who slouched into the drawing-room looking like something any self-respecting cat would have left outside. I wondered slyly if the Marchesa had been responsible for the unfortunate effect of the borrowed plumage. Bottle green was not Miss Drom's colour and the stylish little dress hung on her with all the grace of an old potato sack.

'Ah,' said the Marchesa after pausing just a second or two too long, 'how charming you look.'

Miss Drom ignored the compliment with a scowl. 'I suppose Eddie's told you what happened to us?'

'No.'

'There hasn't been time,' I said defensively. 'Besides, I'm sure our gracious hostess doesn't want to be bothered with our little troubles.'

'Little troubles?' sniffed Miss Drom, giving the pair of us a most suspicious glance. 'I get kidnapped by a gang of criminals and you call it a little trouble.'

'How dreadful,' said the Marchesa brightly.

'They were asking a million pounds ransom for me,' said Miss Drom, not without a touch of pride.

'Really?'

'Eddie and I managed to escape from them but they're bound to be looking for us now. That's why we wanted you to take us to the police.'

'I see.'

'However,' Miss Drom went doggedly on, 'now that we're here, I think the best thing would be for us to ring the British Embassy in Rome and let them deal with everything. The ambassador is a friend of my father and it will be much simpler explaining things to him than to the Italian police.'

The Marchesa turned away to the drinks table to pour out some more martinis. 'I'm so sorry, my dear,' she said with a charmingly dead-pan face, 'but our telephone has been disconnected. I was explaining to Mr Brown here that the villa is really closed. I am only here on a fleeting visit.'

Miss Drom frowned. 'Isn't there another telephone we could use?'

'I'm afraid there isn't. May I offer you a martini? We are so isolated here, you see. There isn't another house within – oh – fifty kilometres.'

The sweet smile which accompanied this rather surprising piece of information found no reflection in Miss Drom's bleak countenance. A true specimen of the bull-dog breed, she showed no signs of being deflected from her purpose by the embarrassment of putting a total stranger to a great deal of trouble. 'In that case, Marchesa, I wonder if you would mind running Eddie and me down to the nearest police station in your car?'

Poor Marchesa! You could see how distressed she was by this threat to our romantic assignation. I watched her admiringly as, with the prettiest of pouts, she parried Miss Drom's demands. 'But, it is so late!' she protested. 'See, it is already dark. And you look so worn out, my dear. Couldn't it wait until the morning?'

Miss Drom's bottom lip stuck out obstinately but I chipped in before the two women finished up at each other's throats. 'Of course it could!' I laughed merrily. 'What a perfectly cracking idea!' The sparkle faded a bit as I turned to Miss Drom. 'We're perfectly safe here in the Marchesa's delightful home, aren't we? Monkey Tom can't possibly have the least idea where we are, so what difference will a few hours make? We'll feel much more like tackling things in the morning after we've had a good night's sleep. And then, I'm sure the Marchesa' – I treated the aforementioned lovely to another of my suave bows – 'will drive us to wherever we want to go!'

'Of course!' agreed the Marchesa quickly. 'In the morning I will drive you to Rome, if you wish, straight to your Embassy.'

'How extremely kind!' I dragged my eyes away from the

Marchesa and appealed to Miss Drom. 'Now, what about it, eh? That's the perfect solution if you ask me.'

Miss Drom's jaw was set like reinforced concrete. 'I'd sooner go to the police station tonight.'

'Well, you can't!' I snarled.

'Why not?'

Oh, damn and blast the woman! 'Because it's getting dark, that's why!'

'That's no reason.'

'The lights on my car do not work,' said the Marchesa suddenly and turned away to pour herself out another drink.

Well, even I thought that that was a most injudicious statement to make though I could understand that the Marchesa was being driven to desperate measures. Get the police involved in this kidnapping business and our one night of illicit love would go straight down the drain. Still, I couldn't help preening myself. The poor girl had really taken *quite* a fancy to me!

Meanwhile Miss Drom was busy registering the utmost incredulity. She'd no manners at all, of course. 'That sounds extremely unlikely,' she said bluntly. 'However, we'd better go and have a look. Luckily, I'm quite good at that sort of thing.'

'I'm sure the Marchesa doesn't want you poking round her beautiful car,' I said spitefully, but the situation was beyond hope.

The Marchesa ruefully acknowledged that her bluff had been called. 'Very well,' she said, a taut little smile hiding her bitter disappointment, 'if you wish to leave that badly, I suppose I cannot stop you. I was only thinking of your welfare. I'm sure you ought to rest that poor foot of yours. However,' – the brave little thing tried to make it sound all frightfully gay and only I knew that underneath her heart was breaking – 'one thing I insist upon: you are going to have a hot, nourishing meal first. No,' – she held up a restraining hand as Miss Drom's trap sprang open once again – 'I insist! Heaven only knows how long the police will be asking you questions. Hours and hours, probably. Believe me, you are going to need all your strength. Now, you two help yourselves to drinks while I go and make a nice supper for us.'

I was all for accompanying her but she stopped me.

'Try and get her to change her mind, Eddie,' she whispered. 'Otherwise . . .'

Otherwise . . .

I could cheerfully have strangled Miss Drom. As soon as the Marchesa had gone I stormed over to the drinks table and tipped what was left in the martini jug into my glass. 'Well,' I said to Miss Drom who had perched herself fastidiously on the edge of the most uncomfortable chair she could find, 'that was a nice exhibition! Charming!'

'She's trying to keep us here,' muttered Miss Drom.

'Of course she is. She happens to be an extremely generous, warm-hearted woman. Good God, considering all she's done for us, I think the very least you could do is meet her half way. What possible difference could waiting till the morning make? You heard her say she was all alone here. She's probably nervous about spending the night in an empty house.'

Miss Drom gave vent to a contemptuous snort. 'Her? Nervous? That's a laugh! I'm telling you, she's up to something.'

I got very indignant about that. 'You've got a mind like a cesspool!' I said haughtily.

Miss Drom, however, was thinking along different lines. 'Well, doesn't it strike you as suspicious, Eddie, the way she picked us up in that car of hers? That road didn't lead anywhere. That's why she turned right round and brought us back the way she'd come.'

'How do you know the road didn't lead anywhere?'

Miss Drom glared at me impatiently. 'Because I saw the sign, of course.'

'What sign?'

'The one down the road. A red circle on a white background. They always stick one of those up on the Continent when you can't go any further.'

Miss Drom, for once in her life, seemed to have spotted something I'd missed. I really must get my eyes seen to.

'Why didn't you tell me about this before?' I asked.

'I haven't had a chance, have I? And look at the way she never asked a single question about where we'd come from or what had happened to us. Well, wouldn't you in her shoes? And, if she was so damned anxious to be helpful, why didn't she do what we asked and take us straight to the police station instead of bringing us all the way up here? Oh, she's up to something all right and, if you weren't such a fool, you'd see it. And what about her saying her car lights had gone wrong? That was a bare-faced lie if ever I heard one. Well, I soon made her change her tune about *that*! And what about there being no servants here, not even a caretaker apparently? I've never heard anything so ridiculous in my life! Just look at the place! Hot water in the bathrooms, bedrooms all ready and not a dust sheet in sight. Oh, for goodness' sake, Eddie, use your common sense! Does this look like a house that's supposed to be shut up? And who shuts a country villa up in the summer, anyhow?'

I'll say one thing for Muriel Drom – she can flog a subject to death with more efficiency than anybody else I've ever met. She went on and on until she'd almost got me convinced that my darling Marchesa was the queenpin of an international white slavery gang. It was only the sight of Miss Drom herself that reassured me. Whatever the Marchesa might or might not be up to, it certainly wasn't the forcible abduction of young ladies for immoral purposes. She'd have left Miss Drom in the gutter where she found her if it had been.

None the less there were aspects of the Marchesa's behaviour which were, to put it at its mildest, eccentric. I wasn't worried about her insistence that we should stay the night, of course. I flattered myself that I knew the explanation for that all right. But the way she had acted down by the lake was beginning to look rather odd, especially when I'd had Miss Drom pounding my ear about it for fully three-quarters of an hour.

'She's taking rather a long time,' I commented when I could get a word in.

Miss Drom snapped this up like a hungry shark. 'It's another ruse to keep us here!' She stood up. 'Eddie, I think we ought to leave now. At once. While we've got the chance.'

It was quite dark outside and the last thing I fancied was groping my way on foot down the mountainside, with or without Miss Drom for company. We still hadn't got a brass lira between us and, during the last half hour, I'd been growing hungrier and hungrier. And what would the Marchesa think? I still couldn't believe that someone as beautiful as she was could possibly be mixed up in any fishy business.

I hummed and hawed, huffed and puffed, hesitated.

'If you would care to come into the dining-room, dear friends, dinner is now served.'

Twelve

There was no getting round the fact that the Marchesa was stalling for time though I was blowed if I could see why. Miss Drom had obviously made up her mind that she wasn't going to spend the night in the villa – come hell or high water – and the Marchesa's clumsy delaying tactics only served to make an unpleasant atmosphere even stickier. As we took our places round the dinner table, however, the courtesies were still just being observed and the two women concealed their exchange of small fire under a smoke-cover of platitudes.

The Marchesa urged Miss Drom to eat. Miss Drom claimed not to be hungry and pushed her spoon rather disdainfully around in the minestrone alla milanese.

The Marchesa wasn't what you might call much of a trencherman herself. She pecked at her food but, unlike Miss Drom, she kept on pecking. Ten minutes it took her before she finished her soup and then, refusing all offers of help (even from me), she disappeared into the kitchen for another quarter of an hour.

All this was just grist to Miss Drom's mill. She resumed her vague and slanderous accusations in a dry whisper, while keeping one eye on the door that led to the kitchen. It put me in a very awkward position. I had to admit that the Marchesa was behaving in a somewhat strange way but – well – we couldn't just up and walk out without so much as a ta-ever-so, could we? Miss Drom, of course, maintained that we could and indeed she'd practically worked herself up to the point of pushing off without me, if needs be, when the Marchesa was back again with a large, exciting looking dish which she announced was saltimbocca alla romana.

It took ages to serve it and then there was an awful fuss about the wine which, being a rough old Chianti, didn't deserve any ceremony at all. When we finally got round to sinking our teeth into the saltimbocca, I thought it was jolly good. Miss Drom put it, and the Marchesa, firmly in their place.

She took one mouthful, paused, and then said brightly, 'It's wonderful what you can get in tins these days, isn't it? No, really, this is *almost* indistinguishable from the real thing.'

The Marchesa went a bright pink and her bosom rose magnificently as she drew breath, but we were spared the outburst because, just at that moment, the stillness of the house was broken by the muffled but unmistakable ringing of a telephone.

The Marchesa deflated.

Miss Drom let her fork drop back on her plate. 'I thought as much!' she said grimly.

One couldn't help admiring the way the Marchesa tried to paper over the cracks. 'Goodness,' she trilled, 'the men must have mended the wires!'

'They weren't broken!' snarled Miss Drom, pushing her chair back and getting to her feet. 'You'd had the phone disconnected because the villa was closed. Remember? Well, come along, Eddie! We are going!'

Reluctantly I stood up too. I was sure the Marchesa didn't want to lose me but I felt I had to go. 'I'm extremely sorry,' I muttered.

'So,' said the Marchesa, her smile no longer quite so melting, 'am I! Now, if you will both sit down quietly in your chairs once more, I will answer the telephone.'

She reinforced this request by producing a small, pearl-handled revolver from the depths of her gold lamé trouser suit and pointing it at us. We sat down, me with slightly more

145

alacrity than Miss Drom because, somehow, I'm never very happy when the weaker sex start waving lethal weapons about.

'Hands on your heads!' ordered the Marchesa, who was beginning to look as though she might have handled this sort of situation before. 'And I advise you to be sensible. One suspicious movement and I shall fire. The first bullet will be for Miss Drom.'

Every cloud has a silver lining.

The Marchesa, still keeping her little pop gun trained on us, backed over to a sort of sideboard and with some fumbling eventually managed to extract a telephone from it. When she answered it she spoke in very rapid Italian which I simply couldn't follow. She was as mad as hell about something, that was for sure, and every now and again she exploded into what sounded like straight-from-the-gutter abuse. Finally she rattled the receiver back on to its stand, flung her free hand up in one of those expressive Italian gestures and sauntered back to the dining-table.

'Scusi!' she said. 'My husband is a stupid pig.'

'What are you going to do with us?' asked Miss Drom.

The Marchesa sat down again. 'You will be finding out soon enough, cara mia.'

I was starting to feel more than a bit of a lemon, sitting there with my hands on my head like a naughty school kid. In front of me the saltimbocca all romana was growing cold.

'I wonder,' I ventured, a damned sight more scared of Miss Drom's reactions than of the Marchesa's, 'if you would mind if I finished my dinner? The condemned man ate a hearty breakfast and all that jazz.'

I doubt if the Marchesa really understood the idiom but she admired the spirit behind it. 'Ah, what courage!' she murmured. 'What coolness! Very well, my friend, but use only your left hand.'

'Thank you!' I said, picking up my fork. 'Actually, I'm so hungry I could eat a horse.'

'And you probably are doing!' sniffed Miss Drom who was never one to shun the hackneyed.

Of course, I wasn't just thinking about my stomach. I hope, dear reader, you know me and my methods better than that. No, I was actually looking for an opportunity to launch a counter attack. A well directed plate or table knife might distract the Marchesa's attention long enough for me to get my hands on that gun. Unless I was much mistaken, she would drop everything if she thought her face was likely to be damaged.

Unfortunately, I am not ambidextrous and a fork sinister thrown at the Marchesa was as likely to scalp Miss Drom as to reach its target. Not that that would have been a total disaster, come to think about it. Still, I bowed to the inevitable and got on with my food.

With Miss Drom glaring at me, the minutes ticked slowly away. I licked my platter clean and looked round for more. There was a sweet course waiting in the kitchen but the Marchesa, rather meanly I thought, wouldn't let anybody go and get it so I had to fill up the odd gaps with the cheese and biscuits which were already on the table. I polished off the Chianti, too, and all in all I was feeling much happier than I had for a long time.

I flicked the last biscuit crumbs off the Marquis's silk sweater and pushed my chair back. 'Any chance of a cup of coffee, Marchesa? I'm quite prepared to go and make it, if you're too busy.'

'You are a little too late, my friend,' she answered quite good humouredly. 'They have arrived, I think.'

We all went on sitting there quietly round the table, ears flapping. Somewhere outside car doors were slammed and there was the sound of people talking.

'Elena! Elena!'

The Marchesa barely turned her head and certainly didn't turn her nasty little revolver. 'La sala de pranzo!' she called languidly.

The dining-room door opened and a man came in. At round about sixty he seemed a trifle old for the Marchesa but I had no doubt that this was her husband. I recognized his style of clothing. In spite of his advanced years, he was a pretty snappy dresser.

He started to speak to his wife, irritably and with no sign of affection. She answered in a mixture of bored indifference and contempt. They were just revving up for a high-pitched slanging match when another man pushed into the room. When I caught sight of him my heart sank. I can spot a Russian a mile off, with or without snow on his boots, and this chappie was almost the prototype of a fairly senior KGB man. There is something about them – the cut of their suits, the thickness of their necks, the expression in their narrowed eyes – which is quite unmistakable.

This one broke up the domestic disturbance with a single word. 'Silence!'

The Marquis and his better half shut up as though somebody had switched them off at the mains.

The Russian eyed them grimly. 'Speak English! You have been told that before. If you can't be bothered to learn Russian, you must speak in a language I understand.'

'I am sorry, Comrade Colonel!' The Marquis shuffled his feet unhappily. 'I was only explaining to my wife what had happened.'

'All necessary explanations will be provided by me. You talk too much, Comrade Marquis, even for an Italian.'

The Marquis cringed under the sneering tone. 'Yes, Comrade Colonel.'

'Go and see to the men. Two of them have been posted as sentries. The others need food and somewhere to sleep. Attend to it!'

'At once, Comrade Colonel!'

'And check your transmitter. I shall wish to send a message to Moscow tonight. What time do you make contact?'

'Tonight at seven minutes before midnight, Comrade Colonel.'

'Well,' – the Colonel examined the Marquis from head to toe – 'what are you waiting for?'

'Nothing, Comrade Colonel!' The Marquis scuttled obsequiously out of the room and the KGB man watched him go with ill-concealed exasperation.

He turned to the Marchesa. 'I wonder how much longer I can endure that husband of yours.'

The Marchesa shrugged her shoulders. 'Don't undervalue him, carissimo. People who are willing to do the menial tasks are hard to find, you know. Your men will eat well and sleep comfortably. That is better than having yet another expert in dialectical materialism, isn't it?'

The Colonel nodded. 'I suppose so.' He pulled his revolver out of his shoulder holster. 'You can put that toy of yours away. I will take over now. Well,' – he swung a spare chair away from the table and sat down – 'what have we here?'

'The girl,' explained the Marchesa indifferently, 'and this man who helped her escape. I had no difficulty in picking them up. Once the storm was over, they were the only people on this part of the lake. They fitted your description and I had plenty of time to get down to the road before they reached it.'

The Colonel leaned forward and helped himself to a piece of cheese off the table. 'Get me a drink,' he said.

'Vodka?'

'No, brandy. It has been a difficult day. I dislike it when things do not go according to plan. They do not care for improvisation in Moscow and I am not looking forward to explaining why we failed to find out that this man here,' – he pointed a stubby thumb at me '– was a subversive element in the gang of kidnappers. What is his name?'

'He says he is called Eddie Brown,' said the Marchesa, pouring out a generous helping of brandy and handing it to the Colonel. 'I haven't asked them any questions. I thought you would wish to do that.'

'Hm.' The Colonel took a long, deep drink and sighed. 'I shall have to ask Moscow what we are to do with him.'

'Couldn't you just kill him and pretend that this escape across the lake never happened?' asked the Marchesa, affectionately stroking the Colonel's furrowed brow while taking care not to get between his revolver and us.

The Colonel laughed bitterly. 'With six men out there and your husband knowing what really happened? I would be firing the bullet into the back of my own neck, dorogaya. Besides, how would I account for the fact that his body is not in the ruins of the house with the others?'

'Couldn't you take him back there now, in the dark?'

'No. The fuses were set for six o'clock. That's more than three hours ago. The place will be thick with policemen by now. We barely had time to get that fat one up from the beach in time to join his colleagues.'

Miss Drom had been sitting through all this charmingly casual and intimate exchange of news in a shocked silence. That was too good to last, of course. She chipped in now. 'Do you mean to say that you've *killed* those men who kidnapped me?'

The Colonel regarded her over the top of his brandy glass. 'Naturally. We strangled the three of them who were waiting for us in the villa. Their arrangements for not being caught by surprise were pathetically elementary. Then we placed a large amount of explosives in the cellar. That duly blew up at six o'clock this evening. Fortunately, we managed to get the fourth man – the fat one who was with you – back off the beach and into the house before it exploded and took half the mountainside with it. You have nothing to worry about, Miss Drom. You have been avenged!'

The chuckle which accompanied this last statement brought me out in a cold sweat. This fat-necked joker was playing it for real.

'But, why?' demanded Miss Drom. 'Why didn't you just hand them over to the authorities?'

Such bright-eyed innocence all but had the Colonel rolling in the aisles. 'Because we do not want the whole world, including your so-celebrated British Secret Service, to realize that you are in our hands. From our point of view, that would be a disaster. Only one person will eventually know that you are well and happy and in the Soviet Union. Your father, of course. He will apreciate that, if he doesn't co-operate fully with us, your – er – health will suffer quite drastically. You understand now the reason for secrecy? If other people – your father's colleagues, for example – knew that you were enjoying our hospitality, your father would immediately be removed from his present position as an intolerable security risk. That would be of no benefit to us at all. So, we have gone to a great deal of trouble to make everybody believe that you were killed in the explosion at the house where you were detained.'

I felt it was about time I stuck my oar in and spread a little doubt and dissension around. 'You've not got much hope of that, have you, chummie? Any forensic scientist worth his salt will spot in no time at all whether there were four bodies or five, however big your precious explosion was.'

He didn't seem in the least annoyed by my remarks. Which made it all the more disconcerting when he got up, ambled leisurely across to where I was sitting and hit me a brutal blow across the side of my head with the barrel of his revolver. Through a red haze of blinding pain I saw him resume his seat and turn quite courteously to Miss Drom.

'Your talkative comrade is quite mistaken,' he said. 'Like everybody in the West, he tends to think we Russians are un-educated savages. We are not. We have a saying in my country: Nicolas II is dead. You understand? It is like your Queen Anne. Well, since we dealt with the Tsar and his family, we have learned a great deal about the problems inherent in the disposal of dead bodies. We know that skilled investigators can determine the number of corpses, no matter how thoroughly they seem to have been destroyed. We are not stupid enough to leave only four when there should be five.'

'Maria?' asked the Marchesa as though she was making small talk over a tea table.

'Maria,' agreed the Colonel. 'Much too dangerous to leave alive after that Palermo business and so useful to us dead. especially with all Miss Drom's personal possessions scattered around her.'

'You mean you've killed a girl to take my place?' gasped Miss Drom in horror.

'Party members are expected to make every sacrifice for the cause,' grinned the Colonel. 'And I'm sure Maria would have willingly volunteered . . . if she had been asked. However, I am glad you are taking such a sympathetic interest in our affairs, Miss Drom. It will help you appreciate the type of people you are now dealing with. We are not a collection of petit bourgeois English crooks who would have been arrested by the police before they collected your ransom money. No, we work with intelligence and system. We leave nothing to chance.

'Take this explosion for an example. Do you not think the police will be highly curious as to why a house, inhabited by a gang of kidnappers, should suddenly explode? Oh, they will be, I assure you! But we have manufactured a number of clues which will provide a satisfactory explanation. We are on the frontier of Alto Adige, you know. The Southern Tyrol. That is the part of Italy that used to belong to Austria and many of its inhabitants wish that it still did. Every now and again these people make a great deal of trouble for the Italian authorities. They protest, they demonstrate and, sometimes, they blow things up. And, also sometimes, we of the Soviet Union help them. Are you following my explanation?

'Well, the house in which you were detained has frequently been used in the past for subversive and revolutionary purposes. By the Freedom Fighters of Alto Adige, amongst others. So, you see, the police will not be too surprised to find that large supplies of explosive were being stored in the cellars. If dynamite is not looked after properly, it deteriorates. The dynamite we installed was in an extremely unstable condition. The police will be able to tell this. It will be accredited to a most unfortunate coincidence that it blew up just when you, Miss Drom, were being detained there.' The Colonel put his empty brandy glass down on the table. 'Believe me, my dear young lady, we have thought of everything.'

'Except me!' I put in before I'd thought about what happened the last time I opened my mouth.

Luckily the Colonel was weary or, maybe, he'd had enough violence for one day. He examined me thoughtfully. 'Except you, my friend. You are something of a puzzle. I shall ask Moscow about you. Maybe they will want you despatched to the Soviet Union with Miss Drom. I have a suspicion that you might be quite a valuable property. If I am wrong, however, it will not matter. We shall dispose of you here.'

So, as prospects go, mine were bleak. I'd certainly no wish to make some bit of Italian soil forever England but even that might be preferable to falling into the clutches of the KGB. I had crossed swords with that bunch of professional thugs before and I knew what to expect if they caught up with me again. I wondered how full a description the Colonel would be able to give his masters back home. Full enough, I feared. My association with Miss Drom would give them a pretty good lead as to who, and what, I was, even if nothing else did. I felt quite queasy. Whichever way the cat jumped, it looked like curtains for little old Eddie Brown. Incredible as it seemed, I was about to be cut off in my prime.

It is thus perfectly understandable that when, only a few minutes later, Miss Drom and I found ourselves locked up together I was a mite niggly. We'd been incarcerated in a disused pantry leading off the kitchen and, if the place had been designed as a top security prison, they couldn't have done a better job. It was a small, square room with walls that looked about ten feet thick. There were no windows; just a couple of tiny grilles set up high near the ceiling and an undersized kitten would have had its work cut out trying to wriggle through them. The only door, constructed of good, solid oak, led directly into the kitchen where four of the Colonel's brutal henchmen were currently stuffing themselves and where they would later be sleeping. Talk about impregnable! Fort Knox wasn't in it.

'I do think,' snivelled Miss Drom as I completed my tour of inspection, 'that you might show some consideration for me instead of thinking about yourself all the time.'

'Consideration for you? What the hell have you got to bitch

about? Once you get to Russia, you'll be treated like a queen! Nobody's going to harm a hair of your head, that's for sure. The longer they keep you alive and kicking, the longer they'll be able to put the squeeze on your old man. By the way,' I added maliciously. 'I hope Sir Maurice's health is good because the day he pops off or even gets himself turned out to grass, you, sister, are a dead duck.'

'Oh, what a rotten thing to say!' wailed Miss Drom, who really didn't show up at all well when the pressure was on. 'I've got a good mind to tell them exactly who you are. It would serve you right if I did.'

'It wouldn't make one ha-porth of difference,' I retorted and kicked the wall. 'I'm for the high jump whatever happens. And do you want to know something else? I wish to God I'd never laid eyes on you or your blasted father!'

'But it's not my fault, Eddie! I didn't ask to be kidnapped.'

I was in no mood for excuses. Besides, if it hadn't been for Sir Maurice, I would still be coasting to a happy old age, teaching Russian in a nice safe comprehensive school. If you ask me, I'd got every right to be bitter.

Miss Drom was weeping and I was just considering remonstrating with her again and making a few pertinent remarks about chins and stiff upper lips when I had one of my ideas. It was the longest of long shots but – what had we got to lose? I thought it over for five minutes or so and then decided it was worth risking.

I squatted down beside Miss Drom who was still managing to force out a few adenoidal sobs and, gritting my teeth, placed a comforting arm round her shoulder. Miss Drom's tear-smudged face turned up to me in blank astonishment. I chiselled out an encouraging smile. Miss Drom's jaw dropped.

'What's the matter with you?' she asked, suddenly suspicious.

Well, for two pins I'd have rammed her ungrateful teeth down her throat, but it was no time for pettiness. 'It's just that, you and I, we're in this thing together,' I said, getting quite a touching break in to my voice. 'It's no time for squabbling, is it?'

'You started it!'

I ignored that. 'We've been in tight spots before – you and I – but we've . . .'

'We wouldn't have been in this particular tight spot at all,' Miss Drom interrupted me rudely, 'if you'd listened to me. I told you we ought to get away while we could but you were far too busy slobbering over that elderly Italian tart, though what you saw in her heaven only knows because she's old enough to be your mother and any fool could . . .'

'Yes,' I said – and men have got the Order of Merit for less – 'well, let's not worry our heads over what's dead and done with, shall we? It's the future we've got to think about now, how we're going to get out of here.'

'You've got a plan?' Miss Drom sat up hopefully and blew her nose. 'Oh, Eddie, have you really? You are quite resourceful, you know, when you put your mind to it. After all, you did hit that dreadful Punchie man over the head with the stone, didn't you?'

I fancied that my contributions over the last few days had amounted to rather more than that but – no matter. 'Listen,' I said, 'you remember what I was saying about them not wanting to harm you?'

'Yes.'

'Well, I was wondering if we couldn't turn that to our advantage.'

Miss Drom's nostrils twitched, almost as if she scented danger. 'How?'

The next bit had to be put tactfully. 'What we've got to do is give me a chance to get away. Then I can go for help. We've probably got several hours before they'll be ready to ship you off behind the Iron Curtain and by that time I'll be back here with half the Italian army.'

'Oh?'

'If not the whole of it!' I laughed. 'But, first of all, you've got to make a diversion so that they won't spot me slipping off. Now, the next time one of them comes in here, you're to be lying over there in the corner. Groaning. Meanwhile, I shall have concealed myself behind the door. Now, the chap will come right into the room and bend over you to see what's the matter. That's when you grab him and get his gun if you can. You start screaming, too. That'll bring the rest of them in at the double and, as soon as they're inside, I whip round the door, slam it behind me, lock it and run.'

For a minute Miss Drom just looked at me in silence. Then she said something which proved she was brighter than I had been giving her credit for.

'You must be mad!' she sniffed.

Thirteen

They don't call me Sugar-Tongue Eddie just because of the shape of my legs. By continually challenging Miss Drom to think up something better I finally got her to agree to give my plan a twirl, though that only led to more arguments over the timing. Miss Drom was all for postponing the attempt as long as possible so as to give any miracles that happened to be in the offing the chance to occur. I, on the other hand, was a powerful advocate for the here and now.

'Look,' I said, 'they're worn out. They've had a hard day and they'll be looking forward to a good night's sleep. If we kick up a fuss and disturb them, they'll be as mad as hell about it. It may make them careless and that's just what we want.'

Miss Drom didn't find that very persuasive. 'If they're careless, they may forget they're not supposed to harm me,' she objected.

'Oh, they won't be as careless as that.'

'I still think we should wait. After all, I've been missing for several days now and I'm sure Daddie will have got a massive search organized for me. Our rescuers may be closing in on us right at this very minute.'

'And, equally, they may not!' I riposted sharply. 'Listen, I don't want to be rude about your father but he's not exactly the world's number one ball of fire, you know. Not by a long chalk. Suppose, which I doubt, they've even got as far as tying Monkey Tom in with your kidnapping. Where does that lead them? Only to a ruined house with five dead bodies, including yours.'

'But lots of people saw us make our escape across the lake. After all, we did steal that float and the owners may have reported it to the police.'

'Even if they did it's a million to one chance that anybody's connected it with your kidnapping. I'll bet people are pinching other people's floats all day long round here. But, just supposing we were traced as far as this side of the lake – so what? From an outsider's point of view from there on we've just vanished into thin air.'

'Somebody might have seen us in the car.'

'And pigs might fly! Can't you get it through your thick skull that we're playing with the big league boys now? That Russian colonel's no idiot, you know. He'll have taken every conceivable precaution. Methodical is the KGB's middle name. The only way to catch 'em napping is to do something right out of the blue. It's the totally unexpected that gets them rattled?'

'But what's unexpected about us trying to escape?' asked Miss Drom. 'I should have thought that was the very first thing they would be on the look-out for.'

That's the trouble with arguing with women. They're so bloody illogical. Recognizing the utter futility of appealing to Miss Drom's reason, I plumped for the emotional approach. The night was getting on and, if we didn't produce some action soon, it wouldn't be worth bothering.

'Patriotism,' I said. 'And unselfishness.'

'What?'

'The trouble with you. Miss Drom, is that you see things from a narrow, purely personal angle. All you're worried about is your own neck. Haven't you ever paused to consider what this is coming to mean to your father and your country? Thanks to you, Sir Maurice is going to be turned into a traitor and all our most precious national secrets are going to be handed to the Russians on a plate. Well, it's a burden I wouldn't care to have on my conscience, I can tell you.'

'But it's not my fault!' protested Miss Drom and got ready to start blubbing again.

'It will be if you don't get up off your backside and pull your finger out!' I told her, not mincing my words. 'You're committing high treason by just sitting there as surely as if you were flogging classified material by the filing cabinet full.'

Miss Drom lapsed into silence as she thought this over. Then her chin went up. 'I shall have to kill myself,' she said bravely.

Of all the egotistical cows!

'Here, steady on!' I stammered. 'There's no need to contemplate anything as – well – drastic as that.'

Miss Drom dabbed her eyes and tried to look noble. 'It's the only way, Eddie. My death will thwart all their plans. Without me, they won't be able to blackmail Daddie into betraying his country.' She gazed unseeing into the middle distance. 'Maybe they'll put a statue up to me in Trafalgar Square,' she murmured.

'What?'

'Like Nurse Cavell,' she explained dreamily. 'She laid down her life for her country, too.'

'Yes,' I snapped, 'all very noble, I'm sure, but let's not give way to despair just yet.'

'Oh, I'm not despairing, Eddie!' Miss Drom was already contemplating herself starring in the film the Yanks would undoubtedly make of her life. 'Actually, I feel quite happy and strangely at peace.'

Blimey – she was writing the bloody script now! I debated with myself whether a good belt round the ears might not bring her back to her senses but I decided I'd better not feed her desire for martyrdom. I proffered a compromise.

'Well, that's fine,' I said, 'but let's see if we can't make a break for it first, eh? If that fails, you can croak yourself afterwards.'

Miss Drom was clearly preoccupied with the progress of a

pathetic little coffin, draped in the Union Jack, as it was transported through the crowds of mourners on its way to a state funeral in Westminster Abbey. 'Very well,' she murmured. 'I know now what I have to do and I shall not waver from my chosen course. There's just one thing, though, Eddie,' – she popped out of her day-dream to settle a practical point – 'I may have to ask you to kill me because we haven't got any weapon. Will you be strong enough?'

'Oh, yes,' I assured her with the utmost sincerity, 'I'll manage somehow. Now, you go and lie down in that corner and, when I give you the signal, start groaning and screaming. OK?'

With conscious grace, Miss Drom took herself off into the corner and sank in a huddle on the floor.

'Are you ready?' I asked.

'Whenever you are, I am!'

Now, as I told you, the room we were imprisoned in had once been a pantry and the walls had had shelves all round them. For some reason these shelves had been removed but in one or two places the remains of the supports were still sticking in the wall. One such fragment was conveniently placed behind the door. It was a splintered block of wood, only about two inches square, set some four or five feet up the wall. I had had my eye on this block of wood for some time as I intended to be perched up on it when our gaolers burst through the door in response to Miss Drom's histrionics. For some reason, which I freely admit I cannot at the moment recall, it struck me that this would be strategically a more satisfactory position than just crouching behind the door at ground level and praying.

After two unsuccessful attempts to get up there I was forced to interrupt Miss Drom's dying duck act and get her to come across and help me. Even with assistance it wasn't easy but in the end I achieved a rather precarious arabesque, spread-eagled against the wall. My only support was a single toe-hold on the block of wood and the couple of millimetres I managed to dig my fingers into the plaster.

It didn't seem much of a platform for the launching of a counter-attack on the forces of darkness and the KGB, but I didn't want to damage Miss Drom's morale by appearing to have made an error of judgement and climbing down again.

Miss Drom went back to her corner.

'Well, go on!' I whispered, not daring to speak too forcefully in case I disturbed the delicate balance. 'What are you waiting for? Start screaming!'

Miss Drom obliged. She shouted, screamed, moaned and beat her hands on the floor while I clung there, wondering how the hell limpets did it.

Our guards out in the kitchen took their time. Which was unfortunate because, as the agonizing pain in my left toe indicated, time was what we could ill-afford to spare. Even Miss Drom's leather lungs were beginning to fail before I heard sounds of welcome activity on the other side of my wall.

'Louder!' I urged Miss Drom. 'Louder!'

She redoubled her efforts and we were rewarded by a heavy hammering on the door and a bawled request in Russian to put a sock in it.

Miss Drom and I, in our different ways, stuck grimly to our task. I comforted myself by thinking it was probably worse when you were climbing Everest and tried to flatten myself even closer to the wall. I could feel a faint trembling starting in my left leg and, if that developed, I should vibrate myself into a very nasty tumble.

The guards were muttering crossly amongst themselves outside and then – oh, joy of joys! – a key rattled in the lock. I couldn't suppress a feeling of intense elation. The mugs were going to fall for it!

Little did I know.

I remember seeing the door from the kitchen begin to open but after that things become confused. One point, however, stands out clearly. The Russian guards were not such mugs as I had thought. Instead of just opening the door and entering the pantry like civilized creatures, the first man kicked it back with such force that I was driven four inches into the brickwork. The door knob got me fair and square and agonizingly in the calf and a hook, which I had not noticed previously, sank up to its retaining screws into my back.

After that it was only a matter of a fraction of a second before I came off the wall. I crashed down with a howl between it and the door. Somewhere, far, far away, I heard the pounding of heavy boots and the unmistakable click as a safety catch was released. I opened one eye and stared inevitably up the barrel of an automatic rifle. I opened the other eye. Through the legs of the man standing over me I could see Miss Drom. She had two armed men towering menacingly over her.

As I had guessed, though, nobody was going to rough her up. I wasn't so lucky. When I didn't comply quickly enough with a sharp order to rise, one huge boot rose into the air, thudded into my ribs and went on thudding with methodical savagery. Rather than just lie there and be kicked through the pearly gates, I struggled over on to my hands and knees. The boot continued to hack away at me but assistance was at hand. Another pair of boots marched up. Then strong fingers sank themselves into my hair and I was yanked roughly to my feet.

The Russians were certainly annoyed at having had their rest disturbed. While two of them checked the pantry to see that we hadn't dug a tunnel through the walls or acquired a secret cache of weapons, the other two worked off their resentment on me. I don't want you to think that they lost their tempers or, indeed, were guilty of anything as half-way human as that. On the contrary, they were admirably cold-blooded and restrained. They had evidently been instructed that I was to be preserved in one piece, for the time being at any rate, so the blows were scientifically designed to inflict the maximum pain with the minimum permanent damage. Those boys certainly knew their job and the state they left me in will serve as a testimonal. There wasn't a mark on my face or a broken bone in my body.

When the key turned in the lock behind them, Miss Drom

hurried across to where I lay slumped against the wall.

'Oh, Eddie!' she breathed. 'Are you all right?'

I managed to nod my head. I was very far from being all right but nodding happened to be easier than shaking. Speech of any kind was quite beyond me.

'Oh, Eddie!' she said again and, helplessly, patted my shoulder.

I was surprised to find that I still had the strength to scream.

For the next twelve hours I just lay there. Every breath I took was preceded by a conscious effort to accept the pain it caused. Miss Drom did what she could and it wasn't her fault that it was precious little. Sometime during the morning the Colonel came in to have a look at me and seemed totally unmoved by what he saw. I fancied I heard him make some cool observation about learning lessons the hard way but I may well have imagined that. He did, however, succumb to Miss Drom's shrill and constant nagging and send in some brandy for me. It arrived in a plastic jug so that we wouldn't get any ideas about using a bottle as a weapon. Somewhere, well hidden, the Colonel must have had a sense of humour.

With Miss Drom's help, I drank as much brandy as I could hold. It wasn't going to cure anything but it did allow me to spend the next few hours without feeling any pain.

It was early evening before I emerged from my drunken slumber. In spite of a considerable hangover, I felt a bit better and even managed to sit up. Miss Drom had saved some soup for me and I swallowed a mouthful or two, more for her sake than for mine. I noticed that she was looking particularly tense and anxious.

'Anything happened?' I asked thickly.

She shook her head. 'Not really. That dreadful Colonel came in about an hour ago to have another look at you. He said you'd live.'

'Bloody sadist!'

'He also said we'd be leaving tomorrow morning, before daybreak.'

'For Russia?'

'I suppose so.' She choked a little but pulled herself together. 'They're expecting to hear from Moscow tonight about what they're to do with you.'

Well, that's the advantage about getting a thrashing like the one I'd received: it stops you worrying about the future.

'I'm sure something will happen before then,' said Miss Drom, resolute in looking on the bright side in spite of all the evidence to the contrary. 'You'll see. Daddie will be alerting just about everybody in Western Europe. The police and the soldiers and all the security organizations. There'll be a reward, too. And descriptions and pictures of us in all the papers and on television. I'm sure somebody must have seen us somewhere. It's just a matter of time.'

I nodded my head again, though it was still not a process to be carried out without wincing. 'Is there any of that brandy left?'

Miss Drom and I both managed to doze off but round about midnight we were wide awake again. I wondered if the Marquis made radio contact with Moscow at the same time every night. I doubted it. That would be just asking for his transmissions to be picked up. In fact, I was a little surprised that they were using anything as vulnerable as a two-way radio at all. It couldn't be their regular procedure. No doubt Miss Drom had upset a lot of routine arrangements.

Actually we had to wait until nearly three o'clock for the next development. The pantry door was opened and one of the guards came in, his automatic rifle at the ever-ready as usual. He was followed by both the Colonel and the Marchesa. Two more armed guards remained in the open doorway. The precautions were flattering but excessive.

The Colonel stared down at me. He had several sheets of paper in his hand and seemed highly pleased with himself. 'Well,' he began, 'we appear to have caught a very desirable fish in our net!' He waved his papers about. 'I have just finished decoding a message from Moscow, Mr Brown. Did you know that we had a large file on you in our archives? I have not been sent details, of course, but I am instructed to look after you very, very carefully. It will not be, I understand your first visit to the Soviet Union though, I fear,' – he grinned – 'it is likely to be your last.' He turned to the Marchesa. 'We should all be well rewarded for this, my dove.'

The Marchesa was looking rather glum. 'Let's hope it is something more useful than a stupid medal,' she snapped. 'You must tell them that my husband and I need more money if we are to keep up our position in society.'

'You will be able to tell them that yourself, my jewel.'

The Marchesa caught her breath. 'What do you mean?'

'Oh, did I not tell you?' The Colonel's grin widened. 'You are to accompany us. Now that we have two passengers, I shall need more assistance on the plane.'

'Why don't you take Arturo?'

The Colonel broke into a chuckle. 'You are asking me to take the husband when I can have the wife? In any case, my instructions are quite clear. You are to come to look after the girl. You do not intend to make any objection, I hope.'

'No, no, of course not.' The Marchesa bit her lip. 'It's just that I have several engagements. It will look suspicious if I am absent.'

'Your husband will say that you are unwell,' said the Colonel, getting a certain amount of enjoyment out of the Marchesa's patent dismay. 'And now I suggest that you get yourself ready. We must leave here within an hour.'

For the first time the Marchesa glanced at me. 'Is he going to be well enough to travel? It is a long journey.'

'His injuries are superficial. By the time we arrive he will be quite recovered and ready to undergo interrogation. Now, hurry! We are using your car.'

He took the Marchesa by the arm and led her through to the kitchen. The various armed guards retreated in their turn and the door was closed and locked behind them.

'Well, that's that,' said Miss Drom with a sigh.

'I'm afraid so.'

'And I never got around to committing suicide, either. I suppose it's no good expecting you to do anything about it now?'

'Not in my condition.' I said and, for once, I was profoundly glad I was incapacitated. The Special Overseas Directorate has a large number of rules and regulations. Some of the nastier ones fitted Miss Drom's particular predicament very neatly. I got some small comfort from the fact that nobody was likely to be enquiring why I had failed to carry them out.

About an hour later they came back for us. The Marquis and the Colonel half-carried, half-dragged me out to the white sports car while the whole contingent of armed guards hovered edgily around. Miss Drom followed, with the Marchesa's pearl-handled plaything in her back.

They bundled me into the front passenger seat next to the Marchesa and, if I'd had the guts, I'd have smiled at the irony of it all. Miss Drom was squashed in the back seat with the Marquis on one side of her and the Colonel on the other.

The Colonel leaned over and tapped me on the head with his pistol. 'One injudicious move from you, my friend, and I shall knock you unconscious. Perhaps you are thinking of opening the side door and throwing yourself out? We have removed the inside handle.'

I looked below and – blow me! – so they had. If I'd had a hat, I'd have raised it to such dedicated thoroughness.

The Marchesa took off and we roared away into the night. It was still very dark and the dipped headlights only lit up the white dusty road ahead of us. I had the impression that we were driving away from the lake and I wondered where in this mountainous part of Italy they were going to find space to land an illicit plane. It would have to be somewhere pretty remote, of course. Maybe the airfield wasn't in Italy at all. We could be driving to Jugoslavia, say, and transferring to an aeroplane there. Would the Jugoslavs be that accommodating? Frankly, I neither knew nor cared.

The Marchesa was driving very fast, even recklessly. As she cut yet another corner on the narrow road, her husband told her sharply to slow down. For a few minutes, she did, but then the speedometer needle slowly began climbing up again. My spirits rose with it and I began working out what I'd do if we were fortunate enough to have a crash from which I emerged as the sole survivor. Given the incentive of survival I was quite sure I could crawl several miles, if needs be, on my hands and knees.

It was getting lighter now as we flew over the ridge of a hill and went screaming down the other side in a scattering of stones and dust. I don't think anybody was enjoying the ride, certainly not the Marchesa if her face was anything to judge by. I was suffering more than most because I just didn't have the strength to brace myself properly as we slithered round the corners. I found myself being tossed about from side to side and backwards and forwards so helplessly that, when the moment of truth did come and the Marchesa shoved the brake pedal through the floorboards, I scored a bull's eye on the windscreen with my head.

It had been inevitable that, sooner or later, the Marchesa would take one blind corner on the wrong side of the road too many. Even at this early hour it was too much to expect that we should have the roads entirely to ourselves. I admit I had been envisaging something like a loaded donkey or a truck or a flock of goats so the huge luxury tourist coach slewed right across the rocky track was as big a surprise to me as to everybody else.

For a minute nobody did anything much except sit there and thank God that they were still alive. Then the Marchesa switched off the ignition and I, with an equally shaky hand, wiped the blood out of my eye and looked at the incredible scene in front of us.

The coach was green and shiny and it was blocking the road completely. The bonnet was open and a large man in a white jacket was standing beside it with a big monkey wrench in his hand. He, too, recovered from the shock and slowly pushed his peaked cap even further back on his head.

The coach must have been stuck there for some time because all the passengers had got out and were now scattered about the surrounding hillside. It looked like a works outing. The vast majority of the passengers were men and they were uniformly dressed in white open-necked shirts. Their way of passing the time was equally traditional. A number of beer bottle crates lay haphazardly in the road and somebody had been slinging the empties against a convenient rock. There was an unmistakable boozy look about the flushed and sweaty faces that were turned towards us.

A grunt of disgust came from the Marquis in the back seat. 'English tourists, of course!' he muttered. 'Look at them! Pig drunk at this time of the morning!'

One or two of them were positively paralytic. As my head cleared I began to register more details: the screwed-up packets of potato crisps, the souvenir bottles of Chianti which were now being downed as the beer started running out, the incongruous straw hats and the stalwart braces holding up some of the blue serge trousers. There, in the dawn's early light, desecrating the noble Italian countryside, were indubitably my compatriots.

It was the Colonel who made the first move on either side. He stood up in the back of the car, waved an imperious hand and shouted. 'Hey, you, there! Get that thing off the road and be quick about it! We wish to drive past.'

I don't know whether it was his manner or his accent or the frustration of not being able to comply with his wishes, but something certainly annoyed somebody and we all ducked as an empty beer bottle skimmed uncomfortably close across the car.

Fourteen

The Marquis, who was undoubtedly the weak link in the chain, got rattled and began pulling his revolver out.

The Colonel was on him like a tiger. 'Stop that, you insane fool! I will handle this. Keep calm – both of you – and keep your mouths shut!'

The coach driver abandoned his inspection of the engine and strolled leisurely towards us. The passengers, too, came crowding round. The sight of the Marchesa evoked some appreciative whistles and complimentary observations on her physical attributes were good-humouredly bandied about.

The coach driver thankfully rested his weight on our bonnet while the Colonel managed to twist his lips into a smile.

'Now, my good man,' he began, having learnt his English, from the wrong text books, 'what is going on here?'

This innocent question provoked a riot of catcalls and jeers and a youngish man who'd been examining our number plates shook his head at the driver.

'You'll get no help from this lot, Harry,' he opined. 'They're bloody Eyeties.' He broke off to leer at the Marchesa. 'Here, how about giving us a kiss, darling?'

'Take no notice of him, love!' somebody else shouted. 'You come for a walk with me and I'll give you something!'

'Aye, the bloody clap, if I know you!'

A third voice joined in. 'Come with me, ducks, and I'll show you me etchings!'

'Is that what you call 'em, Fred? I've often wondered.'

'Hey, there's another judy sitting in the back! Who's that next to her, her old grand-daddie?'

They were pressing round closer now and the white paint-work of the Alfa-Romeo already had several sweaty paw marks blemishing its gleaming surface. It seemed an admirable opportunity for me to do something heroic, but a sideways glance at the Marchesa showed that her right hand, resting negligently in her pocket, had got me covered.

The back chat continued, growing louder and cruder and almost drowning the Colonel's attempts to question the coach driver.

'Well,' rumbled the latter, totally unimpresed by anything or anybody, 'I can't push the bleeding thing out of the way for you, can I? See for yourself – we're jammed right across the bloody road.'

'Cannot these men assist you?'

''Ark at 'im!' roared a shrivelled little chap who wasn't wearing his teeth. ''Oo does 'e think we are? Bloody galley slaves?'

The man next to him chirped up. 'If he wants any pushing done, why doesn't the clever bugger get out and do it himself?'

'That's right, George!' came a boomed approval from the other side. 'Who won the sodding war, anyways?'

'Hey, mister,' yelled somebody else, inspired by a folk memory of organ grinders, 'where's your bloody monkey?'

Taking advantage of the howls of laughter which greeted this sally, the Colonel bent down to the Marchesa. 'Reverse back! Quickly!'

The Marchesa slipped the car into reverse and turned round to see where she was going.

Three or four men had clambered on to the back bumper and were trying to get Miss Drom to accept a swig from their bottle of beer.

'Oh, get on, Elena!' fumed the Colonel. 'Never mind them! Move!'

Obediently the Marchesa shoved her foot down hard on the accelerator and the men leapt clear as we shot backwards for a couple of yards. Then the whole of the rear of the car seemed to collapse. We tipped over to one side and the corner of the body dug with a hideous scraping of crumbled metal into the road.

Before anybody in the Alfa Romeo had recovered his or her wits, they were swarming all over us. The Marchesa's door was ripped open, her arms pinioned to her sides and out she was dragged. Behind me, the Marquis and the Colonel were getting much the same treatment from a bunch of men who, suddenly sober, flung themselves over the back of the car and smothered any attempts either of them may have made to get their guns out.

It was all over before Miss Drom and I realized it had started. We just sat there. The engine had stalled but a thin, sharp-faced man who had remained aloof from the general fracas leaned over and switched off the ignition.

'We unscrewed all the nuts on the back wheels,' he explained and, not waiting for any response, turned away and began issuing orders to the rest of the party. What had looked like a bored and nasty-tempered rabble was now transformed into a swift and efficient squad. The white-coated driver raced back to his bus and clambered up into his seat. With no trouble at all, he got the engine going and swung the heavy vehicle back on the road so that it was facing down the hill. Others were dealing with the Marchesa and her two companions in misfortune. Lengths of thin, strong rope appeared from nowhere and in a matter of seconds the three of them were thoroughly trussed up.

The thin-faced man opened the door on my side. 'Out, you!'

'He can't!' protested Miss Drom, springing to my rescue like an old hen protecting her chick. 'They beat him up.'

The thin-faced man didn't waste time shedding tears over

me. He summoned a couple of assistants. 'Get this bloody cripple into the bus! Back seat, remember!'

One of the assistants hesitated. 'Are you sure you want to take him? We could dump him with the others.'

The thin-faced man scowled. 'I'm sure. He's got some questions to answer before we get rid of him. Get moving!' He pivoted round to urge on the men who were trying to force the wheels back on to the rear axles of the car. 'Come on, come on! It's not got to win the bloody Monte Carlo! Finger tight'll do.'

I was lifted bodily out of the Alfa Romeo and carried over to the coach. Manoeuvring me down the narrow aisle presented more of a problem but, since I was the only one who found it painful, it was soon solved and I was deposited, panting and sweating, in the middle of the back seat. A moment or two later Miss Drom joined me.

'What on earth's going on?' she whispered.

I just stopped myself shrugging my shoulders. 'I haven't the faintest,' I grunted. 'All I know is we've been rescued from the Colonel and his little friends. That'll do me for the time being.'

'But, who are they? Are they Daddie's people?'

'They might be,' I said doubtfully and eased my self round so that I could look out of the back window of the coach.

The wheels had been replaced on the Alfa and the still bound bodies of the Marchesa, her husband and the Colonel were being slung with scant ceremony onto the seats.

Miss Drom was watching, too. 'What are they doing?'

'I don't know.' I had my suspicions but there was no point in upsetting Miss Drom unnecessarily. 'Where's the big white chief?' I asked in an attempt to distract her attention.

Miss Drom slowly shook her head, not in the least distracted. 'Oh, Eddie, look!' She caught her breath. 'They're not going to . . .'

Well, yes, actually, they were.

Half a dozen men, one of them keeping a guiding hand on the steering wheel, had gathered round the car and were pushing it over to the side of the road. Where the drop was. They had a bit of a job getting is across a narrow ditch and over a stony strip of parched grass but, where there's a will, there's a way.

We saw the car tipple over the edge and heard the series of crashes as it bounced down before reaching the rocks below.

'Oh, dear!' said Miss Drom in a shattered voice. 'Well, that settles it.'

The men, after one last look, were racing back towards us at the double. The coach was already moving as the last one piled in.

'It certainly does,' I agreed. 'They must have fallen a good hundred feet. Your kidnapping is producing a rather high mortality rate.'

'No, I didn't mean that – though it was rather awful, wasn't it? I meant the identity of these people. They can't possibly be from the Special Overseas Directorate or from an official organization.'

'Why not?'

Miss Drom gazed at me saucer-eyed. In spite of her recent experiences, she was still pretty naïve. 'When they've just done a really dreadful thing like that?'

I wasn't so sure. 'Those three have just been responsible for five deaths at least.' I pointed out. 'And, if there's one thing any of the security boys in the West would be highly delighted to get rid of, it's a KGB agent and a couple of traitors.'

'Oh, I dare say,' said Miss Drom, the weeniest bit patronizingly, 'but they wouldn't just murder them. They'd hand them over to the proper authorities for a trial and everything. I mean – pushing them over the side of the road like that – it's so uncivilized!'

The occupants of the coach had got themselves settled down in their seats. One or two were reading, others were staring out of the windows at the scenery or leaning their heads back trying to get some sleep. I did a poll count. Unless I'd missed somebody, there were twenty men and two women scattered around the seats in front of us. Add the driver and the two men who were flanking Miss Drom and me and effectively blocking our access to the side windows and that made twenty-five. No – I tell a lie! Twenty-six. I'd forgotten the thin-faced man, who was making his way down the aisle towards us. It was a blooming army!

The thin-faced man sat down in one of the empty seats in front of me.

'Well,' he said, 'I think that went off very well.'

'For some of us,' I agreed.

'You can't make an omelette, mate. Who were they, anyway?'

My eyes opened wide. 'A Russian secret service agent and two Italian communists,' I said. 'Didn't you know, for God's sake?'

He lit himself a big cigar. 'We thought they was Reds but you never know. It could have been the Mafia or any other of these damned foreigners that snatched you. You can't bleeding well trust anybody these days. Look at that rat, Monkey Tom – trying to pull a million quid job without saying a dickie bird to anybody! It makes you wonder what the world's coming to.'

'Well, Monkey's learned his lesson,' I observed with some satisfaction.

'Too right he has, poor old bleeder! Still, we'll give him a slap-up funeral when they release what's left of the body. Some faults I may have, but I don't bear grudges. Well, not against stiffs.'

Miss Drom had been fidgeting impatiently at my side. 'Who are you?' she asked, though you'd have thought a kid of two would have worked that out by now.

The thin-faced man was, quite rightly, outraged by such a display of crass ignorance. 'Who the hell do you think I am?' he demanded truculently.

Miss Drom realized she'd got him on the raw. 'I'm afraid I haven't the least idea,' she said airily.

The henchman sitting next to me couldn't bear it any longer. He leaned across me. 'Here, you watch your lip, girl! You're talking to West Hartlepool Joe – see? – and he's the tops. You don't get 'em no bigger than West Hartlepool Joe.'

'Well, not outside Dartmoor, I suppose,' agreed Miss Drom disdainfully. Appearing to have taken complete leave of her senses, she addressed herself once more to the thin-faced man. 'I have heard of you, of course. Those other cheap little crooks mentioned your name. However, I wasn't impressed by them and I am not impressed by you. If you don't want to get yourself and your cronies into very serious trouble, you'd better take Mr Brown and me to the British Embassy in Rome without delay. I am sure the fact that you did rescue us from that dreadful Russian will count in your favour. Provided you behave sensibly now, I am quite prepared to put a word in for you myself. I think your conduct was unnecessarily violent and cold blooded but there were, possibly, extenuating circumstances.'

West Hartlepool Joe looked at me. 'Is she always like this?' he asked wonderingly. 'Look, mate, you want to put your girlfriend straight on a few of the facts of life. What the heck does she think I have going for me here? There's a million quid in this business. You don't think I'm going to pass that up without a struggle, do you?' He gestured towards the rest of the bus. 'What does she think this lot are? A troop of effing boy scouts? Now, look, the pair of you'd better get this straight. I've been put to a great deal of trouble and inconvenience. What with Monkey Tom trying to cross me and those Russians shoving their noses in, I've just about had it up to here!' He chopped himself dramatically across the forehead. 'I don't reckon on getting mixed up in this kind of job, you know. Me and my boys leave this kind of caper to the mugs, the little guys. I'm a financier, a businessman.'

He was getting quite upset about it.

'I'm sure you are,' I said soothingly, having seen enough of West Hartlepool Joe's business methods to want to keep on the right side of him. 'I suppose, for a million pounds, you felt you just had to risk soiling your hands.'

'Oh, it's not just the money,' he assured me earnestly. 'It's a matter of principle. I'd never have been able to hold my head up again if I'd let Monkey get away with pulling a fast one on me like this. Bloody nerve!'

'How did you find out about it?'

'Oh, somebody talked out of turn. They always do. They thought I was in on it, you see, what with one of my boys supposedly in the middle of things.' He glared balefully at me.

'I'm sorry about that,' I said quickly. 'It was a mistake.'

'Maybe you'll live long enough to regret it,' said West Hartlepool Joe resentfully. 'I don't go much on people taking my name in vain. Especially where money's involved. It lowers the tone of my whole organization, having a lousy two-bit amateur like you going around saying you're my representative.'

I tried to get his mind back on to a less painful subject. 'So you really came over to put Monkey Tom in his place.'

'Too right, I did! I was all set to clobber him good and proper when that other mob moved in. I couldn't make out what the hell was happening at first. You and the girl getting clear across the lake and then them lighting the blue paper under Monkey and his boys like that. We had the devil's own job tracking you down to that villa place and then it cost me a packet to find out when they were going to move you and where. These Eyeties don't tell you something for nothing, you know. Bleeding blood suckers, some of 'em. I'm telling you, these last three or four days I've never stopped. I don't know what my medical adviser's going to say when I get back home. I'm supposed to be taking things easy, you know.'

I expressed my sincere regret for the strains to which he had been subjected and hoped that the loud, disparaging sniffs coming from Miss Drom weren't the heralds of yet another tactless intervention on her part. These noble stands for truth and justice are all very well in their way but you can soon have

too much of them. With a character as full of his own import-
ance as West Hartlepool Joe, laying on the commiseration with
a trowel was the best way of getting results.

'What exactly are your plans for us?' I asked with a flattering show of interest.

'I'm going to collect that ransom for her, of course.' West
Hartlepool Joe jerked his head at Miss Drom. 'I haven't made
up my mind about you yet. I reckon I'm going to have to make
an example of you, just in case any other scruffy little bastards
start getting ideas.'

'Are we going to stay out here in Italy?'

West Hartlepool Joe shook his head. 'Not bleeding likely!
Things are hotting up a bit too much over here. They've
got Interpol muscling in on the bloody act, so I hear, and God
knows how many other effing cops are milling around. They've
been concentrating on Scandinavia but they're sure to be
looking in this direction by now. That explosion at Monkey's
place'll have set 'em all buzzing. So – we're going back to
England.' He pulled a wry face. 'At least we'll be able to
get some decent grub there – and a proper cup of tea.'

'Are you going to fly us back?' I asked.

West Hartlepool Joe scowled at me suspiciously. 'You ask
too many bloody questions, mate.'

'I'm just fascinated by the way you organize things,' I
apologized meekly. 'I've never met one of the top men in
your – er – profession before.'

'That's obvious. You wouldn't be asking such damn fool
things if you had. They'll be watching all the airports, won't
they?'

'I suppose so.'

West Hartlepool Joe's face split in a cunning grin. 'They
won't be watching the Wakes Outing of the Thawnymoor and
District Miners' Benevolent Association, though, will they?
And now' – he cut off my next question with an impatient
wave of his hand – 'you and your girl friend just sit back and
enjoy the ride. Nothing's going to happen to you so long as you
behave yourselves, but one hell of a lot will happen if you don't.

Especially' – he underlined the threat by jabbing a finger at me – 'to you, buddy boy!'

With a warning nod to the two men sitting on either side of us, he got up and pushed his way back down to the front of the coach. There he leaned over and exchanged a few words with the driver before unhooking a microphone and addressing the assembled company over the coach's loud speaker system.

After a preliminary puff or two to make sure everthing was working, his remarks were brief and to the point. 'This is the boss speaking! This is the boss speaking! Now, lads, we've got the Austrian frontier coming up in ten minutes. I repeat – ten minutes. Now, I don't need to emphasize that I'm relying on you to put on a good show, but for Christ's sake, don't go berserk. No slinging bottles out of the windows or anything irresponsible like that. Just stick to what we arranged and it'll be a bloody piece of cake!'

This effort was greeted by a cheer or two but West Hartlepool Joe obviously felt that something was still lacking. He looked dubiously at the microphone and then put it up to his mouth again.

'This is your boss signing off,' he intoned. 'Over and out!'

In spite of West Hartlepool Joe's awe-inspiring prestige, his lads couldn't help exchanging a few smirks as they began to get ready for the storming of the Austro-Italian border. They got down their props from the luggage racks: tin trumpets, fair ground squeakers that shot out in a stiff tongue of paper when you blew them, streamers, football favours, paper hats, rattles, toilet rolls and long striped scarves. Fresh supplies of brown ale were removed from the crates which were stacked up on the spare seats and handed round to all the participants. While a couple of the men affixed a crudely lettered poster across the front window – 'Thawnymoor & District Wanderers for the Cup!' – the coach driver switched on his radio and searched the wave lengths for some suitable accompaniment. Soon we had one of those castrati pop singers howling his unintellegible anguish through a background of amplified guitars and thundering drums.

The coach entered the main street of the village which lay just this side of the frontier. West Hartlepool Joe watched with satisfaction as the windows were rolled down and hell on earth was let loose. The morning hush splintered under the blare of trumpets, the squeak of squeakers and the chattering of rattles. The few local inhabitants who happened to be knocking about found themselves the target of raucous insults, if they were male, and the most piercing wolf whistles, if they were female. Pints of beer were slopped down the sides of the coach and everybody waved and jeered and shouted themselves hoarse. People in the houses flung open their doors and windows as we passed. Some crossed themselves in pious terror. A village dog hurtled out to run yelping and yapping at our rear wheels until a well-directed fusillade of bottle tops stopped him dead in his tracks.

Peering ahead I could see the customs officials streaming out of their block house and watching our approach with astonishment and dread. West Hartlepool Joe was no fool. It was going to take a brave man to penetrate the interior of that coach.

Then the community singing broke out and we arrived at the barrier to the strains of an off-key rendering of 'There'll Always Be An England'.

The frontier guards, predictably, took the easy way out. Ignoring the wad of passports that our driver was waving at them, they raised the barrier and thankfully signalled us through.

We screamed and howled our way across the strip of no-man's-land to where the Austrian officials put up a braver show. They, at least, made us stop and even went so far as to glance at the outside covers of the passports. The noise and the waving redoubled. Miss Drom, who had been keeping her eyes skinned, suddenly made a dash for an open window two or three seats lower down the bus. The man sitting next to her was after her like a flash but she managed to poke her head outside.

'I'm being kidnapped!' she screamed. 'Police! Help!'

A fresh-faced lad in a brand new uniform was standing not ten yards away. He grinned indulgently as he saw Miss Drom being dragged back from the window. He waved and, very much the man of the world, blew her a kiss. 'Gute Reise, gnädige Frau!'

Miss Drom, kicking and biting, was frog-marched back to her seat, having achieved precisely nothing.

'You try that again, lass,' growled her captor as he dumped her down beside me, 'and you'll get the flat of my hand across your gob!'

Miss Drom glared at me. 'I do think you might have made a bit more of an effort,' she complained.

I shook my head. 'In my state of health? Besides, I'm conserving my strength.'

And so, indeed, I was. Having, unlike Miss Drom, more brains than brawn. The best policy, as I saw it, was to play a waiting game. West Hartlepool Joe was very kindly transporting us back to England and it was when we reached those welcoming shores that we were going to have our best chance. This drunken-coach-party ploy might work on the Continent but it wouldn't cut any ice back home. I could just see the British Customs and Passport Control systematically taking us apart and relishing every minute of it.

I lay back in my seat and closed my eyes. And even if we succeeded in getting away now, which was extremely unlikely, where would we be? Surrounded by bloody foreigners yet again. Long before we had made our predicament clear, West Hartlepool Joe and his hordes would be roaring after us like terriers after a couple of markedly inept rabbits. Besides – I yawned luxuriously – I was tired.

Fifteen

We drove for the rest of that day and all through the following night, virtually without stopping. There were brief halts, of course, for petrol and for the occasional mass dashes behind the trees when Miss Drom was closely chaperoned by the two rather shop-worn girls on board. I withdrew with the rest of the gents and was always subjected to a strict and embarrassing surveillance the whole time I was out of the coach. However, I didn't let a little thing like that upset me. I was having a good rest and, although I kept this fact carefully concealed, was beginning to feel much more like my old, vital self. We were fed quite reasonably, too. Cold chicken and ham, sardines and shrimps. The empty tins came in handy for slinging at passing natives who were foolish enough to come within range or otherwise aroused our patriotic ire.

At the various border crossings – into Switzerland and into France – fastidiousness again triumphed. None of the officials on duty felt called upon either to enter the coach themselves or to require us to get out. Their one concern was to get rid of us as soon as possible and they seemed quite happy to take the risk that we might be stuffed to the roof with contraband. I suspected they'd encountered parties like ours before.

I would like to be able to tell you that, as we beetled along the straight, tree-lined roads of France, I was pawing the ground in eager anticipation of the action to come. And I would, if I thought you'd believe me. Depressingly, it was the danger that loomed largest in my mind. That and the fact that I just couldn't see West Hartlepool Joe ever giving us a snow-ball's chance of escaping from his clutches. All in all, I'd have been quite happy to go on sitting in the back of that coach for the rest of my life.

Not that with Miss Drom in the near proximity it was exactly a haven of peace and quiet. The closer we got to the Channel coast, the more she fidgeted around, marking the passage of time by continually digging me in the ribs and asking if I'd worked out a plan yet. There was no satisfactory response to this because, if I said no, she urged me to greater efforts and, if I said yes, she pestered me to find out what it was. I kept telling her I couldn't see what she was getting into such a tizzy about. Compared with the KGB, West Hartlepool Joe was about as innocuous as Noddy. All Joe was after was money and, if the worst should come to the worst, I was sure Sir Maurice would be able to persuade the British Government to provide it.

This defeatist attitude sent Miss Drom into paroxysms of rage which, owing to the presence of the guards on either side of us, had to be expressed in whispers and under-the-breath mumbles. Even thus handicapped Miss Drom succeeded in making her opinion of me quite clear. According to which way the wind was blowing I was either unpatriotic or a coward or I didn't really care for her at all.

The accusations were true and it was only the last one that I found mildly surprising. I had noticed before that in her less foul-tempered moments, Miss Drom appeared to think that our mutual sufferings had forged some bond between us. You will bear witness, dear reader, that never by word or deed had I ever given her grounds for reaching such a conclusion. Maybe I should have made my attitude clearer to her at the time but, frankly, I just couldn't be bothered. Besides, I thought she was just speaking in the heat of the moment and that, when it came down to brass tacks, she had no more real liking for me than I had for her.

It was about ten o'clock, I think, on a bright and sunny morning that Miss Drom's vicious elbow caught me in the ribs yet again.

'We're just going through Arras!' she hissed.

I sat up a bit straighter, yawned and came to the conclusion that I'd sell my immortal soul for a cup of tea.

'We're only about sixty miles from Calais,' said Miss Drom, whose intimate knowledge of European geography never ceased to amaze me.

'Calais? Who says we're going to Calais?'

'Nobody says we're going to Calais! Oh, Eddie, do try and pull yourself together! You're not the only one who's tired and exhausted, you know. I'm merely telling you that we'll be at the coast soon.'

I settled back in my seat again. 'We shan't be there for another hour and a half at least,' I corrected her. 'Now, why don't you shut up for a bit and give me chance to think?'

Ten minutes later she gave me another poke.

'Hell's teeth!' I exploded. 'What is it now? Didn't I just tell you . . .'

'It's the other people in the bus,' she explained spitefully. 'They say your snoring is keeping them awake.'

After that I passed the time staring out of the window.

From Arras we took the road to Le Touquet but at Montreuil we turned north for Boulogne. It was when we'd got through Boulogne and were running out, still northwards, through the suburbs that West Hartlepool Joe made his move. He'd been sitting at the front of the coach but now he got up and came lurching down the aisle towards us.

'You two'd better get ready. You'll be leaving soon.'

'Leaving? Where for?'

Miss Drom was doing the honours, of course.

West Hartlepool Joe didn't tell her. He spoke to the guards sitting on either side of us. 'Now, you know what you've got to do, lads! You two take the man and Dick and me'll see to the girl. If you've got to shoot, aim for the stomach. Have you both got silencers?'

The man next to me shook his head. 'Not me, Joe.'

'Well, never mind. Don't let that worry you if he gives you any trouble. You'll go first and we'll follow with the girl.'

We remained sitting in our places for another five minutes. Then the bus swung off the road and pulled up on a parking space in front of a sort of road-side café.

On a signal from West Hartlepool Joe, the whole party swung into its now familiar routine. Whooping it up, they began to troop off the coach and into the caff. In the middle of the roistering throng, Miss Drom and I were duly shepherded out. No chances were taken. One of my watchdogs left the coach first and then turned to supervise my descent while his companion pressed closely on my heels. I dare say much the same method was used for Miss Drom. Simple but effective.

Once out of the coach, though, things began to happen. The two men seized me by the arms and, laughing and shouting uproariously, propelled me at top speed across the car park and into the café where a minor riot was already taking place. We didn't linger amongst the screaming mob that was besieging the counter. My companions ran me on, through the café and into the kitchen beyond. There was a trap door in the floor already standing open and I was pushed down the steep flight of wooden steps into the cellar below. Almost before I'd had time to recover my balance Miss Drom was stumbling down to join me. Crash! The trap door was slapped down and we heard a couple of bolts being shot home. This was followed by some confused scrapings which I couldn't identify.

'It's a chair,' said Miss Drom gloomily. 'They've put a chair over the trap door and somebody is sitting on it.'

We had a light – a naked electric light bulb placed way out of reach on the ceiling – and we had a couple of superannuated café chairs. There was no window. Not even a grille.

Me, I know when I'm beaten.

'This,' I said, taking the sounder-looking chair, 'is getting monotonous, isn't it?'

Miss Drom vouchsafed no answer. She just stood in the

middle of that grimy cellar, placed her hands on her hips, stared at me and tapped one foot irritatingly on the stone floor.

Well, I made allowances. The last few days had been pretty hairy and nerves were bound to be geting frayed.

'Are you just going to sit there?' she demanded in a voice which was only just under control.

'Oh, come on now!' I said, trying to laugh it off. 'Whatever we do, we're not going to get out of here. Why don't you sit down and stop beating your head against a brick wall?'

Miss Drom spoke through clenched teeth. 'I should like to beat your head against a brick wall! You said that when we got to the coast, you'd do something. Well, we've reached the coast and I'm waiting.' She held the inevitable threat back until the end. 'I don't know what Daddie's going to say about your behaviour, Eddie. I shall have to tell him, you know, and with the best will in the world I don't see that I can present you in a very good light.'

'Well, there's gratitude for you!' I snorted. 'Who planned our escape across Lake Garda?'

Miss Drom remembering her cut foot and all that led to, blushed. 'Well,' she acknowledged with a ghastly coy giggle, 'there was that, and I suppose it wasn't entirely your fault that it failed – though I did keep warning you. But never mind the past – what about the future?'

'I'm working on it,' I said. 'Honestly, I am. The thing is that I was counting on us staying on the coach. I calculated that when we went through the Customs at Dover or wherever, we could . . . Oh, well, what's the use! We'll just have to be patient, that's all. West Hartlepool Joe's only human. He'll make a mistake sooner or later and, when he does, have no fear – I'll be ready for him.'

Miss Drom sat down on the other chair and folded her arms. 'What you need, Eddie,' she said with a sigh, 'is somebody behind you, somebody to keep pushing you. Well, you are rather inclined just to sit back and hope for the best, aren't you? It's a pity because, otherwise, I think you might go a long way.' She eyed me up and down in a speculative sort of way. 'I believe somebody could make something out of you, if they took you in hand.'

As was to be expected, we were kept shut in the cellar until nightfall. I'd warned Miss Drom that this is what was going to happen and I was relieved when it actually did. We were only a couple of hundred yards from the sea. West Hartlepool Joe and his friends bustled us across the road and down over the shingle without giving us the opportunity for one of those daring escapes, with descriptions of which I had been beguiling Miss Drom during our hours of imprisonment. West Hartlepool Joe might even have overheard me because the precautions he took were excessive. Miss Drom and I not only suffered the indignity of having our hands bound, we were gagged as well.

A rowing boat was waiting for us at the edge of the water and I was forced to scramble in at gun point. I got extremely wet. Miss Drom, getting preferential treatment as usual, was lifted in and dumped down next to me. A villainous-looking Frenchman plied the oars and we moved steadily and silently out to sea. We went quite a long way and the waves were getting uncomfortably high before the dark silhouette of a large motor boat appeared ahead of us. Our hands were untied and we clambered up a rope ladder on to the deck.

We weren't allowed to linger there. The guns jabbed away again and we were pushed down into a tiny cabin. Here we were once more locked in and before we had time to remove our gags the engine throbbed softly into life. We eased further out to sea at half-throttle for about ten minutes and then, with a kick like a mule, the boat leapt forward on full power. The porthole through which Miss Drom and I had been gazing blanked out under a solid sheet of spray.

They tell me people go sailing in boats like this for pleasure. Well, one man's meat. It might have been bearable up on deck but in that stifling little cabin it was most unpleasant. The boat hit the waves with a heavy rhythmical thud and rocketed up and down so violently that we had to cling on to the bunks to stop ourselves being flung on the floor. The noise, too, was absolutely deafening but I could put up with that. At least it drowned Miss Drom's voice.

We were going so fast that I calculated we'd be making the crossing in an hour or less, but two hours went by and we were still hammering away with no lessening of speed.

Miss Drom, chalk-faced, struggled over to me and putting her lips close to my ear shouted, ' I feel sick.'

I didn't wish to hear that as I had been attempting to sublimate a few of my own twinges for some time. I knew that if Miss Drom was sick, I should be too. So I beat her to it. All over the bunk to which I was clinging for dear life.

Miss Drom flung me one last look of anguished reproach before turning her head away.

Which gave me further inspiration.

There is just so much the human constitution can stand and I had now reached my limit. I was exhausted, dirty, frightened and feeling very, very poorly. I tried feebly to think what I had ever done to deserve such a fate but, honestly, I couldn't recall anything. I had always tried to do my best – so why was life forever upping and kicking me in the teeth? It was so unfair. Well, I reckoned I'd got the message now. Should I be spared, I was in future going to sit back and take life as it came. No more battling against the dictates of a malevolent fate. No more struggling against the current of life's stream. No more . . .

Oh, God! Sure there was nothing left in my stomach to . . .

It was immediately after this incident that the boat slackened speed and Miss Drom and I sank, completely drained, on to a couple of patches of floor that were marginally less nauseating than the rest. We seemed to be barely moving through the water now and the boat floated languidly up and down with the waves. Up on deck, above our heads, people were moving about. We heard a low whistle. Then an answering whistle. A few more minutes and something bumped gently against us. The door of the cabin was unlocked and we were invited to step outside.

We didn't need asking twice.

Another rowing boat was waiting for us and we clambered down into it, grateful for the darkness that covered our pea-green faces, for the fresh air that filled our lungs and for the prospect of soon getting solid land beneath our feet.

West Hartlepool Joe certainly ran a slick operation. He must have had connections everywhere. The timing was beautiful and all the various operations were carried out quietly and without fuss. We could have done with somebody of his managerial ability in S.O.D.

The rowing boat drove its bows into the beach and we jumped out. I looked round. There were no lights anywhere and no sounds apart from those coming from the sea itself and from our feet as we squelched over the damp sand.

I heard one of the men whisper to West Hartlepool Joe. 'What about footprints, boss?'

Now, why hadn't I thought of something clever like that?

The answer was laconic. 'The tide's coming in. Can you see the cars?'

We were crunching over pebbles now and, then, as we made our way round a sort of dune, there were the cars right in front of us. A Jaguar and an Austin Princess. Miss Drom and I were ushered into the Princess whose somewhat shabby exterior proved to conceal a pretty turn of speed. We found ourselves allocated to almost the same places that we had occupied in the white Alfa Romeo, long long ago in Italy. Miss Drom was in the middle of the back seat with West Hartlepool Joe and one of the men on either side of her, while I occupied one of the folding seats in front of them. Another of the men took the front seat next to the driver.

I noted, without really bothering too much about it, that all the interior door handles had once more been removed. It must be standard abduction procedure these days.

As soon as we were all aboard the car moved off. No lights as we bumped over half a mile or so of rough going. Dipped headlamps as we reached a proper road and began driving smoothly down it. The Jaguar followed us but it must have been a decoy car because after a few miles it flashed its lights in farewell and turned off down a side road.

West Hartlepool Joe switched the car radio on and tuned it in to a VHF police wavelength. We listened to a young lady reading a long list of stolen car numbers.

'Are you risking the A1, Jack?'

The driver half-turned his head. 'It's up to you, Joe. It'll be quicker than effing down these minor roads.'

'What about the cops?'

'Nothing special. I've been listening to 'em all evening. Seems quiet enough.'

'OK. But watch your speed. We don't want picking up for a damn fool thing like that.'

We eventually hit the A1 north of Huntingdon, by which time I was having the greatest difficulty in keeping my eyes open. It was two o'clock. I didn't have to bother peering at my watch as the young lady on the radio kept giving us time checks as she relayed her messages. We were making better speed now, though we hadn't exactly been dawdling before. The driver kept a wary eye out for patrol-cars and pushed the Princess along at just under the seventy-mile-an-hour mark while I wondered if everybody else was feeling as weary as I did. I was facing to the front of the car and I didn't fancy turning round to have a look at the trio behind me. It was the sort of movement that is liable to misinterpretation. Except for the communications chatter coming monotonously over the radio, the car was very quiet. The head of the man in front of me sank slowly down on to his chest. Had the others dozed off, too?

All the good resolutions I had made under the influence of acute mal de mer began slipping away. It's the training, I suppose. Anyhow, I began thinking about escaping once again.

I couldn't open the door next to me without winding down the window and letting in a blast of cold air sufficient to waken a corpse. Could I grab the driver? At seventy miles an hour and with two ruthless men sitting right behind me? Do me a favour! At the very best they wouldn't be more than cat-napping and one untoward move from me and fingers would be on triggers quicker than that.

I tried another line. Could Miss Drom, perhaps, grab a gun or two? I was thinking about trying to turn round and catch her eye when a voice came quietly from the back seat.

'Got a fag on you, Ted?'

'Sure, Joe.'

Well, that exonerated me, didn't it? Nobody could say I hadn't tried. I relaxed, eased myself into the most comfortable position I could find and let my eyes close with a clear conscience.

I woke up into a nightmare as the entire universe spun round – once, twice, three times. I spun with it. Up and down ceased to have any relevance as they succeeded each other with bewildering speed. Of their own accord my arms and legs sprawled out in all directions as I clutched for something solid to hang on to. I had only the vaguest impression of other bodies floating and clawing round about me and the sounds just didn't register at all until the car had completed its final somersault and come to rest more or less upright on its wheels. Only then when, except for a sobbing groaning a long way off, everything was quiet, did I find my ears buzzing with the screams and shouts which must have been uttered several seconds before.

What in God's name had happened?

It took me several seconds to appreciate that I was wedged, upside down, between the seat I had been sitting on and the door. Somehow I managed to get my hands up to the stab of pain on the side of my head and, to my astonishment, I felt the bump actually swelling up beneath my fingers. It took me ages to extricate myself and I remember wondering petulantly why nobody had the decency to come and help me. Eventually I pulled myself back on to my seat again.

I explored my head. It still hurt. My vision seemed blurred so I closed my eyes and took several deep breaths. Things were clearer when I looked round again.

The driver was slumped down in the well by the front

passenger seat with his back to the dashboard. His eyes were shut and he was breathing very slowly in loud, rasping gulps. The man who had been sitting next to him was sprawled awkwardly across both front seats. He wasn't moving either.

We must have had an accident, I thought stupidly, but the implication of what this meant still didn't strike me, not even when I found myself wondering if somebody had sent for the police.

The groaning was still going on and I turned my head round resentfully to see who it was.

The back seat was an inert mass of arms and legs and heads, all entwined and some poking out at unnatural angles. I stared at the hand and arm nearest me and felt ridiculously pleased when I recognized it. That was Miss Drom's hand.

Miss Drom!

Memory came pouring back! We had to get out of here! Quick!

I still didn't seem to have quite the control I ought to have over my muscles but in the end I succeeded in extracting Miss Drom from underneath the two men. It was while I was struggling with this formidable task that I discovered the source of the groans. They were coming from West Hartlepool Joe, which was a pity because it meant that he was still alive.

Miss Drom stirred and opened her eyes.

I gave her a good shake to help her recover her senses. ' Are you all right?'

She blinked like an inebriated owl. 'What's happened?'

'Never mind what's happened! Can you walk?'

'Where am I?'

What a woman!

West Hartlepool Joe was moving and he didn't look half as groggy as he had a few moments ago. The man lying across the front seats was coming round, too. If Miss Drom didn't buck up and pull herself together we should find ourselves right back at square one again.

' Are you all right?' I repeated, giving her a more forceful shake.

'Yes,' she said. 'Yes, I think so.'

'Well, come on then, for the love of God!'

I left her to get on with it while I wound the window down and opened the rear door from the outside. I glanced back before getting out. West Hartlepool Joe – God rot him! – was in the process of making one of those miraculous recoveries you read about in faith-healing magazines. There was no time to waste. I reached back into the car to grab Miss Drom. And do you know what she was doing? Wiping the face of the other man and crooning sympathetically over him. I seized Florence Nightingale by the scruff of the neck and dragged her out.

It was not a second too soon. West Hartlepool Joe had got his eyes wide open now, literally and figuratively, and he was looking at one million pounds sterling slipping through his greedy fingers. His gun was in his jacket pocket and things turned into a race. Could I get Miss Drom away before West Hartlepool Joe shot me?

Now read on!

Miss Drom emerged from the car like a cork out of a bottle. She stumbled onto her knees but, now that I'd got her moving, I had no intention of stopping for a little thing like that. Lugging her behind me, I sped away from the car and the road, heading for a clump of trees.

The night wasn't pitch black by any means but it was still quite dark and we were running over rough and broken ground. I went down first, tripping over some blasted tree root and falling flat on my face. For once in my life, though, Lady Luck was on my side and the bullet West Hartlepool Joe let fly at me went whistling harmlessly through the area where my chest would have been if I'd still been standing up.

'Oh dear!' said Miss Drom as I pulled her down beside me and began crawling on my hands and knees. 'What was that?'

'What the hell do you think it was?' I snarled. 'A bloody mosquito?'

Miss Drom crawled on in hurt silence and then – 'Ugh!'
she squawked.

'Come on!'

'Ugh, how dreadful!'

I caught Miss Drom just before she rose to her feet. 'Keep
down, you idiot! Do you want a bullet through your fat
head?'

'But, Eddie, look at me! Ugh!' Miss Drom fluttered her
hands about in great distress. 'You've led me right through a
cow pat!'

Sixteen

The peals of maniac laughter into which I collapsed can be put down to nervous tension but the unwelcome sound of voices coming from the direction of the car soon dried the tears on my face. The voices meant that somebody else in addition to West Hartlepool Joe had recovered his senses and if either of them was capable of putting one foot in front of the other they'd be right after us. It was no time to linger. We moved off, Miss Drom cleaning herself up as best she could with handfuls of grass.

We hadn't, of course, the faintest idea where we were but, if we lacked a point to aim for, we certainly had one to get away from.

At first we stayed down and crawled along on our hands and knees. After ten minutes or so of this, though, I came to the conclusion that we might as well get shot for men as rabbits and, crossing my fingers in the darkness, I told Miss Drom it was safe to get up. She was only too pleased and, since nobody fired at her, I in turn rose to my full height. We got on more quickly after that but it was still tedious going. We plodded up hills and down dales, over hedges and through ditches. We even crossed a stream and Miss Drom took the opportunity to wash off the remains of nature's bounty. Thus refreshed, she soon found something else to gripe about: she was tired. Couldn't we lie up somewhere and wait for daylight? Well, I happened to be far too frightened to be tired and so we pressed on.

We must have covered miles and miles and yet we'd not come across a house or a road or any other sign of human presence.

Miss Drom had a ready explanation for that, of course. 'We must be going round in circles,' she announced.

It was a thought which had flashed through my mind more than once. 'Don't be a bloody fool!' I said sharply.

'People do, you know.'

'Not,' I informed her crushingly, 'when they are navigating by the stars.'

She glanced up at the cloud-covered sky. 'But, there aren't any . . .'

'Oh, shut up!' I said.

It was at least half an hour after this little spat before we did finally stumble on something to cheer us up. A wire fence blocking our further progress. Miss Drom forgot she wasn't speaking to me and the helpful suggestions came pouring out. Why didn't we just follow the fence in one direction or the other? It was bound to lead somewhere and, really, almost anything would be better than this aimless wandering around in the dark, wouldn't it? She would probably get her head bitten off for saying it but, in her opinion, we were on the edge of some sort of park land. Well, it obviously wasn't just open moor, was it? Or ordinary farmland? Nevertheless, that fence hadn't been put there for fun. It must be enclosing something and so all we had to do was . . .

And that's probably what we would have done if thwarting Miss Drom hadn't become my pet obsession and if the desire to spite her hadn't triumphed over common sense.

'OK,' I said, beginning to climb over the fence, 'if you think that's the right thing to do, you go ahead. Me, I'm going this away!'

Miss Drom wavered, but only for a minute. I didn't think she'd fancy being left on her tod in the midst of all this rampant wilderness.

She surmounted the fence quite well and since the frock really belonged to the Marchesa the bit she tore out of it didn't matter much.

There were faint signs of dawn breaking in the sky. So now, for what it was worth, we knew which way east was.

'When we get to the top of this hill,' I said, in between the wheezes, 'we'll have a rest. Now it's getting light we'll be able to see if West Hartlepool Joe's still on the trail.' I stopped while I dragged some more air into my lungs. 'We'll be able to have a good look round, too,' I added, just as if this was what I had had in mind all the time, 'and maybe get our bearings.'

We reached the summit and flopped down. Miss Drom said the grass was damp. When we got our breath back, we surveyed the scene. Miles and miles of nothing. Where on earth in England could you find so much blasted country?

'Northumberland,' said Miss Drom, unexpectedly adding thought-reading to her other accomplishments, 'is a very sparsely populated county.'

'Who says it's . . .' I began before I could stop myself.

'I was watching the road signs,' sniffed Miss Drom. 'I didn't go to sleep like some people I could name. I knew we were going to have that accident, too. That driver had been nodding over the wheel for absolutely ages. If you'd kept on the alert we might have been able to exploit the situation and we wouldn't be wandering round lost like we are now.'

I stood up and peeled my wet trousers off the back of my legs. 'Come on!' I said and we began slowly to descend the other side of the hill.

There were more trees on this slope and clumps of straggly bushes and bracken which threw eerie shadows in the half light. Miss Drom must have found it creepy, too, because she moved closer to me and was thus in a most favourable position to fling herself round my neck when an outraged bellow tore through the early morning quiet and stopped two hearts beating as one.

Skilfully I swung Miss Drom round so that she was between

me and the patch of bracken from which the sepulchral blast had come.

There was a discontented snort, a scuffling sound and a flash of white. What a good thing it was that I don't believe in ghosts.

I shoved Miss Drom off. 'You nit!' I sniggered. 'Fancy being frightened of a poor little calf!'

'A calf?' Miss Drom turned to examine the innocent white face that was peering out at us. 'Oh,' she said shakily, 'so it is! Aw, isn't it sweet, Eddie? Look at its big, woolly ears!' Miss Drom broke off her sentimental slobbering to toss off what proved to be a very pertinent question. 'What on earth's it doing here, though?'

'Catching bloody pneumonia, I shouldn't wonder!' I retorted. 'Come on!'

'Bye-bye, baby!' cooed Miss Drom.

Baby responded with an even more hellish howl as we walked respectfully past his lair. This time, though, his cry was answered.

I side-stepped Miss Drom as she clutched at me again. 'That'll be his mum, I expect,' I said reassuringly, in spite of the fact that I had rarely heard anything less like a maternal moo in my life.

'She sounds very fierce,' said Miss Drom, looking round anxiously before running to catch me up.

'Good heavens, you're not frightened of a cow, are you?'

'No,' said Miss Drom. 'No, of course not.'

Mama blasted off again. Pure imagination, but she sounded nearer and crosser this time. The pounding of hoofs across the green sward were real enough, though. Well, we had to be getting on so I lengthened my stride. The hoof beats were louder. Miss Drom wasted precious energy by tossing another glance over her shoulder and then surged ahead of me by a good couple of lengths.

I looked back myself. An absolutely enormous, off-white animal with eyes of fire and smoke coming out of its nostrils was approaching at speed and concurrently lowering the biggest pair of horns I have ever seen off a wall plaque. I passed Miss Drom as though she was standing still.

We must both of us have read the same books because we were running – and running fast – for the nearest large tree. Even as I sped along I couldn't help thinking that cows must have changed since the last time I'd left farm gates open and trampled gaily through the ripening corn. Or . . .

' It must be a bull! ' I called to Miss Drom.

That lent wings to her feet all rightie!

I don't know what sort of a tree it was but it was a good-sized one and had several branches not too far from the ground. Mind you, the state I was in I could have cleared twenty feet without batting an eyelid, but it was nice for Miss Drom.

We both of us scrambled up on to the lowest branch just in time to find out what it was like to have ten tons of prime beef hoofing past underneath us. The ground shook, the tree shook, and Miss Drom and I shook. Dear God, it really was a cow! And, to be perfectly honest, not a big one. More what you might call wiry and rather dirty looking. It was also in an absolutely flaming temper about something.

It went quite a way past the tree before it realized that it had missed us. It stopped, pawed the ground and sniffed the air. Then it came streaking back again, bellowing and tossing its head about angrily.

Miss Drom and I shuffled along our branch toward the thick end nearest the bole of the tree while, just below, our bête blanche thrashed about like one demented.

' Go away! ' urged Miss Drom. ' Go away, you horrible brute! '

You can imagine what a lot of good that did.

I advocated a policy of total silence and immobility in the hope that the cow would get bored and push off. We sat like a couple of mice for ten whole minutes and finished up a damned sight more bored than the blasted animal was. Nor is the knobbly branch of a tree the most comfortable perch in the world.

'My word,' I whispered to Miss Drom, rather proud that I still had the cool to crack a joke, 'this bark is worse than a bite, what?'

She didn't get it, of course, but returned to a theme which was only too familiar. 'Why don't you do something?'

Always happy to oblige, I broke a few twigs off and shied them down at our cow. My efforts were rewarded with a renewed outburst of bellowing, much threatening horn shaking and a great deal of tail lashing. Over in its bush the calf klaxoned away in sympathy.

'I never did like cows,' said Miss Drom sulkily.

'Well, hard luck,' I replied and pointed to the horizon, 'because there's a bloody herd of them coming along now.'

There were about twenty of them and they moved faster than any cattle I have ever seen, not excluding in the old cowboy films on the telly. In no time at all we'd got the lot of them stamping angrily around our tree. They were all grubby white in colour and three of them were bulls.

An hour later they were still there, although some of the cows had begun munching away at the grass. They hadn't forgotten us, of course. It was just that they were beginning to find the waiting a trifle tedious.

Two hours later and Miss Drom issued one of her more constructive statements. 'We can't go on sitting here all day,' she said.

It was an hour after that, when the biggest bull had settled down for forty winks with his back against our tree, that the first sign appeared that we were not by the world forgot. Up away on the crest of the hill, down which the original cow had pursued us, appeared the distant figure of a man. Gumbooted and with a stout walking stick under his arm. He appeared to be very interested in our four-footed foes and finally got his binoculars out to have a closer look at them.

Miss Drom and I waved and shouted and were rewarded by having the binoculars trained on us. We'd been spotted, thank God! The man on the hill put his binoculars away and waved back. With his fist clenched.

'Probably a communist,' I said to Miss Drom.

She didn't think that was funny, either.

Time passed even more slowly now as we waited to be rescued. The cows showed no signs of going away and, indeed, I don't think it would have been much help if they had. Given the choice, I preferred being treed by the brutes to finding myself out in the open being chased by them.

'I suppose that man is coming back,' said Miss Drom doubtfully.

'Sure to,' I said.

Actually, it was the cows who either saw or heard the Land-Rover before we did. Heads went up, nostrils quivered, dribbling mouths opened in those ear-splitting brays. The big bull staggered to his feet, rumbling and snorting, and walked over to one of his harem and gave her a good belt in the flanks.

The Land-Rover came bouncing towards us over the open ground. The man with the binoculars was driving and he was looking extraordinarily grim. It took me a minute or two to identify the man in the passenger seat because he had removed his helmet and was holding it on his knees. Well, it's always a pleasure to see an officer of the law, though I thought his presence on this occasion was a mite superfluous.

The Land-Rover nosed gently through the white cows. One or two of them looked willing to have a go but apparently thought better of it and ambled sullenly away. The Land-Rover stopped a few yards away from our tree and the driver switched off his engine and addressed us over the windscreen.

'What the hell do you think you're doing up there?'

I didn't care for his tone. 'Bird watching,' I said.

The driver of the Land-Rover went very red in the face and turned angrily to the policeman. 'What did I tell you?' he growled. 'Bloody students!'

'Look a bit old for students,' said the policeman, examining us without sympathy. 'Could be tramps. They look dirty enough for tramps. On the other hand,' he added fairly, 'they look dirty enough for students.'

'Well, whatever they are, I want 'em charged. Trespassing and malicious damage.'

'Malicious damage?'

The driver pointed an accusing finger at the twigs I had broken off to chuck at the cows. 'What do you call that?'

'Hey,' I broke in, 'that was self defence! You're the one who wants charging, mate! Your cows are public menace.'

'Cows?' The driver gobbled at me incredulously 'Cows?'

The policeman gave me an admonitory shake of his head. 'You want to watch it!' he chuckled. 'I've seen people laid out flat for saying less than that. These aren't cows! They're the most famous herd of wild white cattle in the country.'

'In the world!' the driver corrected him. 'They're part of our national heritage, you lousy young punk! This herd's got a pedigree going back to the thirteenth century and if you've so much as harmed a hair of their heads you'll not live long enough to see the inside of a prison cell.'

The policeman didn't like this threat. 'Now, steady on, old chap!' he said. 'No need to lose your temper. We'll fix 'em for something, don't you worry. Resisting arrest or insulting behaviour, if we can't find anything better.' He gave Miss Drom and me a long professional appraisal. 'Wouldn't be surprised if they haven't both got records as long as your arm.' He leaned back in his seat and chuckled comfortably. 'As long as we get 'em up in front of the bench on some charge or other, his lordship'll do the rest, eh?'

'Aye!' The driver relaxed and chuckled. too. 'He'll do that all right! Remember that Irish poacher we caught? I'll never forget his face when he got six months without the option for a bloody rabbit you'd planted on him in the first place! Oh, well,' – he got his handkerchief out and wiped his eyes – 'I suppose we'd better be getting on with it.' He turned his attention back to me. 'I'll move up so's you can drop down into the back. And don't try anything funny or, by God, I'll chuck you to the King Bull myself!' He started the Land-Rover up and then bethought himself of another problem. 'Here, you've neither of you got foot and mouth, have you?'

Well, of course, we got it all sorted out long before we reached the stage of being sent to prison on some charge trumped up by the jovial policeman and his cross-patch friend. A few telephone calls soon settled everything. I let Miss Drom do the explaining to her father. Contrary to my expectations, he didn't want to speak to me at all.

While Sir Maurice busied himself with setting the wheels in motion in London, Miss Drom and I were permitted to enter the policeman's private residence to tidy ourselves up a bit. Mrs Policeman got quite bewildered. She didn't know whether I was going to seduce her sixteen-year-old daughter or nick the family silver.

In what seemed an incredibly short time a couple of police cars arrived from Alnwick and we were driven the forty-odd miles into Newcastle to catch the train to London. Here, too, Sir Maurice's solicitude for our welfare was much in evidence and we not only had a reserved first class carriage but a pair of cribbage-playing policemen to share it with us.

Miss Drom, confident that her troubles were now over, slept all the way. I kept wide awake, because I had a nasty suspicion that my troubles were only just beginning. I spent a couple of anxious hours rewriting recent history in as favourable light as I could manage. I knew too well what was going to happen, you see. Sir Maurice Drom was going to move heaven and earth to shovel all the blame on my shoulders.

Funnily enough, Sir Maurice was quite gracious when I reported to him in his office the following morning. That in itself should have given me pause but I was so grateful not to have my ears pinned back before I'd got my mouth open that I got over-confident.

'Brown,' he began, quite courteously but without any preamble such as an inquiry as to the state of my health and happiness, 'what was the number of the house you were told to wait outside in Hundemuseumstrasse?'

Although I had been anticipating that the discussion would

be conducted on a more elevated plane. I had prepared myself for all eventualities. '574,' I said smoothly.

'You bloody idiot!'

'Coming from you, sir, that almost ranks as a compliment.'

Sir Maurice was in no mood for witty repartee. 'The number was 475!'

'Was it?'

'It certainly was and, in case you are thinking of claiming that I gave you the wrong number, I have a certified and sealed tape recording of the whole interview.'

'Oh, now pull the other one!' I laughed. 'You're not going to sit there and tell me that I waited outside the wrong house and by sheer coincidence got myself mixed up in your daughter's kidnapping.'

'That's precisely what I am telling you because that is precisely what must have happened.'

'I don't believe it.' My knees turned to jelly and I sat down on the nearest chair. 'You set me up for this business.'

'I did nothing of the sort!' snapped Sir Maurice indignantly. 'You don't think that I would entrust the safety of my only child for one second to you of all people, do you? I had no idea that Muriel was in any danger.'

I waved a feeble hand. 'But – a coincidence!'

'On a scheduled flight to the United States of America I once found myself on the same plane with no less than three men who had all been in my form at prep school. And not only that. We were seated in the plane in exactly the same relative positions that we used to occupy in the classroom nearly forty years before. Coincidences do exist.'

I rallied as best I could. 'Well, you should have let me write all those blasted numbers down when I wanted to.'

'That,' said Sir Maurice, almost sorrowfully, 'is unworthy even of you.'

He was quite right. I turned to a subject upon which I was less vulnerable. 'Well, coincidence or not, you were dead lucky, weren't you? Where would your precious daughter be now, I'd like to know, if it hadn't been for me?'

'Well,' said Sir Maurice with astonishing mildness, 'exactly where she is at the moment, if you really want an answer to your question. We had everything well in hand through the normal channels. These kidnappings have become so common recently that all departments have their own contingency plans drawn up in great detail. Indeed, if you had only stayed in the same place for more than a couple of minutes together, we should have caught up with you long ago.'

'I'll bet!'

Sir Maurice got his cigarette box out and pushed it across the desk to me. 'No, it's perfectly true. We missed you by not more than ten minutes at Lake Garda and we were waiting in ambush at the airstrip from which the late Colonel Chicherin intended to transport you to the Soviet Union. I confess that we had some minor difficulty in picking up your trail after that. We didn't know about that charabanc, you see. We were looking for some more conventional and less conspicuous mode of transport. However, that problem was soon overcome and, once we realized that that rapscallion West Hartlepool Joe was involved, the rest was very simple. The police have had their eye on him for years and they know pretty well all his haunts. We had a watch put on all of them. As soon as you had arrived at your destination – he was taking you to a farmhouse outside Coldstream, by the way – we should have rescued you.'

I let the cigarette smoke trickle down my nose. Gratitude was, of course, something I had hardly expected. 'Well, I didn't know all that, did I?'

'No, no, of course not,' agreed Sir Maurice soothingly. 'No one is blaming you for that side of things. I do think, though, that you might have made more strenuous efforts to let us know what was in the wind before the kidnapping took place.'

'There were difficulties,' I mumbled.

'So Muriel was telling me last night.' Sir Maurice got an avuncular look on his face. 'You two young people seem to have had quite a thrilling time.'

'Yes,' I said.

Sir Maurice waited as though he was expecting me to say more. 'An adventure to look back on in the years ahead, eh?'

'Yes,' I said.

Sir Maurice just stopped himself scowling. He cleared his throat. 'I realize that you find yourself in a rather embarrassing position – er – Eddie, but I hope that you won't let our previous – hm – disagreements intimidate you too much. Let's forget about our official relationship for the moment, shall we? I'd like you to feel perfectly free to talk to me man to man.'

My complete lack of comprehension must have been visible at twenty paces.

Sir Maurice, going puce, swallowed hard. 'Muriel has told me everything,' he said.

'Good. That's saved me putting in a written report.'

'Well,' – Sir Maurice rallied like the old trooper he was – 'I never thought to see you so bashful, my boy! Oh, not that I'm complaining! These matters are talked about far too loosely and far too much in these degenerate days. A certain modest reticence doesn't come at all amiss. However, one must eventually steel oneself to say something, mustn't one?'

One of those natural breaks then occurred in the free flow of our conversation and I took advantage of the pause to pinch another of Sir Maurice's posh cigarettes. He watched me light it in silence. Obviously the next move, whatever it was, was up to me. Well, luckily, I'm rarely at a loss for a word.

'My leave,' I said.

Sir Maurice was galvanized into life. 'Of course, of course!' he agreed eagerly. 'There'll be no difficulty about that once you've – er – settled the date.'

Give me an inch. 'Right,' I said, striking while the iron had gone unaccountably soft, 'I'll take it now. Starting tomorrow.'

Sir Maurice blinked again. 'Come, come!' he chided me with an indulgent chuckle. 'That's a trifle impetuous, isn't it? There are a lot of things to be settled first, you know.'

'Such as?'

'Well, for one thing, I understand that Muriel wants a white wedding and . . .'

I took a very firm grip on myself. If ever I needed an ice-cold head it was now. 'What,' I asked carefully, 'has that to do with me?'

Sir Maurice shuffled through some papers on his desk. 'I hope, Brown,' he growled, 'that you are not going to be awkward about this. I am expecting you to do the decent thing. You are not, I confess, my ideal of a son-in-law but I have never in my darkest moments considered you to be a cad.'

'Decent thing?' I yelped. 'A cad? Look, I don't know what Miss Drom has been telling you but I never laid a finger on her.'

'So Muriel said herself and, naturally, I have no choice but to believe her. However, you must realize, my boy, that you have certainly compromised her in the eyes of society. You spent, I understand, several nights alone together. One' – Sir Maurice braced himself – 'in a bedroom.'

I didn't know whether to laugh or cry.

Sir Maurice went inexorably on. 'I should not, of course, insist on you behaving honourably in this matter were it not for the fact that Muriel has during the last few days grown as fond of you as you must have of her. She is universally loved, I find. She is not blind to your many faults, of course, but she considers – quite rightly in my opinion – that there is nothing wrong with you that the love of a good and pure woman cannot cure.'

The beauty of nightmares is that you do, eventually, wake up from them. This was no nightmare. I tried to break the news gently. 'I can't marry your daughter, Sir Maurice.'

'Why not?'

I ground my teeth. 'I don't happen to like her.'

'What nonsense!' retorted Sir Maurice, suddenly angry. 'Well, she happens to like you and that's good enough for me. I am not, I fancy, an over-indulgent father but in a matter of this delicacy my little girl's wishes are paramount. I am not going to stand idly by and see an insolent young whippersnapper like you ruin her reputation.'

I took a deep breath. 'I am not going to marry your daughter and nothing you can say is going to make me.'

'I'd like to break your bloody neck!' roared the irate parent. 'What am I supposed to tell Muriel?'

'I could suggest several things!' I roared back.

'You unmitigated rotter!' screamed Sir Maurice, jumping to his feet and pounding his desk with his fists. 'You unprincipled libertine!'

Another minute and he'd be pounding me. I decided it was time to withdraw before things started getting too violent. I stood up, too. 'Sticks and stones may break my bones,' I informed him with a certain dignity. 'And now, if there's nothing else, I'll be pushing off. I expect you've got your usual busy day ahead of you.'

This reference to the minutiae of his existence seemed to steady him. He sat down again and, with a thin, bleak smile on his lips, opened a file and glanced through it as though to refresh his memory. The smile widened. 'Ten thousand pounds,' he said quietly.

Well, at least I did him the honour of considering his offer carefully. Ten thousand pounds is not a sum to be sniffed at. Unfortunately a very vivid picture of Miss Drom kept getting in between me and the money.

'Not even for a million,' I said regretfully.

Sir Maurice's manner had changed. 'You misunderstand me, Brown,' he said briskly. 'I am not proposing to give you ten thousand pounds. I am asking you to give it me.' He looked up. 'It's the money you were supposed to deliver to our Viennese contacts. I should like it back now, if you please,' – the smile became crocodilic – 'just to keep the books straight.'

'You must be joking!' I blustered. 'You know damn well I haven't got it. Monkey Tom took it off me. He thought it had come from West Hartlepool Joe.'

'And Monkey Tom is dead. How extremely inconvenient for you. Were there any other witnesses to this unlikely transaction?'

'There were three,' I muttered resentfully, 'but they're dead, too – as you flaming well know.'

Sir Maurice had now got me right where he wanted me and he was beginning to enjoy himself. 'Where such a large sum of money is concerned, the unsupported testimony of an interested party doesn't carry much weight, does it?'

'Are you accusing me of stealing the blasted money?'

'I think you'll find the board of enquiry – under my chairmanship – will find you guilty more of carelessness than of dishonesty. That way the directorate will be able to retain your valuable services for the next' – he scribbled a few quick calculations on the corner of his blotter – 'two hundred years. Oh, dear! That does seem a trifle excessive, doesn't it? I'm afraid you'll have to have more than fifty pounds a month deducted from your salary.'

I don't have to have things spelt out for me. 'I'll bet you could find a way out of this predicament for me,' I said grimly, 'if you really put your mind to it.'

Sir Maurice's eyes met mine in perfect understanding. 'Do you know, my boy, I really think I could. It wouldn't be easy, of course, but for a member of the family . . .'